UNQUENCHABLE CRAVINGS: WAGER ON LOVE

Hard to Catch Series Book 3

Natasza Waters

ISBN-13: 978-1-0688241-0-4

Cover design by Dawné Dominique
Printed in the United States of America

For Mika

CONTENTS

CHAPTER ONE

Nathan sat on the sandstone patio that surrounded the sparkling swimming pool, talking with his old friend on the phone. At six a.m., the Nevada spring morning infused the air with warmth. He lifted a ceramic mug to his lips and downed a gulp of hot, black coffee.

"We're outbound tomorrow, buddy," Ian Kelly said.

When he retired from the Navy, Nathan removed the uniform and assumed civilian status. Ian, his swim buddy and best friend from the day they stepped on the Grinder for BUD/S training, couldn't share much.

"Where you headed?" Nathan asked.

"Looks like Al-Tanf."

He nodded. "Syria, huh? This is your last deployment, man. Keep your fucking eyes open."

"That's the plan. It's been a long time coming. But retirement is just six months down the road. Can't wait to wake up next to Angela and see the kids every morning for the rest of my life."

Nathan had spent twelve years on the SEAL teams. He'd tried to convince Ian to get out at the same time, but his buddy wanted to hit the twenty-year mark for a pension before hanging up his Trident.

"Soon as your ass is back on US soil, you're bringing the family to Vegas for a retirement celebration."

"You know it. Some of the boys from Delta Squad want to come, too."

When Nathan left the Special Forces, Ian assumed his position in SEAL Team One, Delta Squad.

"Just tell me when. I'll block off the rooms at the Royal Jade."

Ian's pension would amount to fifty percent of his wage, which wasn't enough. Nathan wanted to introduce him to

Vince Laker, the man who owned the resort. Without question, he'd bring Ian onboard in the security operations department. They'd talked about it before. Ian and his wife were open to the idea.

"And with any luck, you'll be a free man by the time I get home."

Nathan sure as hell hoped so. He and Bonita separated a year ago. "We finalized the divorce settlement. Waiting for her signature." Paroled after five years of hell.

"Man, I remember your wedding day. Didn't I say you were crazy to marry an actress, especially her?"

"Yeah, I know." Nathan's gaze roamed across the leafy palm trees skirting the backyard. "Could have worked."

"Like hell!" Ian laughed. "She screwed around on you six months into the marriage. I don't know how the hell you lasted this long. You didn't love her. I told you, you'd end up here."

He grinned. "Thanks for the reminder."

"Don't mention it. Where's the barracuda now?"

"Filming her latest movie in LA. She's living in the Malibu residence."

His housekeeper, dressed in black pants and a white cotton blouse, laid a plate of fresh fruit on the teak side table next to him. "Your breakfast, Señor Selkirk."

"Thanks, Maria. Looks great."

"Who gets the beach house in the divorce?" Ian asked.

"I signed it all over to Bonita, except for this place. I don't want anything but my freedom." They owned four homes. One in Malibu, an apartment in New York, the Vegas residence, and an estate in Italy.

"Do yourself a favor and stop being a gentleman. Go introduce yourself to that woman you've been stalking every Tuesday for two years."

Nathan shook his head and gulped another swallow of java. "I'm not stalking Jane. I admire her from afar. That's the way it's gonna stay. She certainly doesn't need me to screw up her life."

"You've never met the woman, but you can't stop talking

about her. You're in love, Nathan. And it's about goddamn time. So you better tie up those Texas-sized bootstraps and do something about it before I get back. I want to meet this woman who's had you twisted up in knots. Anyway, I'm spending my last day of freedom in bed with my wife until the kids get home from school, and then I'm taking them out to dinner. I gotta zero-three-hundred flight into bad guy territory."

"Don't run to your death, buddy." The phrase known by all SEALs meant that once you breached and gained entry to the target, being slow and methodical, especially in close-quarters combat, kept a team guy alive. "And give Angela a kiss for me."

"You bet your ass. On both. I don't want you kissing my wife. You're way better looking than me."

He chuckled at Ian's comment. A guy who'd always kept the team laughing even during the hardest times they'd ever faced. "Love you, man. See you in six months."

Ian disconnected, and Nathan finished his coffee in the tranquil setting of his backyard. Tuesday was always a good day, especially when Jane St. Eval showed up at the Royal Jade with her landscaping crew.

Unfortunately, Ian would never meet her. Nathan had kept his distance for good reasons. The commitment to his marriage vows, regardless of Bonita's adultery, ranked high on the list. But mostly because Jane reflected a natural beauty that attracted him the moment he'd seen her. There was just something authentic, uncomplicated, and sincere about the woman. Breaking the barrier he'd maintained would only ruin her life.

****

Mr. Liam Peters, Chief of Security Operations, led the newly hired Mr. Crocker into the expansive, windowless room. The Royal Jade's security center maintained constant surveillance of the casino resort. Dressed in casual business attire, personnel exchanged information in a streamlined environment meant for one purpose: to stop illegal activity and monitor the safety of guests.

Las Vegas drew millions of visitors each year. The Royal Jade, owned by Vince Laker, ranked in the top tier of Sin City. A destination with Jade's reputation drew con artists by the hundreds. Fraudsters went to great lengths, creating new and inventive ways to cheat the odds.

Security staff rarely sat idle. Card counters to professional thieves roamed the resort, hiding themselves among the throngs of legitimate tourists. The unscrupulous stole identities. Hackers used high-tech devices to create bogus casino accounts, then disappeared into the ether with thousands of dollars.

Liam reached the middle of the operations room and faced his newest employee, who'd dressed in a dark brown suit and beige silk tie.

"This is the Security Operation Center, Mr. Crocker. You'll work in this room once you've finished your on-the-job training with one of our senior staff members."

Mr. Crocker gazed at the stacked monitors covering every wall, including the low-profile desks, sitting end to end and ten rows deep. "There's a lot going on around here."

Surveillance covered nearly every corner of the resort and surrounding grounds. Security officers maintained a watchful eye on the casino floor and exit routes.

Liam allowed Mr. Crocker to observe the environment for a moment.

"Your initial position will entail monitoring the exterior and interior main valet entrances. We section the resort off into quadrants, and eventually this area of responsibility will be yours."

Somebody from behind them shouted, and three men ran toward the east exit door.

"What's going on?" Mr. Crocker asked, focusing on a monitor where two employees stood, peering at the screen.

Liam quickly scanned the live video. "Sports bar," he said. "See that young man? Brown hair, jeans, and a brown button-up shirt? He's the son of an oil tycoon. He's been here before. Hot under the collar, has plenty of money, and once he drinks, he's out of control." He offered Mr. Crocker a rueful gaze and a shrug. "Spoiled brat, in other words."

"I understand."

"The motto around here is *'Our days start with a question mark.'* Anything can happen at the resort. Whether it's a medical incident or criminal activity, it's going to flow through this room. Your eyes have to see it first. Response time is immediate. Beside the managers and surveillance team in this center, seventy-five security men and women work the resort at all times."

"What's happening over there?" he asked, squinting at an adjacent desk with four monitors hanging above a single workstation.

Liam turned to see who had Mr. Crocker's attention. The familiar wide shoulders and trimmed blond hair belonged to a respected man that everyone at the Jade knew.

"Ah, yes. We'll go there once Mr. Selkirk has left. That will eventually be your workstation."

"Who's he?"

"He—is everyone's boss. Mr. Nathan Selkirk is the Director of Operations for the entire resort. Basically, he's Mr. Laker's second-hand man."

"Mr. Laker owns the Royal Jade."

"Correct. Nathan and Mr. Laker have known each other for years. Mr. Laker relies on him to keep this place running with above-average service and safety."

Mr. Crocker tipped his head as he watched Nathan. "He looks kinda familiar."

"He probably does, but it's his wife who's popular."

"His wife?"

"He's married to Bonita Williams."

"The actress?"

"Yes, the *actress slash socialite slash*—pain in the ass."

The new employee surveyed their boss, who stood observing

the monitors hung above the workstation. "What's he doing?"

"Well—" Liam buried a grin behind one hand. "It's Tuesday, Mr. Crocker."

"And?"

Nathan Selkirk zoomed the camera in on the garden beds at the busy main entrance. A woman kneeled in the dirt. Her gloved hands dug into the loamy earth, pulling a few weeds unfortunate enough to pop their heads to the surface.

"Mr. Selkirk consistently checks in with the center operations, but without fail, you'll see him on Tuesdays at that station. When he arrives, you will discreetly remove yourself until he leaves."

Nathan manually panned the camera, then crossed his arms. The landscaper wore a pair of stonewashed jeans and a pale blue T-shirt, tightly knit to her tall, lean physique. A thick ponytail of long auburn hair swept her shoulder blades as she worked.

Mr. Crocker caught on fast. "Didn't you say he was married?"

"*Was*, being the keyword. Bonita Williams belongs to a prestigious Hollywood family with a long history of award-winning actors. Because of her pedigree, she expects immediate attention. Short-tempered and brittle, she's made a name for herself as being difficult on film sets and around here," Liam divulged. "I don't know the history between Nathan and his wife, but Bonita has been openly affectionate with a young and upcoming actor these days. There's a rumor that Mr. Selkirk and she separated, and the divorce isn't long to follow."

"What's he like?" Crocker asked, eyeing Nathan Selkirk's imposing stature as he watched the landscaper. "He's a big guy. I wouldn't want to tussle with him."

"No, you wouldn't. He's in his late thirties and keeps himself in prime physical condition. Nathan joined the Navy and served for several years. Retired SEAL, I believe. After leaving the Forces, he applied his specialized skills to the gaming industry. He stood out, and Mr. Laker promoted Nathan to Director of Operations. You'll like him. He's direct and fair. Doesn't pull any punches. He expects everyone to work as hard as he does."

Nathan picked up the phone on the workstation desk and placed a call.

Liam continued the operations room tour, but his new employee kept darting glances toward their boss.

A few minutes later, a server approached the landscaper on the monitor. The woman turned and smiled.

"Beautiful lady," Mr. Crocker noted as Nathan zoomed the camera focus once again.

Liam agreed. "I've spoken to her once or twice. Her name's Jane, and she's an amiable woman. Two years ago, she won the contract for Royal Jade's landscaping, and ever since then, every Tuesday, Mr. Selkirk shows up to watch her for a while, like you see here. Of course, you'll ignore it like everyone else."

"If Mr. Selkirk monitors all the operations, maybe he's just auditing her work."

Liam approved of Mr. Crocker's assessment, although it was incorrect. "Possibly."

A casino server exited the main entrance carrying several glasses and a chilled pitcher filled with liquid on a tray, delivering it to the landscape crew. Jane called her team over, and they emptied the jug. Nathan watched as Jane nodded and smiled her thanks to the server. The camera zoomed in. Her pleasant features and pale green eyes appeared in a picture-in-picture box at the upper right portion of the monitor.

"He sent the refreshments to her crew, didn't he?" Mr. Crocker asked.

"Assuredly."

"So, he's got a thing for her?"

"Don't know, Mr. Crocker, and no one is going to step over the line and question him. He often strolls in and speaks with staff or monitors the casino floor. But you can count on his presence on Tuesdays around this time."

"You would think he'd be panning the pool area for buxom beauties."

"Dealing with A-listers and their highbrow attitudes is taxing. Mr. Selkirk is a down-to-earth kind of man. If he has a moment, I'll introduce you." Liam glanced at his watch. Ten a.m. Mr. Crocker's familiarization tour would last a full eight hours before assigning him to a senior security specialist, giving him a chance to opt out before his training began in earnest.

"I suppose Mr. Selkirk comes from money," Crocker stated.

"Not at all. People say Bonita hitched up with Mr. Selkirk, thinking he would be the next Vince Laker. He does own shares in some casinos, including the Royal Jade, but he hasn't made his move to take them over."

"Maybe she's divorcing him because he didn't climb the capitalist ladder fast enough."

Liam chuckled. "Personally, I think Mr. Selkirk initiated the divorce. Regardless, we'll all be glad when she doesn't come around anymore. We don't see Bonita often, but when she comes, it's with an entourage and that yappy, primped dog of hers that fits in her purse. I don't think Mr. Laker will care that she's out of the picture, even if she brings in LA customers and their money. She has an enormous following on social media. Bonita thrives on her notoriety, but she can't act worth shit."

The camera panned out again as Nathan kept the woman in the center. She kidded around with a young crewmember, pointing at his chest. When he looked down, she flicked his nose with her glove and shook her head, laughing. The kid grinned, then listened as she motioned with her arm to the lush flowerbed filled with greenery and colorful annuals to their right.

"Selkirk looks pretty intimidating," Crocker said.

Liam kept any further comments to himself as he and Crocker watched a tempered smile cross Mr. Selkirk's otherwise stern-looking features. The man rarely smiled, but when he did, it was like now, watching the landscaper.

On the left side of the monitor, a situation unfolded that jump-started Liam's pulse.

Nathan Selkirk saw it too because he shouted, "Don't do that."

Liam unfurled his crossed arms with a snap, rushing toward

the workstation.

Grabbing the edge of the computer desk, Nathan leaned forward. "Jane—no!"

It happened so fast, neither Liam nor anyone else could do anything to stop it. The landscaper took a couple quick steps backward to analyze her work, but she'd walked onto the driveway. A sweeping turn in the road lined the garden. A taxi whistled around the curve toward the main entrance, ignoring the posted speed limit signs.

"Shit. Call an ambulance!" Liam yelled a second before the cab nailed the brakes, but he was already too close. The impact tossed Jane upward and away from the taxi. She landed hard on the pavement.

Nathan bolted for a side door to their right, knocking over one of the security officers who got in his way.

Liam leaped into a run to follow. "Get the house medical team down to the main entrance. A cab hit a contractor," he shouted as he crossed the room. With the new hire on his tail, Liam reached the door Mr. Selkirk had used. "Come with me. You indicated you had pre-med on your resume. Maybe you can help."

Liam gripped the release bar across the metal door to detach the locking mechanism. Shoving the door with his shoulder, he accessed the back stairwell. The security operation center sat one floor above ground level. Taking the stairs two at a time, he quickly reached the bottom and jumped the last three steps to the cement floor. He thrust the emergency door open. They weren't far behind Mr. Selkirk.

****

Nathan used his shoulders and arms to cut through the crowd of people, four layers deep, surrounding Jane. One of the Royal Jade's security men created a ten-foot buffer between the onlookers and her still body. The gangly taxi driver, with a wild mop of hair, paced back and forth, shaking his head. When

Nathan cleared the last layer of gawkers, he halted, and his breath caught in his throat.

Jane lay on the ground, eyes closed, arms outstretched, and limp. He took the last steps and kneeled by her side. Placing two fingers on her slender neck, he checked her carotid pulse.

Still alive.

One of Jane's crew members, wearing a ball cap with *Green Appeal* embroidered across the top, crouched on the other side of her body. "Did someone call an ambulance?"

Moments ago, Nathan watched her tease the young man in the camera.

"They've been called," he stated, not shifting his gaze from her tranquil features.

"An ambulance is on the way, sir," someone said, squatting beside him.

Nathan glanced across his right shoulder to see his Chief Security Officer. "Thank you, Mr. Peters."

A man in his early thirties, who Nathan had seen with Mr. Peters in the ops room, gently nudged her crewman over, then checked for a pulse.

An older man of Mexican descent, who Nathan knew as Jane's second in charge, kneeled by her head and swept his hand over her hair like a concerned parent. "Aw, *cariño*," he murmured in Spanish.

"How bad is it?" Nathan asked. The Jade's new employee methodically checked her limbs.

After a cursory check, the intern carefully slid his hand beneath Jane's head. Blood coated his fingers when he removed his hand.

"Oh, God," Nathan groaned, closing his eyes for a moment.

Continuing, the young man checked her torso, arms, hips, and then legs. "I can't feel any broken bones, just the head trauma, sir."

"You have medical experience?" Nathan asked, not taking his eyes off her slack features.

"Two years pre-med."

"Open your eyes, Jane." She appeared to be asleep and peaceful.

"Her pulse is slow," he answered, straightening her arms against her sides. "I can't tell if there's internal damage or minor fractures. It's better she stay this way until the EMTs get here. We don't want to take a chance on worsening her injuries."

Nathan heard the long, bereft call of the sirens as they approached. Tenderly, he brushed her cheek with a curled finger, and his chest knotted.

He bent closer, his lips almost touching her ear. "Jane, don't give up. I need to see your smile," he whispered, curling his hand around her fingers. As if responding, her dainty fingers squeezed. His gaze darted to her face. "She squeezed my hand." The security intern peered at him with that look doctors often give—the one with doubt written all over it. "She did."

"Maybe."

An ambulance rolled up to the resort entrance, its haunting sound halted mid-wail. Seconds later, the EMTs crouched beside Nathan as the security intern gave a sitrep on the accident and her head trauma.

"Sir, we need you to back up," the paramedic said, addressing Nathan.

"Of course." He nodded and stood, watching their every move but not shifting far from her side.

"Do you know who she is?" the older emergency attendant asked, glancing up at him.

"Her name's Jane St. Eval."

"Are you family, or know her next of kin?"

He glared at the EMT. "Just put my name down." Nathan dug into his inner suit pocket and retrieved a resort business card. The ambulance attendant looked like he wanted to ask something else but decided against it. "Take it. I'm Director of Operations here at the Jade. This card has my contact info. I'll follow you to the hospital."

"Does she have insurance? I can't find any ID," the paramedic asked, gently patting her jean-clad hips.

Every contractor they hired had liability insurance, but he didn't give a shit about red tape at the moment. "She's covered. If not, I'll take care of the medical bill. Just get her to the closest hospital."

Nathan peered at her crew. Jane's second-in-command gave him a quick nod. "She has no *familia*."

The attendants secured a foam collar around her neck and slid the spinal board under Jane, then carefully lifted her onto the stretcher.

"Blood pressure's low," the EMT noted to his partner as he secured an oxygen mask over her face and adjusted the gauge.

Nathan walked beside the stretcher, holding Jane's hand. Before they lifted her inside, he leaned over. "Hang on, sweetheart. I'll be right behind you."

He took a step back as the paramedics shifted the stretcher into the ambulance and closed the doors.

"Sir?"

He turned to see the security intern. Nathan wasn't good at masking his expression, and the guy took a wary step back. "It's Mr. Crocker, correct?"

"Yes, sir." The man shifted his gaze to the ambulance. "Head trauma can be as mild as a slight concussion. She could wake up on the way to the hospital."

"It can also be serious," he growled. He'd seen enough blood and injuries while working in the teams.

"Yes, sir, that's true. Does her contract have any family records attached? Can I call someone for her?"

"Mr. Peters." He turned his attention to Jade's Chief of Security. "Pull her file. I don't believe there are any emergency contacts, but double check. Text me with the information." He glared at the young man who'd stepped up to assist Jane. "Thank you, Mr. Crocker, for your help."

"Yes, sir."

Nathan hurried into the casino, headed for the parking lot and his vehicle. The only thing on his mind was the woman he'd protected by keeping his distance for two long years.

CHAPTER TWO

Nathan bolted across the gaming floor and shoved open the door leading to the parking garage. His heart barely beat in his chest, cold with apprehension. Inside his vehicle, he started the BMW i8.

With tires screeching on the smooth concrete, he accelerated through the above-ground garage and exited onto the busy street behind the resort. He caught up with the ambulance a mile from the hospital.

While waiting in the emergency room, he filled out a pad's worth of paperwork. Many questions remained unanswered. She lived on Matson Drive and he had her phone number. He filled in her date of birth. A New Year's Day baby, but the thirty-two years since taking her first breath were transparent to him. The resort conducted cursory background checks on contractors and their crews. No criminal charges, no misdemeanors, not even a traffic ticket marred her name. Her crew wasn't as clean, but even those were youthful indiscretions.

Nathan figured she loved the color blue because she often wore T-shirts in different shades, but there wasn't a space for that on the form. He leaned back in the chair, tapping the pen on the clipboard, his jaw tightening. Other worried loved ones or people with minor injuries waited in the cheap vinyl-bound chairs, filling half the seats. He didn't fall into the category of a loved one or family member.

Jane didn't know him at all.

Nathan watched her come and go almost every Tuesday. He looked forward to that day. The first time he'd seen her, Jane's smile pressed a lasting image in his mind, like a flower preserved between wax paper. Headstrong and determined, he'd watched her uproot a hundred annuals she'd just planted because she didn't like the outcome.

Six months after she started her contract at the Royal Jade, he'd been jogging at a local park. Taking a breath, he'd glanced up to see her briskly walking towards him on the gravel path.

For a change, the brim of a ball cap didn't shadow her incredible eyes. Jane's thick hair rained loose in soft waves, and she wore a rose-colored tank top instead of a T-shirt smudged with dirt. Meeting his gaze, the woman he couldn't stop thinking about smiled at him.

They only exchanged a few words.

"Nice evening for a walk," he'd said. Nathan had tossed the pleasantry at her because his mind had drawn a blank.

She'd slowed her pace to a crawl, then stopped. The wind blew the hair from her face, and he saw the flash of gold studs in her earlobes. *"Fresh air is good for the soul. Enjoy your run."*

Their eyes connected for a lingering moment, then she continued her walk. He'd turned to watch her leave. Since that day, her voice and pale green eyes invaded his dreams.

Some people might consider him a stalker because he watched her on Jade's security cameras. Quite the opposite. He watched her from afar so he wouldn't poison her world. To him, Jane seemed as natural and beautiful as the gardens she landscaped.

Living in Las Vegas came with perks and pitfalls. He brushed shoulders with beautiful, rich women all the time. Some married. Some single. But he'd never been unfaithful to Bonita. He'd made a commitment, although marrying the actress had been a mistake. Soon, he'd have the divorce. It couldn't come fast enough. His ex-wife could torment someone else instead of him.

Their wedded bliss hadn't lasted a day before her character changed dramatically. Bonita never stopped complaining, insisting he build his own resort and carve his name on the Las Vegas strip. With unreasonable expectations, she dared him to compete against Vince Laker, who owned five-star resorts on the boulevard.

He'd met Bonita at an event for VIP guests at the Jade. Vince

Laker talked him into pursuing the woman. The casino mogul convinced him that marrying into the right family couldn't hurt. Despite his instincts, Nathan proposed to her after dating for a few months. She had her own money, which she splurged on partying, shopping, and luxurious trips with friends. Wasn't long before their opposing expectations and her constant harping about his professional goals became toxic.

After five years, the torment had finally come to an end.

"Mr. Selkirk?"

Nathan's attention snapped to the doctor addressing him. "Yes, how is Jane?"

"I'm Dr. Nelson, Neurology Department. The admissions desk said you've put yourself as Jane St. Eval's next of kin. Are you her husband?"

"No. I'm not."

"Are you family?"

"She doesn't have any."

"I see, well…"

"Jane is my responsibility. Did she wake up?"

"Yes, Mr. Selkirk, she did. We closed the wound on her head with fifteen stitches, but unfortunately, the swelling caused by the accident has resulted in complications."

His pulse accelerated. "As in?"

"Because of the neurological injury, she's lost the majority of her vision. I don't believe it's permanent," he added hurriedly. "But it will take time for the inflammation to subside. She'll be hospitalized until we're certain there are no further complications, then we can release her to an assisted living facility or she can go home. Either way, she'll need help. Does she live with you?"

"No, she doesn't, but she'll have help. I'll arrange for someone to stay with her."

"That's good." The doctor pressed his lips together and gave him a reassuring look. "Ah, there is one other thing." Dr. Nelson paused, as if considering his words.

"What is it?"

"Right now, she's actually quite angry."

He didn't know Jane, but he'd witnessed her tenacity and the high standards she maintained with herself and the landscape team. He wasn't surprised. "Probably at herself, correct?"

"It appears that way. We can't seem to get her to settle down, and she needs to rest. I can't give her any sedatives because of the head trauma. At least, I don't want to. If you would like to see her, you can, and maybe suggest that her road to recovery would be better served without agitating herself any further."

His heart banged in his chest. "I...uh.... Sure, I can do that."

"Thank you. We've moved her to Ward E. She's in room three-oh-eight."

He scanned the emergency room, forcing his pulse to level out.

How the hell could he calm Jane down? He might make things worse.

****

Nathan found Jane's room and leaned against the door frame, biting down on a grin because he'd heard her halfway down the hall.

"I can go home. I feel fine," Jane argued with the nurse, who busied herself checking the IV tube.

"Jane, you have to be monitored for a few days to make sure no other symptoms arise."

"I'll let you know if I have symptoms. Just point me in the right direction, and I'll get a cab home. I have animals to take care of."

The nurse didn't lose her patience, which told Nathan she had some experience in the field.

"I'm sure there's someone you can call," the nurse suggested calmly. "I'll bring a phone in a little while and you can make arrangements."

"Why don't you just show me where my pants are and I'll be on my way? I don't want the hassle of dealing with health insurance. It's nothing but a pain in the ass, so kick me out."

The nurse adjusted a stand next to the bed that monitored Jane's vitals. "It's taken care of. Now, you have to do your part and heal."

"By who?" Jane's voice rose at the nurse's unwillingness to give an ounce of hope that she could escape her current predicament.

He nearly laughed when Jane thumped her clenched hands on the bed and lay back on the pillow, sighing loudly.

"I hate hospitals."

The nurse glanced over at him and her eyebrows arched, seeing him leaning on the doorframe. "Sir, you can come in." She smiled, but the look held more than just a friendly *come-on-in*. More like a *come-get-me-after-work* look.

"Who's there?" Jane asked.

"You have a visitor," the nurse explained. "A handsome one. If I were you, I'd stay right where you are."

"I don't know anyone who's handsome." Jane's head turned toward the doorway. Gauze covered her eyes, and her pert chin jutted upward. "Are you a doctor? If so, squiggle a John Hancock on a release form and let me go home."

He entered the room and slid the beige guest chair to her bedside. Instinctively, he reached for her hand but stopped himself. "No, I'm not a doctor, Jane. And you need to stay put."

"Your voice sounds familiar." Her forehead wrinkled. "Are you the guy that hit me?"

"No. I'm just checking on your condition."

"They won't let me out of here. Think you can spring me from this place? I feel fine."

Persistent woman, Nathan thought. "I think you should stay."

"So, you're on their side, huh?" She folded her arms over the blue hospital blanket. "I have a headache and a sore hip. It's not life-threatening."

"You also lost your vision, Jane. You're better off here, where the hospital staff can monitor your injuries. When they're satisfied it's safe, you can go home."

Someone had removed the band from her hair, and Jane ran her fingers through her long, thick auburn waves, collecting the strands on top of her head.

"Who are you, then?"

"My name's Nathan."

She tilted her head toward the sound of his voice. "I don't know anyone named Nathan."

"I work at the Royal Jade."

"Oh, I see. Well, don't worry. I'm not suing anybody for millions of dollars. I suppose you want me to sign something."

She pulled the bed sheet a little higher, but not high enough. His gaze slowly fell to her lovely neck and the rise of her breasts beneath the thin hospital gown.

"I'm not worried about an injury claim. I'm concerned about you." Then he realized his explanation wouldn't make sense.

"Worried about me?" She shimmied up the bed a little, then winced. "If you don't know me, why would you be worried?"

"Yeah, well—" He cleared his throat. "I saw the accident. Just wanted to make sure you were all right."

"What do you do at the casino?"

"I..." If he revealed his title, she'd assume he was here to get the Royal Jade off the hook for any incidental claims. "No one special, just one of the floor guys."

She fiddled with the bedsheet, twisting it around her index finger. "Floor guy?"

His clarification had to satisfy her curiosity without sounding like a lunatic, which he might well be.

"Security. I work for security at the resort."

"So you saw my stupid-ass move, huh?"

"Just bad timing, Jane. You've stepped onto the road hundreds of times."

"What?" she whispered warily.

"I've seen you there before," he explained quickly. "Working in the gardens. You're a contractor for the resort."

"I am." She tsked. "Can't believe this happened. I should have known better." She shook her head as if disgusted with herself.

"Think you can stop giving the nursing staff a bad time and hang out here until you're able to go home?"

"I don't have a choice, do I?"

"Not really. Berating yourself over the accident won't help." His heart beat with an uneven cadence. He was talking with her, sitting next to her, finally. "Is there anyone I can call for you?"

She nibbled on her bottom lip, then shook her head.

"No one—a boyfriend? Spouse?"

"No." She lightly touched the back of her head and grimaced. "No boyfriend. But I need to call someone to feed my animals. Do you know my crew? Did you see any of them?"

"Not here, but I'm sure they'll come. Tell you what—Mr. Laker would want the resort to deal with your health insurance. Make things easier, and—"

"You know Mr. Laker? *The* Mr. Laker." Her brows notched together. "You're not just a floor guy," she said warily.

Jane's faculties fired on all cylinders, which gave him hope that she'd heal quickly. "We all know Laker. He's a hands-on kind of boss."

"If you're on a fact-finding mission, then tell him I'm not suing. I take full responsibility."

"Jane, you had your signage on the roadway. The cabbie didn't see it. As for your animals, why don't you let me take care of them? It's the least the resort can do." Hiding behind the resort wasn't what he wanted. He understood her hesitancy. A strange guy shows up, claiming he's from the Royal Jade, and says he's concerned. Nathan wouldn't buy that excuse either.

"You sure you're not a lawyer, Nathan?"

"Definitely not a lawyer."

"Do you have a last name?"

He cleared his throat. "Selkirk."

With her eyes bandaged and temporarily blind, she'd have to rely on the sound of his voice to decide whether to trust him. He also hoped like hell she didn't recognize his name.

"Hello, Mr. Selkirk, I'm Jane St. Eval." She reached her hand out to him, her arm pointed two feet to the right of where he sat.

He'd already held her hand while she lay unconscious on the pavement. "Nice to meet you, Jane." He grasped her hand in both of his and noticed her trimmed fingernails and callused palms. "The resort feels at least partially responsible. We should have a security officer on duty when you're working in the gardens at the main entrance. Those damn cabs come screamin' into the area. It's too dangerous for you. I'll make sure—" He caught himself in time. "Management will assign a security member to keep a lookout until you're finished with your work from now on."

"My traffic control signs meet industry standards, but I've thought about getting larger ones. I kept putting it off. Guess I paid the price for procrastinating." She exhaled a deep breath. "Thank God it wasn't one of my crew." She rubbed her temple with her fingertips in a slow, circular motion.

"Are you in a lot of pain?" When she relaxed her arm on the bed, he palmed her forearm.

"Enough, but I deserve it for being so stupid."

He liked that she hadn't removed her arm from his grasp. "Get some rest. Doc says the quicker the swelling goes down, the sooner your sight will return."

Her face pinched with concern. "What if it doesn't?"

"It will. Believe me. I've had a few concussions. It takes time, but you'll heal."

"How did you get a concussion?"

Her curiosity probably had more to do with figuring out if she could trust him than wanting him to hang around. He'd take what he could get. Every damn second of it. "I got my bell rung a few times in my twenties."

"Doing what?" she asked.

"During my service in the Navy."

"Sailor to casino floor guy. That's a strange leap. Dishonorably discharged?"

He laughed despite doing a piss-poor job of instilling confidence by the tone of her voice. "Um, no. I served for twelve years. Joined up after graduation."

She shifted and winced. "Why'd you leave?"

"Retired. Special Ops takes its toll. I made the choice not to have a lifelong career as a SEAL, unlike some of my teammates. Tried to convince my best friend, Ian Kelly, to leave and come with me to Vegas, but he wasn't ready yet."

"Never met a Navy SEAL before."

She didn't seem overly impressed like some women. "Well, now you have." He cocked his head, and a grin slipped across his lips that she couldn't see. He didn't mind staying a little longer. "Did you grow up here?"

"No. I moved here five years ago and started my business. My contract with Royal Jade was a huge break." She licked her lips, then swallowed. "Is it possible I'll lose the contract over this?"

"No, Jane. That won't happen. Are you thirsty?"

She nodded.

To his right, an unopened container of juice with a plastic straw on top, sat on the standard hospital overbed table. "How about some orange juice?"

"Anything."

He removed the wrapper from the straw and peeled back the foil cover on the juice container. She held out her hands.

"I've got it," he said, brushing the end of the straw against her lips.

Jane's hands slid over his fingers. He stopped breathing, but his pulse went into overdrive. In seconds, she emptied the container. Standing this close, he saw a faint splash of freckles beneath the blush of her cheeks.

"Thank you." She dropped her hands to her sides and rested her head against the pillow.

He deposited the empty juice container on the table. "I'll find you some more."

"Thank you, but I'll wait."

She sounded tired, but at least she wasn't angry anymore. "Try to get some rest." He brushed a few strands of hair from her cheek. Her lips parted a little, and he quickly removed his hand.

"I'll be back later to check on you."

He was halfway to the door when she said, "My animals. Don't you want my address?"

Shit! "Yes, of course. Figured admin would have it on file." He knew exactly where she lived, but admitting that would raise more questions.

"But you don't have the key to my townhouse."

He scanned the area for her clothes. "I don't see the clothes you were wearing anywhere." Usually, the hospital staff shoved people's belongings into a bag that accompanied the patient.

"There's a spare under the big rock to the right of the front door. I live in Henderson. 5555 Matson Drive. Unit ten. Last townhouse on the right."

Hiding a key in an obvious place wasn't smart. "That doesn't sound like a safe place to hide a key."

"I don't have anything to steal. I'm not worried about it."

He pursed his lips. "Is the cat food under the sink?"

"Yes—it's... Wait a minute, I didn't say I have cats." She cocked her head in his direction.

"You look like a cat person."

"I do?"

He'd assumed it was cats because if she had a dog, it would have been with her when they'd met at the park. "Doesn't matter if it's a gerbil. We'll take care of it. See you later, Jane."

"Mr. Selkirk? Tell whoever takes care of my girls not to leave any doors or windows open. Peony and Piper will make a break for it."

He stopped next to the bathroom door and turned a look over his shoulder. "I'll do that."

"You know—when I was on the pavement, someone spoke to me. I thought I was dreaming, but he told me not to give up."

She'd heard him.

Jane tilted her head when he remained silent. "That voice sounded like yours."

"There were a lot of people around you. Brain trauma can cause strange effects."

"Probably," she murmured. "Thank you for coming, Mr. Selkirk. And just so we're on the same page, I don't believe you're a floor guy. Let Mr. Laker know I won't sue the resort. I'm to blame."

He believed her, but didn't care if she did or didn't sue. "I'll do that, and my name's Nathan."

She rolled onto her side to face him, tucking her hand under her cheek. The thin sheet folded around the curve of her hip and defined her slender waist. "Thanks for taking the time to drop by."

He'd stayed too long and resisted the urge to stay longer.

"I'll see you soon, Jane."

Nathan left satisfied that her injuries weren't fatal. Offering to lend a hand with her cats wasn't stepping over the line. He'd notify Vince Laker, but Royal Jade's insurance would cover any medical bills her own insurance wouldn't. Nathan's job as director of operations oversaw issues like these. He'd make sure she was safe and then fade into the background.

CHAPTER THREE

At four o'clock on the eastern edge of Henderson, Nathan found the townhouse complex where Jane lived. An older, lower-income neighborhood. He parked his car in front of her address and strolled up the cracked cement walkway to the front door. Turning over a rock the size of a bowling ball, he found the key and unlocked the door, stepping into the entry that wasn't much bigger than a few floor tiles' width.

Two white cats ran toward him, then stopped when they realized a stranger stood there instead of their beautiful keeper. The pure white Persian seemed less timid and took a few extra paces, wrapping herself around his leg, giving him a quick meow. The other cat had a sleek, shiny coat and kept a wary eye on him from a distance.

"Hungry, girls?"

He reached down and swept his hand over the Persian's thick fur. The cat responded with a throaty purr, and she took another turn around his ankles. A staircase to his left, just past the entrance, led to the second story. A small living room sat to his right. He headed down the narrow hallway toward the back of the unit.

At the end of the hall, he found a tiny but pristine kitchen with white cabinets. Three white walls and one bold blue accent wall to offset the starkness. He found the cat food under the sink and topped up their dishes sitting next to the patio door. Nathan filled the water bowls as well. Both cats came running when they heard the kibble hit the ceramic dishes.

While the cats ate their dinner, he wandered into the living room, which was considerably smaller than his walk-in closet. She'd decorated in yellows, deep browns, and beige. A comfortable, well-used leather chair sat below a floor lamp, craning over the empty seat. To his right was a large desk heaped with paperwork and a laptop computer.

No TV in sight, but paperbacks crammed the built-in shelves. *So, you enjoy reading.* He peered at the titles, mostly mysteries, and a few classics. Continuing to survey her literary choices, he found a collection of romance novels on the bottom shelf and tipped one out of the collection.

Opening the novel, he landed in the middle of a steamy scene. With a grin, he squeezed the book back into its slot and saw more of the same genre nearby.

"Erotica, huh? Interesting."

He wondered whether she'd enjoy storytime if he read her a book.

Earlier, she admitted she didn't have a boyfriend, and his pulse had skipped with a few excited beats. Tracing his index finger across the spines of her romance novels, he imagined turning her fiction into reality.

The thought brought an intense roll to his gut and a sizeable swelling behind his zipper. Most of the time, she wore work boots, jeans, a ball cap, and dirty gloves, but it didn't matter. Compared to Bonita's bleached hair, filled lips, and boob enhancements, Jane was a royal flush compared to his ex. Bonita never left her bedroom without a full face of makeup and designer clothes.

His gaze wandered around the humble home, and he'd give his soul to see Jane with her hair mussed, wearing a simple robe, greeting him in the morning with a sexy smile.

He laughed at himself. Her natural beauty pressed all the right buttons. As much as he wanted to ignore his attraction to Jane, it constantly strobed in the back of his mind.

Although he'd done nothing but watch her for two years, that didn't mean he didn't dream about her or think about her a lot. He did.

During his first year of marriage, Bonita screwed around on him. She'd apologized, and he'd accepted. More affairs followed, but on the rare occasion when Bonita wanted servicing, usually after downing a bottle of vodka, he'd fulfilled his husbandly duty to keep the peace.

Where he laid his head at night wasn't a home. He and Bonita stopped sleeping in the same bed six months after they'd married. But when his wife drank too much, she always found her way to his bedroom door. A while back, during one of her screaming jags, she'd threatened divorce. Nathan jumped at the opportunity and agreed. Instantly.

A week later, he'd literally dropped the pen on the dining room table after signing the separation agreement his attorney sent, and Bonita wanted to fuck him. The woman couldn't separate the drama-doused movies she acted in from real life. He'd made a monumental mistake by marrying the actress, but the charade was over.

Nathan surveyed Jane's simple living room, sparse instead of cluttered, so far removed from the elegant décor at his residence. A few framed photographs caught his eye. He walked to the wall separating the hallway from the living room to have a closer look. Jane and two friends, a blonde and a brunette, arms draped over each other's shoulders, smiled at the camera. He squinted to see the name of the hotel behind them.

"The Empress."

The brick building, covered in ivy, looked distinctly English in architecture. He scanned the other photographs. The same women hammed it up in front of a wax figure of Queen Elizabeth. In the next picture, they stood on a dock. Behind them, a large vessel sat alongside with the name Victoria Clipper painted on the bow.

"Huh." Further down the wall, he came across a picture where the women were jammed in with a mob of people. They'd painted their cheeks with red and white maple leaves. He backed up a step and looked at all the pictures. "A trip to Canada," he surmised.

He scanned the room, seeing it as a whole. The lodge pole couch with a heavy American Indian blanket thrown over the armrest added a rustic décor. The few pieces of colorful artwork that covered her walls were definitely modern Native American.

He wandered up the stairs, following more photographs of places she and her friends had visited. Mount Rushmore. The Washington Monument. New York. When he reached the bedroom, he stopped, wondering whether to enter. The door stood ajar. White cotton sheets, brilliant red pillows, and a red throw graced the queen bed. Everything was in its place—neat and tidy.

Two framed pictures sitting on a small dresser caught his eye. The first showed two crosses covered in yellow roses, rising from a snowdrift against a mountainside. Despite its beauty, with the sunset and blue sky in the background, the photo served as a poignant reminder that she'd lost two people from her life. Two people she cared about. A news clipping sat in the second frame. Nathan picked it up and read the headline: Avalanche takes two and leaves one. A grainy photo of the same women and Jane sat mid-column.

Revelstoke, B.C. He read the article explaining the accident. The women had remained trapped for three days; her two friends expired within forty-eight hours, but Jane lived long enough for rescuers to save her life. They'd been skidooing in a popular area when the mountain let go. Jane looked the same then as she did now. Maybe that's what brought her to Nevada.

He glanced down at the white Persian, who wrapped herself around his pant leg again. Nathan bent and picked her up, the cat purring instantly. He walked over to the bed and sat down.

"So, your mistress has an adventurous soul."

The cat purred louder as it flexed its claws against his chest. The other cat jumped onto the bed and rubbed up against his back. Guess the kibble made him family.

"You girls are lonely, aren't you? She'll be home soon." He placed the Persian on the bed, and both cats curled up for a nap near the pillows.

With her animals fed, there wasn't much else he needed to do. Nathan checked the back door to make sure it was secure and left the townhouse. He would have brought Jane some books, but she couldn't see, so that wouldn't help. He grinned with a better idea.

****

Nathan headed home to change. Reaching the driveway to his residence, he stopped on the street. Behind the gated entry, he saw Bonita's white Porsche parked by the garage.

"Fuck."

She'd been living in Malibu for the last three months. What the hell was she doing here? Instead of facing a round of melodrama and however many gin and tonics she'd downed, he did a quick U-turn.

After grabbing a bite at the Jade and picking up Jane's gift, he arrived at the hospital around eight p.m.

"How's the most beautiful patient in the hospital doing?" he asked, then slammed his mouth shut before more compliments rushed out. He pulled the chair beside her bed.

"Mr. Selkirk, did someone feed my girls?"

"I think they miss you, and it's Nathan, remember? How's your head?"

"Feels like a thousand ball-peen hammers striking at once. They gave me some pain relievers, but they're not helping to relieve anything."

"I brought you something. Thought it might help instead of you laying there looking at the inside of those bandages for hours."

"Okay." A delicate smile curled her lips. "Anything would help. I'm going stir-crazy here. Are you sure you can't ask the doctor to let me go home?"

"Not yet." He curled his fingers over her hand, guiding it to the book reader.

"What's this?" She touched the edge gingerly and let her fingers trace over the keyboard at the bottom.

"I'll show you." He guided her finger to three buttons and helped her select a story. A male automated voice began reading the novel.

A smile thrust itself onto her face, and she nodded. "That's great, thank you so much. I'll give it back when they take these silly bandages off."

"No need. I bought it for you. I downloaded a few mysteries and some classics."

"Seriously, you can let the resort know I'm not suing. This isn't necessary."

"They..." He paused. "It's nothing. And—well, there's another genre in there too."

"Another?" Her brow furrowed.

"Yeah, but you might want to keep the volume down on those or use earbuds. I bought you a pair."

"What?" She barked with laughter. "Oh my God, you went to my place and snooped in my bookshelf."

"I'd call it reconnaissance, not snooping," he said while grinning.

Her cheeks blushed, and he backed away, sitting in the guest chair. The urge to kiss her was far too potent.

"Who are you, really?" she asked. "After you left earlier, my nurse described you. Not only does she want a date, by the way, but she thinks you're an executive, which would explain why you're here."

With one sense temporarily debilitated, her other senses had kicked in. "I told you, I'm no one special. Just concerned."

Jane crossed her arms and pursed her lips. "I don't believe you."

He chuckled. "Until those bandages come off, guess you'll have to trust me. In the meantime, I can read one of those spicy books you like."

A smile revealed Jane's straight, white teeth. "I'd like to hear that."

He took the eReader from her lap and selected a story. "I'm up for that if you are." Nathan was having too much fun kidding around with her.

"I'm joking," she drawled.

"Uh-huh, I'm not."

She burst out laughing and lay against the stacked pillows. "All right, mystery man, go ahead. Embarrass yourself."

"Compared to what I've seen in Vegas, doubt that." He leaned back in the uncomfortable chair. Lucky for them, the other bed in the semi-private room remained vacant. Opening the story, he dove into the novel. "Lacy jumped up from her beach towel, forgetting that she'd untied her tiny bikini top earlier. Too late, she stood in front of Matt with her taut breasts and hardened nipples, glistening with suntan lotion for his full viewing pleasure."

Jane placed a hand over her mouth to hide a wide smile.

"Sounds like Matt's a lucky guy." And he continued to read.

****

Jane rolled onto her side and fluffed the pillow. She listened to the deep tone of Nathan's voice as he read the novel. He said he worked for the casino but didn't specify his position. There was no doubt in her mind that he was the person who had spoken to her after the accident.

She kinda loved his comforting, low timbre. Sexy, if she wanted to be truthful about it. Because Jane didn't have her sight, the nurse filled in the blanks by describing him as seriously handsome. But more importantly, he sounded like an honest man. When he'd wrapped his large hand over her fingers, the innocent but confident contact had washed away her anxiety.

Nathan continued to read the erotic tale. It was a sexy, lighthearted story, but coming from his lips made it so much hotter. When he read the love scenes, he didn't stutter or sound embarrassed. His voice dropped a little lower and became huskier, as if the sensual story affected him. She licked her lips, and he paused a moment, taking a breath. The only sound was the tick from the equipment monitoring her vitals.

"Ah, maybe this wasn't such a good idea," he said.

Her cheeks puckered with a smile. "Can't stand the heat?"

"Not when I'm reading it to you."

Her heart beat like a drum. If he was as good-looking as the nurse said, why didn't he have a wife? Maybe he did, but he had to make sure Jane wouldn't sue the resort. "If you want another change in profession, you should consider narration." His warm chuckle made her skin tingle.

"I'll remember that."

She didn't startle when his finger traced her cheek with what seemed like a genuine touch of concern. "I appreciate the reader and your visit, but shouldn't you be with your family? It's late, isn't it?"

"If I had one, I would be."

He seemed like a guy who could take a joke. "So I can tell the nurse you're free for a date."

"Not interested in the nurse."

Her fingers itched to touch the angles of his face. "She'll be disappointed."

"Don't care," he said, his voice husky. "Jane?"

"What?" she answered, happier than expected when he'd returned to keep her company.

"Maybe I should read *'War and Peace'* instead."

"I think...whatever you read is fine." His visits brought a welcome distraction from the hospital's monotonous atmosphere. Footsteps. Trollies. Buzzers.

His fingers threaded through her hair. She loved the scent of his aftershave. Present but not overpowering. A sweet but smoky nuance. As if he'd read her mind, Nathan lifted her hand and pressed her palm against his sharp jaw. Gently, she slid her fingertips across his skin and across the coarse stubble of whiskers.

"Jane, we need to take your blood pressure," a woman said.

She heard the tinny sound of a cart rolling across the floor and the crackle of Velcro.

"Blood pressure, huh?" Nathan commented. "It might be a little high right now."

She felt his cheek tighten in her palm. "Good timing," she said, smirking.

"Good thing they don't want to take mine." He chuckled. "I think that's about all the reading I can stand for one night. Get some rest. I'll see you tomorrow."

"Night, and thanks for taking care of my cats. And the eReader," she blurted.

A warm kiss brushed her forehead, and goosebumps rushed across her skin.

"You're welcome."

"Is that your boyfriend?" The nurse wrapped the blood pressure cuff around her left arm.

"No, he's a mystery. Never met him before."

"Whoa, some mystery."

"What does he—" She paused, not knowing whether she wanted a second opinion. Maybe he was better as a mystery, but curiosity got the better of her. "Another nurse said he was cute. Tall. Broad shoulders. She described him as an executive type."

Jane recognized the sound of the ball being pumped to inflate the cuff and felt the band squeeze her arm.

"Hmm, I wouldn't call him cute. More like drop-dead gorgeous. Wouldn't describe him as an executive either. Not in a clean-cut, politician way. I have a girlfriend who married a Marine. You know that rugged, confident type? Your mystery man reminds me of him, but he does wear a suit."

Plenty of Americans served their country. Nathan said he'd served in the Special Forces. "I know he works at the Royal Jade, where I have one of my contracts."

"What do you do?"

"I'm a landscaper. I keep the grounds green and colorful."

"Nice. I think I'd like working in the fresh air. Even when it's blistering hot. Plants don't scream when you yank them outta the ground, either."

Jane grinned. "No, but they do sting and bite sometimes."

"Yeah, I guess so. So do kids when you give 'em a needle."

They both laughed.

The cuff stopped tightening around Jane's upper arm and then slowly released.

"Once your eyesight comes back, you'll like what you see. He has those intense kind of eyes that pierce your soul."

She doubted she'd find him attractive. Hardly any man attracted her attention. "From his hands, I think he's big and probably very strong."

"You're right," the nurse said. "Seriously broad shoulders, and it's easy to see he works out."

"I like his voice. He sounds—kinda hot."

The nurse unwrapped the cuff from Jane's arm. "I don't think you're too far from the mark there, either."

"Really?"

"No question," she said, then fell silent. "Hmm."

"What?"

"Your blood pressure is low. Do you know whether you're normally that way? Some people are."

"No, I used to be pretty constant, maybe 117 over 80. Something like that."

"It's a lot lower than that."

Jane pulled the bedsheet over her right shoulder. "Please don't tell me I have to stay more than another day. I'm going crazy here."

"From what I heard, you've got some interesting reading to bide your time."

She blushed and rolled her lips together. "Not to mention a vivid imagination."

"So a gorgeous man you don't know shows up, bringing expensive book readers and reads you erotic romance. Why the hell doesn't shit like that happen to me?"

"I know. Doesn't make sense. It'd be just my luck to get hit by a car and then stalked by a serial killer."

The nurse laughed. "I don't think that's the case."

"He seems nice enough, but I think he's here to make sure I don't sue the resort."

"Maybe, but I don't get that vibe from him. You know, you

can just tell sometimes."

Naturally curious, especially about Nathan, she asked, "Why do you say that?"

"The way he looks at you. As a nurse, I've seen that look many times from worried husbands. He's definitely concerned."

"He said his name is Nathan Selkirk."

The nurse drew a sharp breath.

"What? Do you know who he is?"

"Um. No. Nope."

"You do too. Don't lie."

"Sorry, hun, but I can tell you he's a handsome man women wouldn't easily forget."

"Meaning?"

"About six-foot-four and not an ounce of gangly. He's all muscle." She fingered the tape covering the IV in Jane's hand. "I'll let the on-duty physician know about your pressure reading."

She wanted to get the heck out of here and heal at home. "Do you have to?"

"Yes, I have to." She checked the bandages on Jane's eyes. "Can you see any light yet?"

"Actually, I can. A little."

"I'll dim the lights. Rest, and if you can't sleep, ring the buzzer." She slid the call button into Jane's palm. "I can give you a mild sedative, but only a mild one."

"Thanks. What's your name, by the way?"

"Karen. I'm on duty for another ten hours. Night shift for the next few days."

Jane saw a slight darkening beyond her bandage when Karen lowered the lights. "I seriously want to get out of this place."

The nurse patted her arm. "You and everyone else in here."

****

Nathan waited while the wrought-iron gates automatically yawned open at the entrance to his property. He'd considered going back to the Jade and sleeping there, but with any luck,

Bonita had retired for the night. He drove past green lawns and cultured bushes toward the high-end house built ten years ago. A clear statement of architecture meant for the rich, with off-white stone walls and lighting to augment the multi-peak roofline.

When the judge completed their divorce and he knew for certain that the residence was legally his, he'd sell the monstrosity. He didn't need nine bedrooms and fifteen bathrooms. Fucking ridiculous.

When it came to their assets, he'd played it like a guy with a winning hand, but in this case, he shoved all but one chip at Bonita. Take it all but the Las Vegas residence. They had a prenup. Part of the agreement stated he'd receive three million and this home. He didn't need or want the money. He'd sold his fucking sanity and his soul. Time to reclaim both.

One of the six-car garage doors slid open, and he parked inside. He turned off the engine but didn't move. Besides his motorcycle, some outdoor sports gear stored on a single shelving unit, and a couple of garbage cans the garage was as pristine as the interior of the extravagant home.

He remembered his parents' garage stacked floor to ceiling with cardboard boxes. Dad's tools covered the workbench. Bikes, two freezers, and the smell of oil always lingered in the air. With all his siblings, there were plenty of hand-me-downs. Old toys that Mom wouldn't get rid of waited for the day she'd have grandchildren. Nothing went to waste.

At thirty-nine, Nathan doubted he'd ever have kids. Bonita freaked out when he mentioned starting a family. She thought it would end her career. Ruin her body. In the back of his mind, he'd been certain divorce, not children, was in his future. He'd been right.

Making his way into the designer kitchen with an eight-burner gas stove and top-of-the-line appliances, he saw an empty gin bottle sitting on the counter and three slices of lime on a cutting board.

He tossed the bottle into recycling.

Their housekeeper worked from six until four. A friendly middle-aged woman who'd emigrated from Mexico years ago. Maria had silently put up with Bonita's tirades because she needed to feed her family of six children. Unbeknownst to Bonita, Nathan gave their housekeeper a ten-grand bonus every Christmas. He'd have to make sure he found her alternative employment once he sold the place.

Instead of grabbing a beer, he headed for his bedroom in the east wing of the vacuous house. Hanging up his suit, he changed into workout pants and a T-shirt. He exited by the back entry and into the balmy evening, walking across the cobblestone path edged with in-ground lighting under the covered breezeway. A blast of cool air struck his face as he entered the workout building.

Top-of-the-line fitness equipment filled the space. Durable and versatile, Nathan used most of the pieces during each hourly session, including the weights and cardio equipment. In the morning, he ran five miles around and through his neighborhood. He left the SEAL teams behind, but not his physical fitness.

After stretching, he tackled the weights. Ten minutes into his workout, the door opened.

"You're home late," Bonita said, leaning against the wall with a crystal tumbler clutched in her fingers.

He eased the bar onto the supports and sat up on the bench. "Didn't expect to see you again."

Wearing a pair of designer jeans and a V-neck red blouse, she swept her blonde hair over one bony shoulder. "I want to talk. Been waiting for you all day."

She didn't appear completely shitfaced. "Thought you were working on a film."

"Finished it." She swallowed the liquor and set the empty glass on the table next to a stack of white towels. She strode across the room and straddled the bench, facing him. "I wanted to tell you myself, but as usual, the paparazzi caught wind of my relationship."

Nathan had seen the photos of Bonita with her co-star, probably in his early twenties. "Hope it works out."

Her eyes squinted. "Don't you care that someone else loves me?"

This wasn't the first time she'd fucked around on him. After the first couple of times, he stacked her indiscretions like he would firewood.

"Bonita, you and I never had a marriage. Least, not in the way I imagined."

She'd used his past service in the teams like she'd gone through those years as his wife. She hadn't. Bonita wanted brownie points from her fans by pretending to understand what military wives dealt with, especially the Special Ops spouses. A huge mistake on her part, because social media lit up with the partners of serving members and called her out on her bullshit.

Savvy to the negative backlash, she quickly changed gears and started a campaign for his position in the resort industry. Her husband, the up-and-coming success story. Bonita's public image took priority over everything.

"You never loved me," she accused. "All you cared about were my connections."

Vince Laker cared, but he didn't. "You had expectations that differed from mine. We should have figured that out before we married."

"I honestly loved you. I saw your potential, but you wasted your time. You're more dedicated to Vince than me."

He sighed and rubbed the back of his neck. "Is there a point to this conversation? You're involved with someone else."

Her mouth twitched. "So are you. I don't know who she is, but I know there's someone. I found comfort with other men because every time I tried to fix us, you pushed me away."

"Is that after the first or second time you screwed around on me? I've never touched another woman during our marriage, Bonita."

Her nostrils flared. "We could have taken the world by the balls, but you threw it away. I don't understand why."

Nathan wasn't sure whose balls she was talking about. "There's nothing to understand. We come from different stock. Have different priorities. You live your life through trending gossip and the next film. I wanted a family. You didn't. I don't give a shit about fame. You use it to breathe. There's nothing to regret. We're not compatible."

Tears rimmed her eyes. "People are blaming me for the divorce. Vicious rumors about me fucking other men."

He chuckled. Bonita didn't give a shit about their marriage —she only cared about her image in the headlines. "They're not rumors. You *did* fuck around on me. Several times. I don't care how you spin the story. People get divorced all the time. It only takes fifteen minutes for folks to become captivated by the next big controversy."

"At least do me the decency of telling me who she is."

Yeah, right. As if he'd allow Bonita to use Jane, innocent of everything except for his admiration, as her excuse for the divorce.

"You want to point a finger at someone? Point it at me." He laid back on the bench and gripped the bar to press a few more pounds. "You've got a new boy toy. Move on."

"But he's not you. None of them have been you, Nathan. I want to try again. I'll honor our vows, I promise." She gripped his knee. "Please."

He grunted, bench pressing the hundred and seventy-five-pound weight. He had to wonder whether her newest fuck-buddy dumped her after the movie finished filming.

"Please, Nathan. Talk to me." She lay her hand on his leg and caressed his thigh. "I don't want to give up on our marriage."

After five reps, he eased the bar onto the supports. "Listen, sweetheart, you've got a million adoring fans and scripts piling up. You shouldn't give a shit what a few tabloids write. And you sure as hell don't need me."

Outside the fitness room, her yappy terrier barked at the door.

"Men are always trying to get in my pants. Millions of people adore me. Why don't you?"

Jesus Christ! Her narcissism burned hot tonight. She couldn't stand the idea that someone didn't swoon at her feet. Bonita glared at him, wanting an answer. She had a reputation for being a heartless and demanding woman. She used empathy as a tool of the trade when it suited her. While some actors who'd reached fame gave back to their communities, Bonita bought a new Porsche and took a three-month holiday in the tropics. He'd searched for qualities—any qualities she might have—to ignore the rest and keep their marriage afloat. Didn't happen.

The teammates he stayed in touch with considered him crazy for marrying the woman. They'd been right. Ian Kelly, his swim buddy and best friend, tried to talk some sense into him before he'd put a ring on her finger. He should have listened.

By the time he caught wind of her first affair, he already knew their marriage had little hope of surviving.

She wanted to know why he didn't adore her. The truth sat on the tip of his tongue, but he wasn't raised that way. "I had plenty of opportunities to be unfaithful. But I made a vow to you. I kept that vow. You didn't. We're separated. Sign the divorce papers."

She balled her hands and screeched. "Fuck you, Nathan. You don't give a shit about my career and the damage this will do. You're a heartless bastard."

Striding across the gym's rubber flooring, he sat on the WaterRower. Bonita slammed the door behind her.

He shook his head. "Exit stage left."

CHAPTER FOUR

"**G**ood morning, Jane."

Drifting in and out of sleep, the man's voice jolted her awake. It wasn't Nathan.

She stretched and sat up. "Owww." Her left hip voiced its disapproval, and her neck hurt like hell, too.

"Little sore, huh?" He prodded her neck with his fingers. "I'm Doctor Nelson."

"Hi, Doc. So, you're releasing me today, right?" His hands pressed on her hip, and she tried not to wince.

"Not today, Jane. You're lucky you didn't break any bones. I understand the taxi hit you pretty hard."

"It felt hard, believe me," she said, while his hands gently pressed her shoulders back against the pillow.

"Your blood pressure is of concern, though."

"Can't be that bad. Other than my vision, I'm good to go, right?"

"Let's find out." He placed a cuff around her left arm. "How severe are your headaches?"

"Nothing I can't handle. Doctor, I'm pretty sure my insurance company wants me out of here."

After the cuff deflated, the doc was silent for a moment. "I don't deal with those matters, but there's no issue that I know of." He removed the cuff. "Jane, I'm going to order an MRI for you. There's no good reason for your pressure to be this low."

"I feel fine."

"You would until you tried to stand up, and then you'd pass out. I'll come back after I get the MRI results."

Once the doctor left, the overpowering need to use the

bathroom hit her. The nursing staff had put her in a diaper that she dearly wanted to remove. Relieving herself like a toddler wasn't happening. A short walk to the bathroom couldn't hurt. She'd just have to feel her way along the wall until she found it. Jane swung her legs off the bed and pushed herself to a sitting position.

When her feet hit the floor, she lost her bearings, gripped in a severe dizzy spell. Before she crumpled into a heap, someone wrapped their arms around her waist.

****

Nathan walked down the hallway toward Jane's hospital room. She'd been on his mind all night. He should have just slept in a chair beside her bed.

After their conversation, Bonita had dove into another bottle of gin. Three sheets to the wind, she'd hammered on his bedroom door around two in the morning. He endured a barrage of yelling, tears, and then the sickening sensual plea to let her in and make love to her.

By not responding, she slammed every door she crossed until she'd finally reached her own room.

Falling asleep seemed far away as he'd laid in bed, staring at the white vaulted ceiling, worried about Jane, but exhaustion finally closed his eyes. In his dreams, his mind wandered to the moments they'd shared. Spending a short amount of time with her solidified the notion that they had an unforgettable chemistry. One he needed to ignore.

Halfway through the night, Nathan woke with a stiff cock. The more he tried to think of anything else, the more her smile invaded his thoughts. What the hell was it about Jane that squeezed his heart into a tight ball? He had no choice but to maintain a friendly but distant relationship.

Sunlight poured into his bedroom, forcing his eyes to open and revealing the backyard with its glistening swimming pool. Too late to take a morning run, he showered and left the house by seven a.m., heading for the hospital to see Jane before work.

When he stepped into her hospital room, she swung her legs over the edge of the bed. That looked like progress and he smiled, but it didn't last long as her legs buckled.

"Jane!" He lunged across the room, catching her before she hit the floor.

He lifted her onto the bed. Two nurses ran into the room.

A nurse named Anna reached the bed first. "Oh my, she tried to get up, didn't she?"

What the fuck was going on? Nathan glared at the brunette while the other nurse checked Jane's vitals.

"Why did she collapse?"

"Low blood pressure," the blonde RN named Nicki answered.

"From what?"

"We're not sure. The doctor has ordered an MRI."

"Mr. Selkirk." He snapped his attention to Anna. "You don't have to leave, but if you could give me some room so I can take her blood pressure again." He moved to the other side of the bed and held Jane's right hand. The normally rosy hue on her cheeks had paled.

"Pressure's dropped even farther. Call the doctor," Anna stated, her voice considerably tighter.

"What's the matter?" he asked.

Nicki glanced across the bed at him. "Mr. Selkirk, if you could wait outside."

"Tell me what the hell is going on?" he said harshly. She stepped aside, and he read the pressure. Seventy over fifty-five. "Holy shit."

A minute later, the on-duty physician rushed into the room. Nicki gave him a quick summary.

"She needs an MRI now," the doctor instructed. "Take her downstairs." The physician finally noticed him. "This will take some time. You can wait, or we can call you when we know more."

Nathan stepped out of the way as the nurses prepared to roll Jane's bed from the room. "She's out cold. You must have some idea."

The doctor scribbled something on Jane's chart. "Not sure. That's why she's going down for an MRI."

Two hours later, they rolled Jane back into her room.

"Where's the doctor?" he boomed. He hadn't budged from the guest chair, using his cell to answer emails and call his admin assistant, Barb, to tell her he'd be in later.

"He's coming, sir." A nurse he hadn't seen before maneuvered the bed into place against the off-white wall.

"Jane?" He quickly stepped to her side, but she didn't answer.

Seconds later, the doc from Emergency, the one he'd spoken to when she was first admitted, walked through the open doorway. "Dr. Nelson. What's happening?"

"The MRI revealed what's causing her low pressure. The swelling in her head has increased and is pressing against a major artery in her brain. It's cutting off the oxygen. We can treat it a couple of ways."

"I don't give a shit. Just treat it," he said, interrupting the physician's diagnosis.

"Mr. Selkirk, we will, but you need to know the options before we go ahead. Neither is without risk."

"Options?" They wanted *him* to choose?

"We can operate and release some of the swelling, but any time brain surgery is involved, it's extremely dangerous."

"What's the other option?"

"It's slower, but with medication, we can try to bring down the swelling. It's a tipping scale. The longer her oxygen remains at a diminished level, the higher the risk of brain damage. Either way, there's a high risk of permanent damage."

Nathan's heart twisted into a knot. He rammed his fingers through his hair. Jane's future was in his hands. What would she choose? "Is she awake?"

"No, she's in a mild coma."

"How mild? Can she hear me?"

"It's possible, but she wouldn't be able to respond."

"Let me try. I want to talk with her."

The neurologist nodded. I have another patient to see. I'll be back shortly.

For two long years, he'd kept his distance. All that lost time. He leaned over and pressed a gentle kiss on her soft, sleeping lips. The hospital staff had removed the bandages, and he wished she'd open her eyes.

"Wake up, Jane." He placed his mouth next to her ear. "Sweetheart, we haven't shared more than a few hours together." He drew back and gazed at her tranquil expression. "The doctor can help you, but there's a risk either way. Medication, which is slower and could mean some damage the longer you stay this way, or surgery." He tipped his forehead against hers. "No matter what happens, you'll be safe. I'll make sure of it." He held her hand. "God, why you?" She'd survived an experience that most couldn't, and now this. "I know you're a fighter. Fight now. Tell me what to do." He waited, his heart getting heavier by the second. "I think you should have the surgery." He felt a small squeeze on his fingers. He almost missed it; it was so slight. "All right, the surgery."

When he looked up, Dr. Nelson stood beside him with a rueful smile. "I think so too. It's her best chance."

****

The surgery took ten hours, and although Nathan returned to his office at the Royal Jade, his thoughts remained with Jane. Just about every emotion passed through his heart. At five p.m. his cell rang, and he snapped up the phone.

"Mr. Selkirk?"

"Doctor, how is she?"

"She's stable. The swelling has receded considerably, and after she goes through the recovery room, she should regain consciousness and we'll assess at that time."

He breathed a sigh of relief. "Thank you. When can I see her?"

"Wait until tomorrow. And, of course, because of the surgery, we had to shave her head."

"I see. She won't like that much."

"Most women don't. Have a good evening."

After visiting Jane's townhouse and feeding the cats, Nathan spent the night in his office. He worked late, catching up on paperwork now that he knew Jane was out of danger. He opted to sleep on the leather couch in his office rather than go home.

His cell lit up every five minutes with texts from Bonita, demanding he come home.

She had thousands of young fans who thought she walked on water. The actress set fashion trends and spent most of her free time posting on social media. Filming two movies a year had given him a little peace while she'd stayed on location.

He'd spent five years in a bogus marriage with a woman who had as much substance as the shit her yappy mutt left all over the backyard. Finalizing their divorce couldn't come fast enough.

After reviewing the casino's quarterlies, Nathan loosened his tie and lay on the couch. A casino never sleeps. The sound of footsteps in the hall or murmurs of people talking broke the silence. Employees worked round the clock in many departments.

Neon lights from the never-ending glow of the Strip leached through his floor-to-ceiling windows, bringing him out of a restless sleep around three a.m. He dragged his legs over the edge of the couch and wandered to gaze out at the early morning activity on the world-famous boulevard.

The City of Sin had provided a good life for him in some ways. His fierce green eyes reflected back at him in the window. With his tie gone and his crisply ironed shirt rumpled from sleep, he saw a different man than he'd been ten years ago. He stared at his reflection, his jaw rigid. He'd accomplished a lot since arriving, but he'd also made mistakes.

From time to time, Nathan pondered if he had made an error by leaving the SEAL teams. But if he hadn't, he wouldn't have met Jane.

She worked hard, etching out a living like so many others. Jane had a simple life, but he never meant to be part of it.

What did he expect from her? Nothing in his life had changed except for his imminent divorce, which would free him from Bonita's pompous world, although his wasn't much better. Getting close to Jane only heightened his curiosity.

Would she remember when she saw him for the first time? Would she recall the evening they spoke to each other in the park? His brow creased with indecision. Maybe he shouldn't give her that chance. After the hospital released her, he'd hire someone to care for her and remove himself from the picture.

His world revolved around the Royal Jade. Not only the day-to-day operations but also rubbing shoulders with the wealthy. He worked long hours. Her day ended at four. Sunshine and Mother Nature defined Jane's existence. The resort's operation consumed his time. As a bachelor, there was no one to let down.

Yet his attraction to Jane burned. Like a moth to a lit kitchen window, his heart fluttered endlessly, wanting inside.

Morning arrived with a stiff back, and he groaned. Soon as Nathan's eyes opened, he cleaned up and headed straight for the hospital. Before he reached her room, he heard her voice.

"They cut my hair off. God, what the hell?"

"They couldn't get to your brain through your ear, Jane," a woman replied.

"You're a laugh a minute, Karen."

He stopped in the doorway, suppressing a grin. "So, I see she's back to being a pain in the ass."

Jane's chin shot up at hearing his voice, but her eyes remained closed.

Karen turned with one eyebrow raised. "How'd ya guess?"

"Don't come in here, Nathan," Jane ordered.

He shook his head and smiled at the nurse, who shifted the guest chair next to the bed.

She gave him a quick wink and a pat on the back. "She's doing fine."

A thick bandage wrapped around Jane's head, but hospital

staff had removed the one covering her eyes.

"Nathan—leave."

"What? Why?"

"Just leave."

"Jane," he growled. "Hair grows back. Don't worry about it."

"Leave."

"Nope."

She pulled the covers over her head and rolled onto her side, facing the wall. "Leave," she mumbled from under the sheets.

"Not going to happen, Jane." He grabbed her hip and carefully rolled her onto her back. He laughed, seeing she still had the sheet firmly tucked over her head. "Jesus, woman, I've seen you covered in dirt and dripping with sweat from all the hard work you do. Do you think I give a shit that your hair is gone because they had to save your life?"

A mumbled "yes" came from under the blanket.

What a character! He laughed and grabbed the sheet. Even though she held on tight, he pulled it down to her chin.

"Nathan, what's the matter with you? Go home. Go to work. Go wherever it is that you came from."

"Can't work. Can't sleep. Open your eyes, sweetheart."

"No." She growled and tried to yank the sheet up again.

"God, you're stubborn, aren't you?"

"Yes, go away," she blurted.

The rosy color had returned to her cheek, which he grazed with his finger. "Open your eyes."

"I can't see anything. All I can see is light and fuzzy images."

"That will change soon, but you won't see anything unless you open your damn eyes."

Her long lashes fluttered and revealed those beautiful pale green irises. His heart twisted into a tight knot. "Hey there."

"Why do you keep coming back?" she asked, looking in his direction but not focusing.

"I told you."

"I don't believe you. A floor guy at a casino can't deal with medical bills, and mine must be out-of-this-world expensive.

Don't think my insurance covers brain surgery."

"Jane, the Royal Jade has insurance, and it covers contractors. So relax."

"A floor guy wouldn't know that. You had something to do with working this out. The question is, why would you do that for me? I don't know you."

"No, you don't, but you can trust me. Everything is going to be okay. I promise I have your best interest at heart." Turning his back on her wasn't an option.

She blinked and exhaled out her pert little nose. "The doctor said you decided they should operate."

"You were in a light coma. I told you the choices. Whether it was a reflex or not, I don't know, but you squeezed my hand when I suggested the operation."

She pursed her lips. "I would have done the same thing."

A hospital worker pushed a service cart in front of the door and slid a tray of food from the slats, then entered the room. "Breakfast is served," he said brightly.

Jane wrinkled her nose. "What's on the menu?"

"Sustenance," the guy said, shifting the overbed table next to Nathan and setting the tray down. "Bon appetite."

Nathan positioned the mini-tabletop over her lap. Jane fingered the plastic cover on the tray. "What is it?" she asked.

He removed the top for her. "Looks like peaches, toast, and, ah, scrambled eggs with bacon."

"I'm not hungry."

He picked up the spoon. "Maybe not, but you need to eat, so open wide."

She spit out a laugh. "You're gonna feed me." Her voice climbed an octave.

"You want to get out of this place or not?"

She rolled her eyes. "Sure hope they don't serve spaghetti for lunch, or I'll end up wearing it." She opened her mouth, and he slid half a peach slice onto her tongue. "Huh, not bad," she said, then swallowed the fruit.

Without more complaints, she downed the entire breakfast.

He tucked the napkin into her left hand, and she wiped her mouth. "Thank you for being my babysitter."

Nathan shifted the table away from her lap. "You're welcome." Her eyes moved but never settled on him. "I'm heading to work. You need anything when I come back for lunch?"

She crossed her arms. "I didn't ask you to come back for lunch."

"No, but I'd hate to see you covered in pasta sauce."

Her smile made his heart do crazy shit.

****

Every morning before work, Nathan dropped by the hospital and returned for lunch and dinner. After the evening meal, he stayed and read to her until she fell asleep. Most nights, he slept in the chair beside her bed, holding her hand. The nursing staff left them alone, quietly working around them. He knew all the nurses' names by the end of the first week.

He overheard Karen telling another RN what a surprise Jane would have when she could finally see who her guardian angel was. Karen hadn't questioned him, but he was sure she recognized him.

While Jane slept, he found Karen sitting at the nursing station.

"Can we talk?" he asked.

The brunette looked up from the binder she wrote in. "Sure, but if you're wondering if I've told Jane who you are, I haven't."

Folding his hands on the counter, he nodded. "That's probably a good idea."

"Is it true?" she asked, then closed the binder. "Are you and Bonita divorced?"

He glanced at the other hospital staff working at their desks. "Pretty much."

She smiled. "Good. I hate that egotistical bitch. Those Hollywood mags talk like she's the next comin' of Christ, but she

49

rubs me the wrong way."

Nathan grinned. "You're an excellent nurse and a great judge of character. Anyway, Jane doesn't know who I am. For her safety, it should stay that way."

Karen's eyebrows arched. "You don't want Jane involved with the media nonsense, do you?"

"No, I don't. The focus is usually on Bonita, but photographers follow me too. I usually spot them before they spot me, but not always."

"Jane's going to find out who you are eventually. Not to mention, she likes your company. None of my business, of course, but I kinda think you like hers, too."

Her admission warmed his insides. As much as he liked this nurse, he couldn't trust anyone. "It's complicated, and I don't want Jane to worry about anything except getting better."

Karen nodded. "I get it. If I see anyone that looks like paparazzi hanging around, I'll let you know."

"Appreciate it." He dug in his wallet and handed Karen his business card. "I hope Jane won't be here for much longer."

Karen took the card and tucked it in her uniform pocket. "All her vitals are good, but her eyesight hasn't returned yet."

"Do you think there's permanent damage?"

Karen shrugged. "The doctors thought she'd have her sight back by now. Brain injuries are hard to estimate. They'll do more tests in the coming days." She tilted her head. "You're a real sweetheart for sticking by her side. Even with all the staff, hospitals can be awfully lonely when no one comes to visit."

"Does that happen often?"

The edge of her eyes squeezed with a sympathetic expression. "Too often, unfortunately."

"Thanks for taking such good care of her."

"That's my job," she said brightly.

He made a mental note to order flowers, have Jade's chefs put together platters, and have them delivered to the nursing staff tomorrow evening.

He returned to Jane's room and sat in the vinyl chair. They'd talked about everything from politics to favorite hobbies. There was nothing fake about Jane St. Eval. He loved her honesty, her eyes, and her quick humor.

On the tenth day of what she called her incarceration, he realized without a doubt what he'd always suspected would happen. His admiration of a woman he'd watched for so long from afar had strengthened into a connection he couldn't sever.

Jane stirred and reached out her hand. "Nathan?"

"Right here," he said, cupping her fingers between his.

Her eyes remained closed, and she drew their joined hands to her cheek, then fell back to sleep. Shit! In her sleepy state, her innocent action of finding peace in his presence cracked his heart wide open. Since the accident, time had flown by. Hours had turned into days. Her bruises and aching bones had healed, but her eyesight hadn't returned.

She needed him. At least for now.

****

A week after her operation, Dr. Nelson said Jane could engage in mild exercise, and they added a walk to their daily routine. After each meal, Jane coiled her arm around his to keep her bearings, and they strolled the hallways, then sat outside in a small courtyard with benches for patients and visitors.

Friday evening was the busiest, but two people left the garden as they arrived. Nathan led her to a wood bench. He watched Jane tip her head back, soaking in the warm evening sun.

"My eyesight isn't improving," she said. "I'm screwed, aren't I?"

Nathan slid his arm across her straight shoulders and tucked her to his side. "You're not screwed. Doc said everyone heals at a different pace."

"I don't know what I'm going to do, but I need to figure something out. Make plans."

He heard the worry in her voice. Nathan swept his palm up

and down her arm. "What kind of plans?"

"Without my eyesight, I can't run a landscaping business. Miguel, my foreman, has been managing my contracts while I've been in the hospital. I could head back to Colorado. I know people there," she said wistfully.

He didn't like that idea. "You know people here, too. Give it some time, Jane. Your vision will return. You're still healing. Don't engage a challenge until you're ready."

She leaned her head on his shoulder. An unspoken sign of trust that he lapped up like a thirsty dog.

"Is that a SEAL thing?" she asked.

He chuckled. "Yeah, I guess it is. It's a good rule to live by."

"I hate this. Just when I thought I was finally getting somewhere, fate drop-kicked me out of bounds." She lifted her head and rolled her shoulders. "I'll figure something out. I always do."

With the sun's warmth on his hand, he caressed her bare neck and admired her profile. She wasn't a mystery anymore. The woman claimed a little more of his heart. Nathan dreaded the day when moments between them like these would no longer happen.

"Everything's gonna work out."

He'd omitted telling her about Bonita. His divorce needed one signature and a courthouse stamp to complete the paperwork. The subject of his position at the Jade didn't rise again. In turn, Jane didn't share the tragic events of the avalanche, and he didn't ask.

He suspected the hospital would discharge her soon. His comings and goings had gone relatively undetected. A few people recognized him, but with the rapid change in patients, no one connected him to Jane except the nurses.

At the moment, she was protected from any consequences resulting from his divorce. But once she left the hospital, could he really keep his distance anymore?

"Okay, break is over," he said. "Let's get you moving."

"How about if you steal a stretcher, I'll jump aboard and you sneak me out the back doors?" she said, standing up and facing the exit.

He laughed, but his pulse hopped to attention. "How about you stand still for a second while I cover your bare ass?"

She gasped, and her hand flashed to her backside, realizing the hospital gown had come undone.

"Oh, my God. I'm sorry." She fiddled, trying to find the ties.

What the hell was she sorry for? The woman had an ass that made his mouth go dry. With unsteady fingers, he shoved her hands aside and secured the cloth ties.

"Fixed." When he straightened to face her, Jane's cheeks burned a deep red.

"Thanks," she mumbled.

He placed her hand on his crooked arm. "Believe me, it was my pleasure."

She spit out a laugh. "Wagon's ho, mystery man."

CHAPTER FIVE

Two weeks after her admission to the hospital, the doctor gave Jane the green light to be discharged. When Nathan arrived at the hospital to pick her up, she stood outside the front entrance. One of the orderlies must have dropped her off.

"What are you doing?"

"Nathan?" She turned her head, her eyes looking in his direction but not focusing.

He wrapped his arms around her waist. "Yeah, do you have anyone else hanging around you practically twenty-four hours a day?"

"Very funny. I'm waiting for my cab."

"A cab?" He took a step back and shook his head. If independence needed a picture, they'd use her as a cover girl. "This way."

"This way, where?"

"My car. Come on." He took the overnight bag from her arm and guided her toward the parking lot, her hand gently gripping his forearm.

Nathan opened the passenger door when they reached his BMW. She touched the window, the car's frame, and the seat to get her bearings, then eased herself inside.

"I'm closing the door," he warned.

Jane kept her hands in her lap, and he shut the door.

"How are my girls?" she asked, reaching for the seatbelt when he got behind the wheel.

"Fat and happy." He started the engine.

She grinned. "I smell your aftershave and leather. What kind of car is this?"

"One with four wheels."

She snorted. "Compared to my ten-year-old half-ton with the distinct odor of manure, it smells expensive."

Nathan laughed at her description. "My aftershave or the car?"

"Both, smartass."

Thirty minutes later, he pulled up to the curb in front of her townhouse and shut off the engine.

As soon as the front door opened, the cats came running. When they saw her, the meow song started immediately.

"Hey, girls." She reached down, and they rubbed themselves against her arms. She wrapped her hands under their bellies and picked them up, tucking them against her chest.

Both cats pawed her face as if to say, "Hey, we missed you."

"I'm going to make some palatable tea. Would you like some?" She placed the cats on the floor. "The stuff in the hospital was awful."

He dropped her hospital bag by the entry closet door. "You're cut off from hot elements until your sight returns. I'll make the tea."

"Deal. I'll open the windows and let in some fresh air." She took a few careful steps with her arm outstretched until she grasped the railing. Feeling her way, she climbed the stairs. He had the urge to follow, but figured she'd want to do this herself.

He filled the kettle with fresh water and set it on a stove that needed a one-way trip to the dump, then opened the back door to let the breeze blow through the house. The cats had followed their mistress upstairs, so he didn't worry about an escape. The spring day brought the Nevada desert air into the kitchen. He turned to see Jane making her way down the hall, watching as she felt her way around and got used to everything in her current state.

She sat on the well-worn couch, curling her legs under her ass. "It's good to be home," she said, her brow wrinkling. "I was thinking..." Her voice dropped to a whisper. "Maybe this is all payback."

During their lengthy conversations, Jane had told him she'd

been raised by foster parents. She'd described them as a kind couple with four biological children who never adopted Jane. They didn't show up at the hospital, which probably meant they'd washed their hands of her once she'd left their home. The guys from her crew had visited a couple times, but no one else. Without her sight, she had to be scared.

"Jane, there's no such thing as karmic debt." He crouched in front of her.

Tears glistened in her eyes. "That's not true; there is," she argued quietly.

"Accidents happen." He paused, wondering if he should broach the subject. "I saw the photos on your dresser."

She nodded and bowed her head. "Kate and Celia." Her forehead creased. "We were friends since kindergarten. We went through everything together." Jane stretched her shapely jean-clad legs out on the couch.

He gently cupped her hand. "Do you want to tell me what happened?"

"It was my fault."

"I know you think that, but I doubt it."

"The girls and I went through every milestone of life together. We could finish each other's sentences. Liked each other's boyfriends, and if we didn't, we'd dump 'em." Her voice rang with bitterness. "We went to college together. Traveled. We argued, and we made up. Kate and Celia got married. Kate has a little girl, and Celia has a boy. We remained close but once they had their own families, we didn't spend as much time together. I badgered them to come with me on the skidooing weekend. If I'd just left it alone, if I'd gone alone…" She shook her head, tears gathered in her eyes. "They hung on for so long, Nathan, but then the cold was too much. We hardly had any air and no strength left to dig ourselves out. I held them in my arms as they passed from this world." She looked in his general direction. "I don't understand why I didn't die too."

"There's no answer to that." He gently brushed a tear from her cheek. "Is that why you came to Nevada?"

She nodded. "I couldn't stop thinking about the accident. I couldn't move on. Despite being a big city, Denver constantly reminded me of my friends wherever I looked. So, I ran away."

"You didn't run away, Jane. You started over, and that's what anyone would do."

He'd done the same. After high school graduation, he had no direction. He joined the Navy and tried out for the SEALs. Hardest fucking thing he'd ever done, but after twelve years of service, he'd moved to Las Vegas and used his skills to land a job at the Jade. He and Vince Laker hit it off, and before long, he'd become Director of Operations. Nathan had reinvented himself a few times over.

The kettle whistled, and he returned to the kitchen to make their tea. By the time he came back, she'd fallen asleep. The doctor said she would probably do that a lot in the healing process. He covered her with the colorful blanket with native designs, then sat in the chair across from her, sipping the hot tea.

Maybe they could both start over. He'd lived the last five years dealing with Bonita's drama. Her friends and family were just as caustic as the actress. Shallow people with their concentration focused on the next big film, the next party, or what was in fashion. He was sick of that bullshit.

The cats jumped onto the couch, finding a comfortable spot close to their owner.

Spending time with Jane didn't take any effort. Together, they were a seamless fit with many of the same values.

Living with Bonita and her kind had sucked him into a world he never wanted but became a part of anyway. Carefully crafted illusions. Bonita's ilk lived in a make-believe realm filled with flash and greed. All the things that ego sucks on to exist.

He watched the slow, peaceful rise and fall of Jane's chest as she slept. His bond with Jane seemed to cleanse his soul. He swallowed a lump of concern.

Vince thought the time had come for Nathan to take a piece of Vegas. His mentor dared him to become a casino owner. But there was a lot of time and politics involved in not only acquiring but also owning a resort, which meant no space for things that counted in a relationship.

A knock at the door pulled him away from the pros and cons of involving Jane in that life, unsure which side was winning.

****

Lanna took a double take at the man who opened the door. "Hi. I'm Lanna Freeson from the Nurse's Aide Foundation."

"Hi, Lanna. Come on in. Jane is sleeping." He stepped back to let her inside.

"That's good," she said, eyeing him. What an extraordinarily good-looking man—big, brawny, not to mention sexy as hell. Her nipples tightened with attraction. She offered the guy a friendly smile while her eyes took a slow stroll down his physique. "I understand she has head trauma and she's blind."

"That's right. Temporarily. Whatever you can give her a hand with, I'd be grateful, but let her decide when she needs the help. She's very independent."

"Most people are. They don't take losing a sense like sight easily. She'll be fine, I'm sure." Lanna scanned what she could see from the front entry. Low income, yet here was a guy like *this* in the patient's home. Interesting. "My contract summary says she's a gardener."

"A landscaper. Jane owns the business, and we contracted her at the Royal Jade."

"I see. So you represent the casino?"

He gave a sharp nod.

She swayed her head a little to the side and added an impish grin. "Well, I'll make sure she receives good care. If you'd like, I'll call you this afternoon." *Please tell me to call you.*

He reached into his pocket and pulled out a business card. "This is my number. Keep me updated."

"No problem," she said, giving him another smile.

With a benign look in his sharp green eyes, he headed down the paved walkway to the street and got into a silver BMW sports car that had to be worth big bucks.

Very interesting. Lanna nosed around the townhouse, then finally looked in on this Jane St. Eval. What a pathetic name. It sounded like a two-bit soap opera star. The sleeping woman had pretty features, even with the bandage wrapped around her bald head.

The chick had to have something to eat in this little hovel. Lanna plunked her backpack on the tiny kitchen table, then rummaged through the fridge.

"Bare bones," she said with a sigh. The closet-sized pantry produced a little better fare. Lanna grabbed a bag of chocolate chip cookies from the shelf and stuffed an unopened bag of Doritos in her knapsack.

Fifteen minutes later, she heard movement from the living room.

"Hello," she called out.

"Hello? Who's that?"

"Hi, Jane. My name's Lanna. The Royal Jade hired me to assist for a while. I'm a nurse."

"Oh, did Nathan call you in?"

Hmm, did they have something going on? She'd have to find that out before ousting the chick from the picture. "I'm not sure, Jane. Can I get you anything? Are you hungry?" She returned to the living room and stood in front of the woman. Jane looked around thirty, with green eyes and high cheekbones—pretty. Obviously, she couldn't see a damn thing because she stared at the bookcase, four feet to the right of Lanna.

Jane swept the blanket aside. "No, I'm not hungry. I need to do some shopping. The fridge is empty."

No shit! "I'll help you with that. Why don't you get yourself together, and then I'll take you to the market. You have a car, right?"

"A truck. The keys should be in my purse. But I'm not sure where that is."

She'd already scoured the contents. "No worries, it's by the front door." She watched Jane wander down the hallway and work her way up the stairs. While Jane got ready, Lanna scouted around downstairs. Nothing worth pawning unless you were an avid readaholic.

"These photographs on your wall," she asked when Jane returned. "Did you take them?"

"Yeah. I love photography. Not that I have time to do it anymore."

"I don't recognize where they're taken."

"Victoria. Ever been to Canada?"

Luckily, the firm she temp'd for didn't do a thorough background check. "Nope." With her rap sheet, no country, especially Canada, would allow her to enter.

"Did you say my purse was at the front door?"

Lanna watched the woman struggle to find her bag and rolled her eyes. "Little to the left, Jane."

"Uh, thanks," she said, grasping her leather bag and slipping the strap over her shoulder. "Shall we go?"

Time to toss in the empathy card. "You're sure you're up to it?"

Jane felt around for the knob on the front door. "I've been cooped up in a hospital for two weeks. I need to stretch my legs."

How did a chick with a shaved head get a guy like Nathan? Maybe they were related somehow. The man's rugged good looks hadn't given away any tells. But that fab, expensive suit draped over his rockin' body and the hot car were definitely worth sticking around to find out who he was.

"All right then. Let me know if you get tired and we can come home. You shouldn't push it too much."

Lanna took a last sweeping look around the townhouse, in case she'd missed anything she could pawn, as she detoured through the living room before joining Jane on the stoop.

"I feel pretty good," Jane said.

Until you accidentally trip on the stairs.

Lanna played nursemaid and lets-be-friends, talking with Jane as they shopped. At least she'd get a few free meals outta the woman if nothing else panned out.

"Did you see Nathan?" Jane asked while they stood in the cashier lineup, waiting their turn to load the groceries onto the belt.

"Um, no, he wasn't there. I just had instructions to come in," she lied.

"Oh," she said, sounding a little dejected.

Time for some recon. "Is he your boyfriend?"

"No. He works at the Royal Jade, and he's kind of been hanging around since I had my accident."

Lanna dumped the groceries onto the moving belt. "Hanging around?"

"At first, I thought the resort sent him to make sure I wouldn't sue, but of course I wouldn't do that. Then he just kept coming every day." She shrugged. "His name's Nathan Selkirk. Guess I could call him a friend."

Shit! She hadn't bothered to look at his card. "Did you say Nathan Selkirk?"

"Yes. Why?"

Jackpot! "Oh, no reason. I just thought I recognized the name, but nah." Selkirk, Jesus, could it be the same guy who was married to that actress? She had to find out. Things were looking up.

After a few more stops, they arrived back at Jane's townhouse, and Lanna's ward disappeared upstairs for a nap. Standing on the front stoop, out of hearing range, Lanna called Nathan. He answered on the first ring.

"Yes," she said. "Mr. Selkirk, it's Lanna calling."

"How's she doing?" Concern coated his voice.

"No issues. I took her grocery shopping, and she's having a rest now. We got to know each other, which puts the patient at ease, especially with the loss of her vision."

The title on his business card read *Royal Jade Casino Resort. Director of Operations*. That sounded like a decent job.

"Good. I'm almost finished here. I'll be there in about an hour."

"You're coming back? My contract states twenty-four-hour

care."

"The resort covered the bases. It's not necessary, at least right now. I'll take care of her in the evenings."

Jane might call him a friend, but if Nathan only acted on behalf of the resort, he sure as shit wouldn't babysit.

"All right, well." How should she work this? Think. Think fast. "She mentioned the accident happened at the Jade."

"That's right."

"Sounds to me like she's having second thoughts. Can't blame her, but Jane is considering suing the casino." Not true, but if caught in a corner, she could say it had been a misunderstanding. It couldn't hurt to throw a few screws into the relationship.

"Sorry?"

"I think she's lost a lot of work because of the accident and wonders whether the casino would take that into consideration."

"I see. We are culpable to a point. There should have been extra security where she worked."

"Just thought I would mention it. The Jade is a premier resort. Must have plenty of insurance. Not my concern, but I thought I'd pass it along."

"I'll talk with her."

Nathan disconnected the call.

Back in the house, Lanna's keen gaze wandered around the sparse kitchen. She'd sown the first seed of trouble in the landscaper's life. Jane wasn't worth much, but Nathan looked like a guy with a thick bank account. She smiled to herself, then grabbed her backpack, leaving through the front door without bothering to lock it. She couldn't wait to get home to Greg. He'd be very interested in all of this. Tonight, they'd do some planning.

CHAPTER SIX

"Jane?"

Nathan shoved open the front door to her townhouse, surprised it was unlocked; then again, maybe not. She said she didn't worry about break-ins, but she should worry about her own safety. Jane lived in a decent, low-income neighborhood. That didn't mean scumbags avoided the area.

"Nathan?" she answered from the living room.

"Hey, how's my patient?" He entered the room to find her curled up on the couch, wearing a silk green bathrobe, and the eReader in her lap.

"Just doing a little reading. Well, kind of." She slid her finger along the bottom of the reader and pressed the second button to pause the automated voice. "I'm good. You don't have to keep checking in on me." She looked up, but in the wrong direction.

"Where's the nurse?"

Jane shrugged. "Don't know. I took a nap and when I got up, she was gone."

He hadn't given Lanna instructions to stay until he returned. She probably had other patients. "Jane, if you're having second thoughts about suing the casino, you need to let me know."

"What?" Her expression crinkled with confusion. "No. Why do you ask?"

Had he completely misjudged the woman? Maybe his feelings for Jane had clouded his normally good judgment.

"I want to make sure you don't feel you're being manipulated somehow."

"Manipulated?" She broke into a grin. "Are you manipulating me, Mr. Selkirk?"

Her eyes shone with a smile. What the hell was going

on? Why would the nurse lie to him? While getting to know Jane, she'd never asked him for anything. Or hinted that she'd changed her mind about an injury claim. Her character beamed with straightforward values. If she said she wasn't changing her mind about suing the Jade, he believed her.

Nathan crouched next to the couch and clasped her hand. "No. I'm concerned and, if honest, enamored. By you." He'd spent the entire day putting out fires at work, using auto-pilot mode, but all he really thought about was getting back to Jane.

"Yeah, the hairless wonder," she drawled.

He leaned over until his breath brushed her cheek to let her know he was close. "I told you, I don't care." Jane inhaled but didn't exhale. "I'm not going to kiss you, sweetheart, because I'm going to leave that up to you. But I'm right here."

She raked her teeth over her top lip while releasing a stuttered breath. His pulse pounded, waiting for her next move.

A sweet grin swept across her perfect lips. "Do you want me to kiss you?"

How many times had he reminded himself to keep this professional? Keep her safe, then draw back when her sight returned. He palmed her soft cheek. The only time he'd kissed her lips, she'd been in a coma.

"Too much," he admitted.

Her palms drifted up his chest until she reached his face and slid her thumb over his bottom lip. The simple touch skyrocketed his pulse, but her gentle kiss boiled his blood. Nathan lingered, his heart thundering as pure bliss slithered into every corner of his body. He'd caved to a kiss, thinking it would relieve the pressure, but it didn't.

Regrettably, she drew back. "Never kissed a man sight unseen before."

He considered admitting that she *had* seen him. Once.

"Maybe that's a good thing." Before he lost control, he said, "Why don't we get you dressed and go out for dinner? I'm not a great cook."

"I am."

"You can prove that some other time. Being holed up in here isn't good for you." He removed the blanket from her legs and helped her stand, feeling her warmth against his chest, which had an immediate response below his belt.

"I don't mind takeout, and even blind, I think I can put something together."

"You need a good meal that isn't served on a tray. Come on." He paused. "Unless something's wrong and you're not telling me. That sure as hell better not be the case."

Jane plopped a hand on her right hip. "What was your rank in the Navy, because you sure can sound bossy?"

He knew she hated the hospital and would do anything to stay out of the place. "Sweetheart, you're avoiding the question."

"And you're being overly protective. Aside from bumping into walls, I'm great." Jane stepped back and stretched her arms toward him, wiggling her fingers. "Take me upstairs, Mr. Selkirk."

He swallowed, but someone had stuffed a pillow down his throat. She'd gotten upstairs by herself already. What did she need him for?

"Um, sure."

****

Jane's lips tingled from the kiss. Whenever Nathan was close, her pulse raced with a frantic beat. His voice made her body quake with desire. The thrill intoxicated her.

Was she really standing in her bedroom with a gorgeous man, according to Nurse Karen, willing to let him dress her? "Where're we going? What should I wear?"

Crazy, sexy thoughts raced through her mind, and she couldn't contain them. She heard the closet door slide open.

"Whatever you want to wear," he replied.

Had he turned to look at her? Loosening the belt at her waist, she let the robe slip to the floor, pooling around her feet. He'd been on his best behavior. A total gentleman. Either he was a friend or…

"Uh…" He cleared his throat. "Jane." He exhaled heavily. "Man, gardening keeps you very fit, doesn't it?"

"I'm not going out like this, I assure you," she said, grinning. "I don't know what bra and panties I grabbed from the dresser earlier. For all I know, I mixed red, blue, and white and look like a barbershop pole.

He cleared his throat again. "Umm, no. You matched your reds perfectly. Are you sure you can't see?"

"Just a little light and movement." With heightened hearing, his steps on the low-pile carpet seemed to move closer.

"I can see just fine," he said in a low timbre, his warm breath tickling the sensitive skin on her neck. Large hands palmed her upper arms, then gently squeezed. "Jane, you're driving me insane."

Nearly blind, her other senses pooled their resources. The bulge in his pants pressed against her stomach. Jane tipped her head upward. Her eyes saw nothing but a blurry image.

Without asking, she placed her hands on his chest and slowly wandered, crossing a silk tie and a cotton shirt. She let her fingers roam to his broad, muscled back, covered with a suit jacket. "I can't see you, but I can feel you."

His fingertips grazed her collarbone, then skimmed her shoulder. Goosebumps rose across her skin, and her nipples tightened behind the lace bra.

"What? Um. Clothes. You need—"

She slid her palms up his chest. "You're very tall, aren't you?"

"Got an excellent view from up here," he said, his voice rough. "Darlin', I need to get you dressed before I do something I won't regret, but you might."

This man had protected her since the accident. She'd spent every day with him. While their friendship grew, so did the hectic beat of her heart. When he'd dared her to kiss him, she hadn't hesitated.

"Like losing control?" she taunted.

Nathan's mouth crashed against her lips. His nimble fingers

released her bra, sliding the fabric across her breasts, then letting it drop to the floor. The tips of his thumbs brushed leisurely circles around her nipples. Her head rolled back as her need eclipsed everything but his electrifying touch.

Nathan swept a muscular arm around her waist and behind her thighs, then lifted her onto the bed. With fumbling fingers, she unbuttoned his shirt to touch his skin. Bolts of impatience sizzled down her spine.

"God, Jane, I fucking want you."

His tongue lapped at the tip of her breast, suckling and teasing the peak into his mouth while driving her mad.

"Show me," she whispered.

A rustle of clothes and the soft thud of them landing on the floor proved he wanted her too. He kissed his way down her stomach to her mons. Nathan's warm hands removed her panties and gently opened her thighs.

His warm, moist tongue French kissed her clit, and his fingers joined in to please her.

As if he'd been holding back, he suddenly unleashed his desire, his tongue flicking her bundle of nerves. Her breathy gasps seemed to spur him on. Racing toward an orgasm, she tried to pull away, but he wouldn't let go of her hips, holding her captive.

"Nooo. Please, Nathan. I need—oh shit."

His muscled body slid up her skin. "What do you need, babe? Tell me," he said against her throat.

"You. All of you."

Nathan rolled to her side, and she heard the release of a zipper, then the rustle of clothes. The rip of cellophane followed and a second later, his thick crown eased against her opening.

The weight and closeness of his body sent excited shivers through Jane. His kiss burned with passion.

"Jesus, sweetheart. I want to make you come."

His deep timbre heightened her lust. Raising her hips and palming his powerful shoulders, Nathan read her signals and eased into her core, burying himself to the hilt.

He moaned. "Oh shit, you feel good!"

Her inner muscles contracted around his thick shaft while she sank her fingertips into his hips. Every plunge drove her closer to the edge, where she teetered. His throaty moans and hard cock hurled her over the top, and he came with her.

Nathan gently teased her clit with his thumb as her breathing eased and her pulse receded. He kissed her deeply and kept kissing, still sheathed inside her channel.

She sighed and then laughed. "I just let a man I've never seen before make love to me, bald head and all. I must be losing my mind."

He kissed her cheeks and then her lips. Her gaze settled on a face she couldn't see but wished she could.

"You're beautiful, Jane. Absolutely one hundred percent beautiful to me." He placed a sweet kiss on her nose.

"This is the weirdest physiotherapy I've ever heard of."

He chuckled, then shifted onto his back, rolling her to settle on top of his body. His fingers tenderly strummed her spine. "I didn't expect this. And I'm not sure whether this was very smart so soon after your injury."

"Your resort is really going the distance, you know."

"The Jade has nothing to do with this. It's all you, sweetheart, and it's my desire, not theirs."

His hands strayed down her sides as if memorizing her curves. When she shifted to a sitting position on his hips, his mouth teased her right breast.

She'd made love to him not based on secondhand information from the nurses that said he was hot, but because her sixth sense begged for intimacy with this man. If she was being played, she liked the game. Either that, or he'd read too many erotic romance novels to her in the hospital. Shifting to lie beside him, he cradled her shoulders with one arm, curling her against his side.

"I'm in no hurry, but I'm starving," she said.

"How do you feel? You're not faint, are you?"

"No." She slid her hand up the hills and valleys of his abs, then grazed his face. "Hmmm, powerful jaw, stubbled cheeks that feel quite ticklish on my thighs, by the way," she teased. "Soft, thick hair, long but not too long. What color is it?"

"Green," he answered while laughing. "I'm a headbanger."

"No, you're not. I didn't feel any earrings."

"Took 'em out."

She perched on her hip. "Seriously, I want to know. One nurse said you have sandy-blond hair. Is it?"

"Accurate, I suppose."

"Blond. Huh. I don't like blonds."

A deep laugh rolled from his chest. "Really? You seemed to like me just fine a couple of minutes ago."

"Maybe I did, or maybe I didn't."

With one arm, he rolled her back on top of him. She liked the feel of their bodies touching, skin on skin, and the way his palms cupped her butt cheeks.

"I love your auburn color, especially when the sun shines on it."

"Sure, when I have some. Why the heck did they have to shave me bald?"

"To save your life. Stop worrying about it. Your hair will grow back."

"I'm stuck wearing a ball cap for the foreseeable future. Are you sure you want to go out with me? If you're as hot as the nurses said you are, just think about all the sympathetic looks you'll get."

"I don't care what people think. And I know you don't either. Let's have a shower and grab some dinner."

After their shower, which he insisted they take together, he found the clothes she wanted and helped her dress.

"I have a few scarves in my closet. Top shelf. Maybe I can hide this bandage."

The way he took command and wrapped the silk scarf around her head led Jane to believe the man didn't squelch at a situation he'd never faced before. She might look like a gypsy palming a crystal ball, but since she couldn't audit his fashion skills, she had to trust him.

Standing on the street, Nathan guided her hand to the roof of his vehicle. She hadn't noticed the soft top before. "Convertible?"

He opened the passenger door. "Who needs eyesight? You're doing fine without it."

"Tell me that again when I mistakenly bury my hands in a cactus."

****

Nathan grinned as she identified the things she touched. Fingering the top of the car door, she clutched his left hand, then stopped dead. Her expression shifted to shock. Jane reached over with her other hand and felt his fingers.

"This is on your ring finger, isn't it?"

Shit! He kept the ring on to avoid gossip, but mostly because of the women he sometimes had to entertain at the Jade. Wearing a ring kept things above board. Until now, he'd been careful when holding Jane's hand. Why the hell hadn't he taken it off?

Jane seamed her lips, then quietly eased herself into the passenger seat.

He closed the door and rounded the vehicle. Silence hung heavy when he slid behind the wheel. "Jane, I'm separated. My divorce is almost final. The paperwork is complete." She nodded, but said nothing. "Listen," he grasped her hand, placing her fingers around his ring and wiggled it off.

"What are you doing?"

"What I should have done five years ago." He helped her remove the gold band. "Hold on to that for a second, would ya?"

"Why?"

He started the engine and quickly had them on the highway, headed toward Laughlin.

"Now," he said, lowering the passenger window.

"Now what?"

"Chuck it. Throw it as hard as you can."

70

"Are you serious?"

"Dead serious. Get rid of that fucking thing."

She clenched the ring in her palm and raised her hand. "Last chance," she piped.

He grinned. "Hard. Throw it hard."

Jane let the ring fly from her fingers.

Gone, Bonita was gone. As gone as anyone could be. He leaned sideways and kissed Jane on the cheek. "Thank you."

"For what? I think a semi just drove over your symbol of eternal love."

"For you, Jane. I'm thanking God for making you." He tore down the highway, feeling truly free. Despite the traffic-filled road ahead, a promising future lay wide open with Jane.

Nathan steered them to a popular Italian restaurant in Laughlin. After the four couples ahead gave their names, he stepped up.

"Selkirks, for two."

By Jane's smile, she hadn't missed the plural he added to his last name.

"Umm, yes, Mr. Selkirk," the hostess answered. "It's an hour wait, but uh..." The woman paused. "You're Nathan Selkirk, aren't you?"

Nathan sighed. Figures he'd run into someone who followed Bonita. "Yes."

"I'm sure we can find you and your...guest, a seat as soon as possible."

"Great. Thanks."

With an arm around her back, Nathan guided Jane away from the desk.

"That woman knew who you were," she said.

His lips grazed her ear. "Guess I have some things to clear up."

"You mean, fess up. Don't you?"

Nathan squeezed her shoulder. "You okay to stand? We can head outside and sit on a bench."

"I'm fine with standing. Not so sure about your quick

departure from answering my question."

After twenty minutes of heavy silence, they finally took their seats in a booth. He still grappled with how to express what he had left unsaid.

"It smells so good in here. I'm starving," she said. "If I never taste a bowl of banana pudding again, I'll count my blessings."

"Your other senses are picking up the slack. What are you in the mood for?"

"Answers."

He cleared his throat. "I know, but I'm referring to dinner."

"What do you suggest?"

He didn't miss the wariness in her voice. "Just about everything. It's a five-star restaurant. How about we order appetizers, have a bottle of wine, and figure it out after that? Wait a minute. Nope. No wine for you."

Jane crossed her arms and sat back. "Why not? After the two weeks I've had, I deserve some, don't I?"

"Not yet. You're still on the blood pressure meds. No alcohol, sorry, darlin'."

"You know, when you say *darlin'*, I hear a Texas twang."

He chuckled. "No worse than the million pictures of wildflowers on your walls. You're definitely from Colorado."

"Whaaaat?" She burst out laughing. "Okay, fine."

Jane's laughter lightened his heart and accentuated her unique beauty. Seeing her in person, instead of through the monitor in the security ops room, brought him a thousand times closer to her. Staying away from Jane had become a distant memory.

"I might have too many pics of Colorado fauna, but I am a landscaper after all. Speaking of which, I need to call my suppliers. I know Miguel picked up the orders, and he and the crews have kept up with our contracts, but I need to get back in the saddle. I might end up riding it backwards, but I'm going to try."

He didn't doubt she'd tackle her injury by finding a workaround. "Miguel cares about you. When the taxi hit you, he was by your side, riddled with obvious concern."

"I wish I could pay him more. He's a good man. That's not always easy to find. Once I have a few more contracts, everyone's getting a wage increase. It takes time to earn a reputation. Landscaping is a cutthroat business. There're literally hundreds of people with a pickup truck and lawnmower trying to underbid someone else's contract. I juggle a lot of balls to keep my business going. Being a reliable contractor isn't enough these days."

"How many guys do you employ?" he asked, impressed she could stay alive in such a competitive business.

"Fifteen men and five women. Finding hard-working people is harder than you might think, but I haven't lost a single crewmember yet, which is common in labor jobs."

A waiter, dressed in casual black pants and a blue shirt, took their orders. Once he was gone, Jane leaned forward, her eyes staring past Nathan's shoulder somewhere on the wall behind him. She slid her palms across the table until she found his hand.

"How old are you, Nathan?"

He tongued his front teeth. "Thirty-nine, but the last few have been dog years."

"Why do you say that?"

"I've spun my wheels for a while now, but I think it's time to stop."

"That's good, I guess." She tilted her head. "How long were you married?"

Time to lay it all on the table. "Five years, and that was five years too long."

She raised her brows at him.

"You'd think in this day and age there's no such thing as arranged marriages, but there are. You could say someone convinced me it would be a smart move."

"Are you a father?"

"No." He coughed. "No, my ex wouldn't think of ruining her body with a baby. She's, ah, well, she's an actress." No more secrets. It wasn't fair to either of them.

"An actress, huh? A wannabe or someone popular?"

"Do you know who Bonita Williams is?"

Jane paused. "Um, don't think I do."

He jerked his head in surprise, then remembered she didn't have a TV. "A well-known one, actually. I married her for all the wrong reasons. Vince Laker thought it was a good idea."

"Vince Laker? The owner of the Jade?"

"One and the same."

"Soooo, you're close to him."

"You could say that."

"That would mean you're not a floor guy," she drawled, her lips tightening with disapproval.

"No."

"No...what?" she asked, her eyes narrowing.

"I work all over the resort."

"I can hear the hesitation in your voice. Are you holding back for a reason?"

It had been a good reason at the time. "I didn't want you to think I was trying to con you after the accident. I'm the director of operations at the Royal Jade."

"I don't know what that title means, but I'm guessing high on the food chain."

"Yeah, pretty high." He laughed at her description. "In simple terms, I run the resort."

The waiter returned with their appetizer. "The plate is hot, ma'am," he said, like he was talking to a child.

Her lips seamed with what looked like annoyance. "I can hear the cheese bubbling. I would assume it's hot."

Nathan burned a grin, seeing the waiter's eyes round with surprise.

"Yes, ma'am. Anything else?"

"Yes, I'd like a glass of—"

Nathan jumped in. "Water. She wants more water."

She raised an eyebrow and cleared her throat. "Sure. Water's fine."

Nathan served the fried cheese appetizer onto her plate. Hell, he'd been feeding her for two weeks. Why stop now?

"I can do that, you know."

"You're used to doing everything on your own, aren't you?" He slid the plate across the table until it touched her hand.

"No one else is going to." She fumbled for her cutlery, then tasted the fried cheese. "Oh, my goodness, that's good." She chewed it down. "So, you married an actress and you've got a kickass job. What's not to like about that?"

"I married Bonita knowing I shouldn't, but I got talked into it by Vince. With her connections, he thought it was a smart business move. Was for him, but I can't stand her family or the people she surrounds herself with. My folks are hard-working people who earned everything, and if they couldn't buy it, they grew it."

"Farmers. Right?"

"Yeah. Have you ever been to Texas?"

She shook her head. "I've visited almost every state, but Texas is still on the bucket list."

"Why did you choose to move to Nevada?"

She thought about it for a second. "It was the last vacation the girls and I took together before the avalanche. We had fun in Vegas."

Nathan covered her right hand. "Good memories are meant to be cherished. I'm happy you ended up here."

Her eyes narrowed. "Was it you who approved my contract at the Jade?"

"Hmmm. Yes, but I didn't know who you were then. I looked over everyone's bid. I liked yours the best."

"Really?"

"It's the truth. And then you showed up. Tuesday, May 19th, 10:30 in the morning."

Both her brows raised with that.

"I planned on introducing myself like I normally do with a new contractor, but when I scanned the monitors and saw you for the first time, I stopped myself."

"Why?" she asked quietly.

"Couldn't. Not after watching you interact with your crew and your smile." He remembered that moment. The instant attraction. "I was married, although unhappily, but I was married. And I knew if I talked to you, I'd want something more."

"You've been watching me for two years. I can't believe it."

He sighed. "Yeah, I know it sounds creepy, but I had my reasons."

"No. It's unbelievably sweet and romantic," she said quietly, squeezing his hand. "And I never ever saw you?"

That day in the park, he'd done three shoulder checks after they'd spoken briefly. She'd never turned around. That explained one of two things: she didn't like what she saw, or Jane already had someone in her life. At the time, he'd buried both thoughts. He knew differently now, which left the initial option.

"It's possible," he said, unwilling to lie but deviating slightly to give her time to get to know him.

He'd never been insecure about women. During his years in the teams, he rarely struck out, but he wasn't looking for permanent in those days.

Jane touched the edge of the plate to get her bearings, then laid her fork down. "Are you sure? Because you don't sound sure."

He slid closer to her on the horseshoe-shaped bench seat and palmed her soft cheek. "When I saw that cab round the roadway and watched you fly through the air, I lost my mind. I trampled five guys to get to the front entrance."

Jane clasped his fingers and cupped his hand. "Are you trying to tell me something?"

"You've only known me for two weeks, but I've admired you for two years." He wrapped his hand around the back of her neck and inched her toward him. "I knew what I felt was far deeper than what I wanted to admit. I kept my distance because I had to."

He kissed her, his tongue easing between her soft lips, while his heart thundered with happy acceptance.

"And now?" she asked, after drawing away by a few inches.

"I guess that's up to you. With the barrier gone, all I want is more."

A future with this woman solidified in his soul. Jane was the gal he wanted to spend his life with. His choice. The right choice. Nathan didn't question why he wanted her or his need to protect her, no matter what they faced.

CHAPTER SEVEN

In a discreet corner of the Italian restaurant, a camera shutter clicked nonstop. Little did the couple know that their intimate dinner would become tabloid fodder with pictures endorsing a shocking headline.

"What do you think?" Lanna asked. "That's Bonita Williams' husband, right?"

"Yeah, it's him." Greg shoved her back with an elbow. "You're fucking up the shots. Gimme some room."

Lanna obeyed and put a few inches between them.

Since the age of fifteen, she'd been hanging out with Greg. When his mom's boyfriend laid the boots to him one night, Lanna found Greg moaning on the hood of an abandoned car where kids in Lovelock, Nevada, bought their weed and shit. In those days, she thought she loved him.

They ran away from home ten years ago and survived on the streets of Vegas. At one time, high on Moon Rocks, they'd made a pact to crawl out of poverty. Lanna went to school and earned a nursing assistant certificate. Wasn't hard. She completed the course in a few weeks. With no criminal charges at the time, she aced the background check. Proof of a high school diploma caused a problem, but Greg knew someone who made a forgery.

She found a job at a local hospital making seventeen bucks an hour, cleaning people's asses and puke. Greg worked odd labor jobs but kept getting fired for stealing stuff. Unable to escape the gutter, they ended up in jail for armed robbery. Greg got two years. Charged with a lesser offense, she served five months in prison.

Lanna had a chance to run—start over. But like an idiot, she'd waited for him. Not anymore. This dude, Selkirk, was her ticket to freedom.

The shutter continued to click. "Might be some money in it," Greg said. "I checked online. No proof he's divorced. Rumor is his wife, Bonita, is fucking some actor in LA."

"Pretty sure Nathan's fucking Jane." Wish he'd press those lips on me, Lanna thought. Greg was okay, but he didn't take enough showers, smoked too much grass, and never brushed his teeth. "I saw his fancy car. He's got money."

"Or a shit ton of debt. No pictures online of him and this chick." Greg lowered the camera for a second. "She owns a two-bit landscaping company called Green Appeal. By the sound of her digs, she doesn't have much. I checked out the area. Most of those townhouses are rentals."

Lanna hunched over the table, hunger pains gnawing at her stomach. Greg had given the hostess forty bucks for the seat, but he had no intention of eating.

"Bonita's famous." She watched Nathan kiss Jane like the bitch was the only woman on earth. Jealousy spurred her temper. At sixteen, Greg made her fuck guys so they could survive. Mostly butt-ugly assholes. No one like Nathan ever paid for her services. "A Hollywood tabloid might want the scoop and those photos."

He guzzled the rum and Coke he'd ordered. "Do something useful and call a few of them to find out how much they'd pay."

"Our funds are running dry," she said. Within a week, they'd be on the street again. She hated living in their piece-of-shit van. Greg was on his own if she could convince Nathan to let her stay at Jane's place. It wasn't the Taj Mahal, but it was better than the rat-infested, pay-by-the-week dump where they currently lived in West Las Vegas.

Greg lifted the camera and took a couple more shots of Jane and Nathan. "I'm betting the prick wants to keep his affair quiet. He'll pay." He glanced at Lanna. "Entitled assholes like him don't deserve the money they have."

She sipped from the glass of water the waiter had placed on their table. "Jane's gullible. If I can get her to trust me, it might help our cause."

They watched as Nathan shifted closer to Jane in the three-sided booth.

Greg sneered. "That nutsack really looks like he's in love with the bitch. That's good for us. Won't take much to motivate him to open his bank account to protect his dirty little secret."

"Wha'cha thinkin'?"

"We'll see if he coughs up some dough. If not, we'll move on to another idea. One that will definitely get his attention."

They'd pulled plenty of petty scams before, but this Nathan guy had money. Lots of money. Lanna's lips curled into a smile. "How much do you think he's worth?"

Greg finished his drink. "Question is, how much is *she* worth to him? There's more than one way to cash in on this at the same time."

The couple at the next table kept darting wary glances their way.

"We got enough pictures, Greg. Better blow this place before they see us." She dug a twenty-dollar bill from her jacket pocket to cover Greg's drink. She'd stolen sixty bucks from Jane's purse earlier. Blind as a bat, the chick couldn't tell what was in her wallet.

****

Leaving the restaurant, Jane asked, "Mind taking a walk? The warm wind feels so good."

For a woman like Jane, who spent the majority of her time outside, sequestered in the hospital for two weeks must have been torture.

"I know just the place."

Jane slid her hand down his arm. "Lead the way."

Nathan guided her to the promenade that edged the Colorado River, and they merged with tourists strolling the walkway. "Notice any change in your eyesight?"

"Can't see anyone clearly, but I see movement. I'm turning into a bat, 'cause I can hear everything. People's conversations.

Chirp of a bird, and that loud jet boat on the river."

A sleek boat with three outboard engines motored down the waterway. Pint-sized watercraft ferried tourists for scenic tours and acted as inexpensive taxis between the resorts. Sea-Doos raced along the narrow waterway, zigzagging around the other vessels.

"Give it time. The doc said your sight could return slowly or suddenly. The healing process is different for everyone. Until then, you can hang on to me."

She tipped her chin up and grinned. "You love that idea, don't you?"

"Sounds like you have me figured out." Truth was, he liked it a lot. "Have any contracts in Laughlin?"

"I don't, but I like this place. It has potential," she said, strolling beside him. "It's small and doesn't overwhelm the senses like Vegas."

"True. Laughlin struggles because visitors want the Vegas strip and everything it offers."

"Someone needs to look beyond the gambling. Make better use of the desert around here. Focus on an adventure destination with gambling as a secondary draw."

The setting sun saturated her green eyes, making them even more beautiful. Nathan gazed at the remarkable woman by his side, then scanned the river.

"Uh, huh. So what would you do to make it more inviting?" he asked.

"I'd definitely improve the flora and fauna. A botanical garden, for starters."

"Right up your alley."

She grinned and forked her fingers through his. "The main drag isn't very attractive. Mostly parking lots with a few palm trees. None of the resorts scream *inviting oasis*. Nor do they take advantage of the beautiful vistas. It's always windy here. I'd promote sports like kiteboarding, sandboarding, and river races for extreme enthusiasts. Add endurance events for bikers and hikers. Host competitions like an extreme bike race or dune buggies. Anything to attract a crowd that follows those activities. If someone invested in a new resort and drew visitors, I think the rest of the business owners might renovate. Competition is good for everyone."

"Jesus." He shook his head and gazed at her in awe. "You are so right. It's underdeveloped with endless opportunities."

"Exactly. Sitting dormant, waiting for someone to recognize its potential."

An enormous grin tightened his cheeks. Nathan imagined a fully developed destination resort that incorporated Jane's ideas. His aspirations clicked to green like they'd been sitting at a stoplight.

"You are amazing," he said.

"What?" She slowed her pace, then stopped, while the people behind them altered course to go around.

"I've been paddling in place for a while. I want to change that, Jane. For you. For our future."

Her brow furrowed. "Our what?"

Nathan watched visitors of all ages stroll along the riverside walkway. "Why don't you and I build this town into something incredible?"

"We? How? What the heck are you talking about? Almost everything I earn goes back into my business. I can barely scratch two bucks together to feed the cats."

"Don't need money. I want you as my partner, and your creativity and business sense."

She chuckled. "Business sense? I shovel dirt and yank weeds."

"Come on, let's get a drink and I'll explain."

"I can't drink," she grumped.

"Right. Ice tea, then."

"Me and my big mouth."

****

Seated next to the window in the Cove Bar and Lounge, Jane

listened to Nathan's ideas, her eyes widening with his business plan. A huge plan.

"Nathan, what you're talking about takes enormous amounts of money. Like huge!"

"It's covered."

The man's confidence made it almost impossible not to believe him. "It's covered, he says nonchalantly. Why? Did you thump a leprechaun over the head and steal his pot of gold? You said your family are farmers."

After laughing at her description, he said, "They are. I'm not."

She sat back, feeling a little dizzy, but didn't want to worry Nathan. "If I understand correctly, my mystery man with a chiseled physique, that would be you, has also made prudent investments?"

Nathan's muscled arm slid across her shoulders, and he planted a long, delicious kiss on her mouth. "I'm saying you're my inspiration, but what I really want is to take you home and put you to bed."

That sexy, low timbre got to her every time. "Can't really argue with that offer." She fanned herself with a napkin, the heat rising ten degrees in her body.

Thirty minutes later, they arrived back at her townhouse. Nathan walked her to the front door. "I'll be right back. Have to find a parking spot behind the complex." Street parking was prohibited overnight.

"That sounds like you're staying the night," she teased, fingering the contents of her purse to find the keys.

"Am I assuming too much?"

Feeling around the door, she found the keyhole and inserted the key. "Do I need to question your motives?"

He chuckled as he swept his large palm down her bare back. "Only if you don't believe I want to make love to you."

Earlier, when he'd chosen her clothes, he'd conveniently picked what she called her slutty top. A shimmering red halter blouse with an open back and deep cut front, but it was the man who made her feel sexy.

"Make me a believer then," she dared.

When he returned from parking his car, Nathan didn't waste time leading her up the stairs and to her bedroom.

Her old mattress sank as he lay down, then he traced his finger along the front of her blouse, barely touching her skin.

She squirmed under his caress. "Are you teasing me?"

"Maybe. But maybe I'm not in any hurry. Maybe…"

He burst out laughing when she threw herself on top of him and pinned his shoulders. "I'm a wounded woman with little patience. Don't stir the pot, Mr. Selkirk," she warned, narrowing her eyes.

"Wouldn't dream of it, darlin'." Nathan's warm hands slid to her neck, untied the knot, and removed her top. "Jesus, help me, you are so beautiful."

When his warm lips mouthed the peak of her nipple, her blood flared with heat. She didn't need anything except to feel him naked against her body.

Nathan rolled her onto the mattress, then his lips left a sizzling trail of kisses over her ribs and past her naval. He took his time removing her slacks and lace undies. His tongue licked the sensitive skin around her sex, but not her clit.

"Nathan," she breathed.

"Patience, darlin'."

"Don't *darlin'* me! You spent two weeks reading me erotic romance novels in that sexy timbre of yours. This is all your fault."

She cried out as his tongue darted in and out of her core. The orgasm rushed through her body, making her writhe with pure bliss.

His firm, bare chest pressed against her breasts, and she reached for his shaft, dipping his thick crown into her silky wetness. His groan told her all she needed to know. Jane wiggled beneath his toned body. With both hands, she massaged his erection while her mouth eased over his cock.

Nathan's breathing came in shallow pants. "Shit, Jane."

She urged him to roll over and crawled up his body like a cat ready to pounce. Teasing his shaft with the wetness between her thighs, easing him into her canal just enough to push through the folds, and then sensually withdraw.

He moaned, wrapping his hands around her ass and plunging into her core. "Reading those fucking books to you made me nuts, because I imagined us like this."

She rode him slowly, prolonging the passion. His warm palm slid to the back of her neck and he drew her down, kissing her hungrily.

Suddenly, he gripped her hips to halt her motion. "Sweetheart, stop. I gotta put on…"

"I'm safe, Nathan." She surged forward, shutting his mouth with a kiss and rolling her hips.

"I am, too, babe. Are you sure, because there's nothing I want more than to feel all of you?"

"I want that too."

With a gravelly moan, he drove himself to the hilt. Clenching her inner muscles, she milked his cock, launching him into a fury.

She ground her hips against his body, loving every savage thrust. "Oh, babe, come deep inside me."

Her words sent him reeling over the edge as he plunged his stiff cock in and out of her slick channel. Under her palms, she felt him shudder, and warm cum erupt inside her core.

When his breathing returned to normal, his arms slid around her waist. "God, you just set me off so fast."

His finger circled her right nipple, then he kissed each breast. "Wait here," he said.

A minute later, she felt a warm, wet washcloth gently clean the residual of their lovemaking. No man had ever been that thoughtful. Nathan wasn't just a sexy package, but a gentleman, too.

"Thank you. Hey, um, there's a bottle of Advil in the medicine cabinet. Can you bring it back with you?"

His hand gently cupped her jaw. "Aw, sweetheart. How bad is

it?"

"On a scale of one to ten, it's around an eight."

"Shit. Why the hell didn't you tell me?"

She smiled and wished for the hundredth time she could see him. "You're worth a little pain."

He grumbled as he left to get the pills.

Returning to the bed, he sat beside her and slid a glass into her left hand and the pills into her right. "You had a serious injury, and I'm not taking any more chances. As much as I want you, we're taking a break."

"For how long?"

"Not happening again for at least a week."

"A week?" she squeaked. "Listen here. It's been three years since I've had sex. Another week is overly cautious. Besides, the headache started back in Laughlin."

He took the glass from her hand once she'd downed the pills, then adjusted the pillow beneath her head. "That's even worse. You should have told me."

"I didn't tell you because you'd react like you are now."

"You've got an appointment with the neurologist next week. If he gives the all-clear, then we'll go from there."

"Maaan, you are such a hardass."

Nathan kissed her cheek. "I never thought I'd hold you in my arms. It's all I ever wanted since the day I first saw you. Not going to lose you now just because I'm an impatient bastard."

****

Nathan woke up alone, which he didn't like. Then his other senses kicked in. Sunshine streamed in Jane's bedroom window, and he smelled coffee brewing. He threw on his pants and went downstairs.

"You're up. Good, I was just about to get you," she said, standing by the stove.

He looked at the clock above the sink. Six. "You're an early riser."

"Don't want to waste the day."

She'd made a pretty good attempt at breakfast. Scrambled eggs, sausage, and toast. "This looks damn good, but it's risky. Did you burn yourself?" She shrugged, and an impish smile coated her pretty lips. "Jaaane. Did you?"

"Just once."

"Where?" He lifted both of her hands by the wrists and turned them over. A good-sized blister bloomed on the edge of her right pinky.

"It's fine. I ran my finger under cold water. Not a big deal."

"Do me a favor and stop tempting disaster. It won't be long before your vision returns. Just park the ambitious chores for a couple of weeks, okay?"

She wrinkled her nose but agreed.

He kissed her, his hand sliding to the small of her back, only then realizing she wore nothing but a thong under the apron. At one point, he'd imagined seeing her with mussed hair and a robe, but this was a thousand times better.

She smiled, knowing that he'd figured it out.

His hands strayed to her hips, squeezing her beautiful curves. "Do you promise to do this every morning?"

"Only when you're standing in my kitchen."

Was she saying what he hoped she was? "Darlin', that's a temptation I can't refuse."

"Eat, Mr. Mystery Man."

The nurse was scheduled to arrive at seven. He wanted to be outside, concealed from view, before she arrived. Finished with breakfast, he took their plates, rinsed them in the sink, and stashed them in the dishwasher.

"Jane, when the nurse comes, I want you to do something for me."

She felt around the table, then lifted her mug of coffee. "What exactly?"

"I want you to tell her we had a fight, and you threw me out."

Without taking a sip, she set the mug on the table. "Why?"

"Humor me."

"Fine, but why don't you trust her? You hired her, didn't you?"

"From a firm in town. Yes, but they don't always do in-depth background checks. Last night when we were in Laughlin, she was there with a guy. You had me a little distracted, but I think they took pictures of us."

"The restaurant sounded full. How the heck did you see them?"

"I'm trained to notice things. Yesterday, she called me and said you wanted to sue the resort."

Her brow creased. "I didn't say that."

The cats trotted into the kitchen, and he retrieved the kibble from under the sink and filled their bowls.

"Didn't think you did. But something's up with this woman. Don't worry about it. I just want them to think we've gone our separate ways. For your protection."

"Do you think they're criminals, con artists, or something like that?"

"Don't know, but I'll find out soon enough."

"How?"

The cats curled around Jane's ankles before attacking their breakfast.

"I've got access to criminal databases and friends at the LVPD. If Lanna and her accomplice have a record of illegal activity, I'll find it."

Jane crossed her arms over her ample chest, which looked pretty damn hot with just an apron bib covering her assets.

"Why would they take pictures of us, unless it's for blackmail? Is there something you neglected to tell me?" Her tone darkened. "If you lied about your divorce, then tell me now."

After storing the cat food, he sat at the kitchen table. "It's not a lie."

"Cue the bittersweet strings of an orchestra and *plink, plink, plink* of piano keys promising heartbreak. I hear a 'but'."

Despite being blind, Jane had impressive powers of observation. She couldn't see his expression but heard something in his voice that raised a concern. He had no intention of ever lying to her. He'd withheld information about their brief meeting in the park because he wanted to give their relationship time to cure.

"After I separated from Bonita, for a few fleeting moments, I wanted to march down to the garden and talk with you. Make my move. The *'but'* you hear is an echo of my reservations. I work long hours and exist in the world of hospitality. Rubbing shoulders. Politicking. It's what people expect. The long list of responsibilities as director of operations includes rolling out the red carpet for VIPs. I lead a large team of staff who create an inviting environment, even for people who don't have deep pockets, so they'll return. It's all bullshit, but it's part of the job."

Jane's fingertips depressed the skin on her upper arms as if waiting for a punchline she wouldn't like. "And?"

"After watching you for two years, I concluded you work your ass off by turning the soil, planting flowers, and trimming shrubs. At the end of the day, you wash the dirt from your hands while I change my suit and entertain an oil barren's wife at Vince's request while her husband loses a million bucks in a private card game."

Jane unraveled her arms, then tapped her fingertips on the table. She closed her eyes. "When you say *entertain*, do you mean sex?"

"Hell, no."

"A married man who carries a condom on his person tells me otherwise."

Nathan scrubbed his chin to stop smiling—not that it mattered. Last night, he hadn't used protection. "If you're referring to my preparedness earlier yesterday, it's not what you think. I didn't plan for that to happen between us, nor should you worry that the prophylactic is ten years old. It's not."

"Sooo," she said, her voice sounding like she was about to make the great reveal in an Agatha Christie murder mystery. "You want me to believe that you reject your most attractive customers who seek personalized service?"

He couldn't help it and laughed at her antics. "Exactly. My marriage was a farce, but between her boyfriends, Bonita came knocking. I didn't want an accident to happen and bring a child into a marriage bound for divorce court. Or get an STD from her lovers."

"Okay, that's a reasonable explanation." Seemingly not satisfied, she said, "Rich, beautiful women must have tried to seduce you at the resort, but you're telling me you have a shiny halo and never, ever cheated."

"Plenty of women, but when I make a vow, as in marriage, I don't break it."

Jane's mouth tightened into a slim line. "Jury is out until I know you better."

Wise woman. "The point I was originally trying to make is that I didn't mind the long hours at work because I didn't want to go home. I had a wife who emptied two mickeys of gin per day and threw tantrums every time I walked in the door. But I care now. I want to spend the nights with you. The problem is my responsibilities haven't changed. Not until I make or break it as a resort owner, and that will mean even more time."

Jane sighed and sat back in the vinyl-backed chair. "I hate to tell you this, but after I put away my rakes and shovels, I'm up to my eyeballs in paperwork, billing, and phone calls for new contracts until ten at night. My work never ends. When I lay my head on the pillow, my mind races for another hour."

Evidently he'd simplified her responsibilities, and that was a mistake. "I know how commitment can tear a man away from his family. Saw it all the time when I was in the teams."

"Some couples weathered the storm, didn't they?"

"Sure, but they made a plan and we should, too. Starting with dedicating one day a week to each other. No matter what."

Jane nibbled on her bottom lip, then nodded. "Which day?"

"I'm not finished. Breakfast. Together. Every day. As soon as the judge stamps my divorce, I'm selling my place and downsizing by twelve thousand square feet."

Her eyebrows arched. "Where the heck do you live?"

"Dragon Peak Drive. The place should go for about thirty-four mil."

She coughed and leaned forward. "Say what?"

Nathan clasped her hand. "I'm going to buy something more reasonable. Our lives might be full ahead, but I want you to fall asleep in my arms every night."

Her lips parted for a second and then smacked shut. "I have ten more months on my lease for this place."

"I'll pay off the lease." He gazed out the patio doors at her tiny fenced backyard. "Where do you keep your equipment?"

"I rent a storage unit. Why?"

"And you buy your plants wholesale."

"As close as I can get." She sat back, and Peony the Persian jumped onto her lap. Jane swept her hand down the cat's back, and the feline flicked her fluffy tail.

"Ever thought about growing your own plants?"

Jane continued to stroke the cat's back and received a loud purr. "Of course. But having a nursery means having land. More staff." She shrugged. "Not to mention plenty of liquidity. The only way that'll happen is if I win the lottery." She tipped her head. "Although—a few of my guys think I should start a YouTube channel."

His temper shot through the ceiling. "Not a fucking chance!"

She blinked with shock. "Why? Gardening videos are all the rage. Thousands of views. My guys think I'd make a killing."

"You'd get views. All from guys jerking off, watching you bend over instead of wanting to know how to plant cucumbers. No!" He thrust a flattened hand through the air.

She burst out laughing. "That sounds like jealousy talking."

"Call it what you fucking want. If you need land to start a nursery, we'll take that into consideration when we purchase a new home."

She exhaled and shook her head. "Nathan, have you considered that you're ending a relationship and jumping right into a new one? You know, some people call that a rebound, and those rarely end well."

"Nope, admiring someone from afar for two years is called torture, not a rebound."

She snorted. "This has been a very enlightening conversation, but I see now why Lanna and her friend might be gunning for you. If it isn't common knowledge that your divorce is imminent, they probably think you'll pay them off to keep their mouths shut."

"Yeah, that's my guess. Whatever the scam, it will fall flat. Our future is in *our* hands, but I don't want to disappoint you. That's why we need ground rules."

A genuine smile lifted the edges of Jane's lips. "Maybe you should go on a few dates before jumping into long-term commitments and buying houses."

Nathan stood and rounded the table, sliding his arms around her torso. "Unless those dates are with you, I'm not interested."

"Plenty of wealthy, gorgeous women visit the Royal Jade," she said in a teasing tone. "Since you're every nurse's wet dream, not to mention a retired SEAL, and I understand they have a reputation for playing the field, you should consider all your options before wining and dining a struggling landscaper."

He slid his hands beneath the bib of her apron and palmed her bare breasts, causing his cock to thicken. "Hmm, if I didn't know any better, I'd say you're trying to get rid of me. But there's a problem with that."

Jane tipped her head back, and her pretty lips parted. "As in?"

Her nipples stiffened under the brush of his thumbs, increasing the pressure beneath his belt line. "I don't want anyone but you." Peony took his fingers caressing Jane's breasts under the apron as a game and batted the moving target. "You're pussy is playing with me."

Jane broke into a hearty laugh. "That was definitely the sailor talking."

He plucked the cat from Jane's lap and dropped the feline on the floor. "Let's put you back to bed."

"I thought you cut me off for a week."

Nathan gripped her hand and led her down the hallway, then

up the stairs. "You are. Doesn't mean I can't kiss you until you drift off to sleep."

"I have work to do. I've got two weeks of paperwork to catch up on. Without my sight, I have no idea how to do that."

As she strode up the stairs to the second story, Nathan appreciated the red thong on her gorgeous ass, which the apron didn't cover. What he'd give to climb in bed with her, but he had to situate himself outside and wait for the nurse.

"I'll find an accountant at the Jade and send them over to give you a hand. But for now, you rest." He untied the apron at the back of her waist and slipped the neck strap over her head. Seeing her nearly naked, his cock swelled, and he had no clue how he'd resist making love to her for an entire week. "Get your beautiful ass in bed."

Jane sighed, but followed his order. Laying her head on the pillow, he tucked the blankets around her sides.

"Where's my phone?" she asked.

"On the bedside table. When you get up, keep it with you. If something happens with Lanna or anything else, call me. I put my number in your contacts."

"How am I supposed to find it? I can't see the numbers."

Hmm. "Then I'll call you, but if you don't answer, I'm jumping in the car immediately."

Jane's palm slid down his forearm. "Nathan, you've been amazing, but if my eyesight doesn't return, I won't be your burden."

"With or without your sight, darlin', I'm not going anywhere." He leaned over and placed a healing kiss on her lips. No matter what lay ahead, they'd figure things out together.

Just before seven, a dumpy eighties vintage blue van stopped in front of Jane's townhouse. Nathan concealed himself across the road and took pictures of the plate and the two people inside. Same guy as last night. He watched Lanna enter the townhouse, and her boyfriend gunned the engine and sped toward the stop sign at the end of the street.

Nathan followed at a distance to make sure the guy wasn't

just circling the block. The van drove to an address in a sketchy part of West Las Vegas. When the guy with greasy black hair got out of the vehicle and entered Room Six, Nathan grabbed a few pics of the motel with his cell, then headed home for a change of clothes.

CHAPTER EIGHT

Sitting in his vehicle, Nathan checked his texts. He'd muted the notifications yesterday. Literally, hundreds of messages from Bonita filled his phone. Calm requests asking where he was eventually turned into demands for him to call. Then the accusations followed.

I know you're not at the Jade.

Where are you?

Who's the bitch that stole you from me?

Please, Nathan, don't give up on me.

Answer me, you asshole!

The string of profanities ended around midnight. Nathan thumbed through them all to make sure he hadn't missed an important text from the resort. Then he hooked his cell on the dashboard holder and headed for his residence.

Twenty minutes later, as he rolled to a stop in front of the garage door but didn't go in, he saw a black Audi R8 parked by the front door. Bonita never got up before noon. Whenever she invited friends over, it was always in the evening.

Nathan ascended the stamped concrete steps and punched the code to access the front entry. Stepping into the war zone, he paused, listening for the quick *click* of Bonita's high heels on the marble floor. When she didn't appear, he aimed for his bedroom. Striding down the hallway with paintings mounted in thick gold frames that were hung every five feet and hand-crafted credenzas every twenty feet, he finally passed Bonita's bedroom door.

He paused when he heard a man's throaty groan, followed by, "Yah, baby, suck it like that." She'd brought her newest conquest home. That was a new level of fucked-up.

Nathan carried on down the hallway and turned left into his

bedroom suite. At least she hadn't trashed his room. She'd done that more than once. Unlike the rest of the house, he kept his space simple. Neutral colors on the walls with chocolate brown accents. A desk sat in front of a bank of floor-to-ceiling windows where he sometimes worked during the evening to catch up on outstanding issues.

Two loungers, which he never used, sat near the glass pivot doors that opened onto the pool deck. His private bathroom was almost the size of Jane's entire downstairs. He took a quick shower and strode into the five-hundred-square-foot ensuite to change his clothes. The room, because he couldn't call it a closet, looked like an upscale clothing shop, with his suits neatly spaced on a bar and wall-to-wall hardwood shelves and drawers.

Normally, he ran five miles before work, but he was already late. About to leave, he paused in the ensuite doorway, then did an about face. He grabbed one of his suitcases and tossed four days' worth of clothes inside, then secured the latch.

Nathan nabbed two suits and zipped them into a garment bag.

He left his packed items at the front door and headed to the kitchen to grab his to-go mug. Selecting his pre-programmed setting on the five-thousand-dollar coffee machine Bonita just had to have, he waited for the four shots of espresso and cream, topped up with hot water, to finish going through the cycle.

"Oh! Hey, man!"

A guy with curly blond hair, wearing nothing but a pair of jeans, strolled into the kitchen. So this was Bryce, the new and upcoming Hollywood actor Bonita had hooked up with. He'd only seen the guy once on the cover of a tabloid. The photograph showed Bryce and Bonita swapping spit. Barb, his admin assistant, was a doll, and Nathan knew she'd purposely left the rag on her desk so he'd notice.

The twenty-something guy hadn't moved. His blue eyes watched Nathan warily. "Umm, Bonita wanted a cup of coffee."

He screwed the cap on his to-go mug. "Help yourself. To coffee and Bonita. She's not my wife anymore."

The kid shrugged. "Sorry, man. What can I say? Thought what we had was just an *on-location* thing, ya know, but she called me last night crying and asked me to come."

He sounded like he'd jogged straight off the California coast with a surfboard tucked under his arm. Actors like him didn't need talent. Followers on social media launched careers like his. Production companies wanted to sell movie tickets. A hot new guy like Bryce drew thousands of teenage girls and young women to the theaters.

"Don't sweat it, kid."

"Where the hell are you going?"

Bonita stood in the archway of the massive kitchen, which was rarely used to cook a meal, wearing a satin robe, hands perched on her hips. She must have seen his suitcase at the door.

"Atlanta. Business meeting," he said. He'd done it enough times. She wouldn't question his answer.

She glanced at Bryce, then back at him. "Where were you last night?"

Nathan took a long draw from his to-go mug, then lifted it as a toast to her sanctimonious stance, asking where he'd been, while her bare-chested frat boy stood ten feet away. At first, he found it hilarious, but five years of her constant bullshit hit the finish line. "Bonita—go fuck yourself."

She gasped, then squealed at Bryce. "See what I mean!"

Nathan strode past his ex and through the pristine but cold dining room with a sixteen-seat table, and kept walking till he grabbed his suitcase.

Bonita chased after him, but stopped at the entrance doorway. "Bryce and I are going back to the Malibu house," she shouted from the stoop.

"Wish you the best!" he said, heading down the cobbled path to his vehicle. Hopefully, she wouldn't burn this place to the ground before she left. He tossed his luggage in the back seat and got behind the wheel.

Bonita, always wanting to be seen in the last act, slapped the driver's window with her palms.

"What?" he said sharply, rolling down the window and starting the car.

"You've hurt me for the last time, Nathan. If you leave, we're done. I mean it."

She'd signed the separation agreement a year ago. The divorce papers were at her attorney's office. Bonita could blow her latest boyfriend all she wanted. He'd say they were done.

Nathan threw the stick in reverse, gave her a look that plainly stated, *Don't give a shit,* and did a quick two-point turn, leaving his ex screaming profanities at him. He darted a look in his rearview mirror and grinned as the front gates yawned open.

A few miles down the road, he pressed a button on his cell.

"Call, Jane."

After two rings, she picked up. "Hello."

"Hey, darlin'. I just realized it's Friday."

"Okay," she said. "And that means what?"

"Means a guy who's got a thing for a certain sexy landscaper is asking if she'd like to go out on a date tonight."

Jane's wholesome laughter made him smile, washing away the residue of Bonita's toxicity.

"What did you have in mind?"

"Something you'll enjoy."

"I might be free, but didn't you just finish saying you work long hours? It's the start of the weekend. Isn't that peak time at the Jade?"

Nathan eased his foot on the brake, stopping at a four-way intersection. With no other traffic, he continued toward the highway. "Give the cats some extra kibble. I'll pick you up after work. We'll pack you an overnight bag."

"But I just got home. Where are we going?"

With Jane's temporary blindness, a fun date had to lean on a tactile experience. When they looked back on their first *official* date, he wanted it to be memorable. "Somewhere you've never been before. Now, where's Lanna?"

"Downstairs. I heard her come in just after you left. Told her I was taking a shower. I'm going down there now."

Nathan joined the highway bogged down with taxis, buses, and people driving to work. "If you sense any trouble, make an excuse and tell her to leave."

"I got it covered, Dick Tracey."

"I know you do."

He took the next off-ramp, using a shortcut to a back road that accessed the parking garage entrance at the Jade. He cranked the wheel, slowed for the speed bumps, and parked in his designated spot. Until he knew what Lanna and her partner were up to, he didn't want to tip them off. If there was even the remotest chance Jane was in danger, he'd find a place to rent short-term where she could stay.

Pushing the ignition button, the quiet purr of the BMW's engine stilled. Struck by the danger posed by the nurse and her accomplice, he paused. Wasn't this exactly in line with his concerns about drawing Jane into his circus? It wasn't as if people tried to blackmail him every day, but being connected to him put Jane in a vulnerable position.

With his silence, she asked, "You still there?"

"Yeah, I'm still here." Lanna wasn't the only threat. Bonita had a lot of connections. Until she truly moved on, he had to protect Jane from the fallout.

"What's wrong? I can hear a change in your tone. If you want a healthy relationship, that means open dialogue. So lay it on me."

"I'm analyzing how to shield you from a potential threat, sweetheart."

"Hmm. Want to take a pause on dating until my sight returns? When you shout, '*Take cover,*' I won't inadvertently dive into moving traffic. I'm good at that, you know."

Her light-hearted suggestion made him grin. "How about we keep my blooming crush on you more discrete? I don't want to hide our relationship, but I want you safe."

Jane chuckled. "Once you give the *all clear,* I'll drag you to Jade's rooftop myself."

Nathan exited the car. "I hope you know how much I care

about you, Jane St. Eval. Believe me, I'll be shouting it from the rooftops."

"You're kinda wonderful yourself, Mr. Selkirk. Talk later."

****

After making the bed, going mostly by feel, Jane headed downstairs. Water ran from the kitchen tap, and dishes clinked as they were being placed in the dishwasher. Running her right hand along the wall, when the wall ended, she knew she'd reached the kitchen.

"You don't have to clean my dishes."

"Better than twiddling my thumbs," Lanna said. "Have a seat. I made a fresh pot of coffee. You interested?"

"No, thanks. Had my fill."

"Has Mr. Selkirk left for work?" she asked.

Jane didn't doubt Nathan's concerns. If this chick and her boyfriend followed them last night, they were up to no good. "Don't know. Don't care," she said briskly.

Movement stopped at the sink. "Um, what does that mean?"

"It means I'm a good judge of character, even when I'm blind."

Lanna's blurred image stepped toward the kitchen table. "Really? He seemed nice to me and honestly concerned about your well-being. You wanna talk about it?"

The less she said, the less chance she'd make a mistake and give Lanna a reason to doubt her. "Nothing to talk about. The Jade initiated Nathan's actions. He doesn't care about me. I told him to get out."

"It sure didn't look that way to me. I—I mean, when I met him yesterday. I don't know the guy, but he seemed genuinely worried about you."

Liar. Lanna fucked up. She'd said Nathan had been gone when she showed up. "That's his job. Making people feel important. I guess he thought flirting with me couldn't hurt."

"So you two haven't been an item for a long time?"

"He showed up at the hospital after my accident. Nurses described him as a handsome guy. When he started flirting, I fell for it for about thirty seconds."

"Men are such assholes. I didn't want to say anything, but I think he's married."

Lanna poured herself a coffee and then sat at the kitchen table. Scam artists had multiple avenues to make a buck, and Jane didn't want them plotting a different angle. "No, he's separated, and the divorce is pending. He and Bonita are just keeping their private matters under wraps."

"Oh."

Jane smothered a grin at the nurse's gloomy-sounding response. "Anyway, I'm doing fine, and as much as I enjoy the company, I don't need any help."

"Your home care service covered one week. It's already paid. I could hang around. Keep out of your way, or help if you need a hand. That's my job."

Yeah, right! "Thanks, but I have an entire crew of guys I can call if I need a hand."

The doorbell rang, and Lanna jumped to her feet. "I'll get that."

Jane stood. "Not necessary. That's my senior landscaper. We're having a meeting today."

Lanna followed Jane to the front door. If she wasn't mistaken, her vision seemed a smidge better this morning. Shapes and angles of objects appeared sharper. The dark envelope converging on her sight had lightened. Fingers crossed, this was a good sign.

She opened the door. "Morning, Miguel."

"*Buenos días*, Jane."

Miguel had offered to drive her to the storage unit for the meeting. "Thanks again, Lanna."

The woman didn't answer and headed down the cement path to the sidewalk. Hopefully, that was the last she'd see of the nurse-slash-crook.

"The boys are excited to see you again, cariño. We have

missed you, but there's been no problems. I have taken care of everything."

"I know you have, Miguel, and I'm grateful." She spotted a red lump on the entryway table. She grasped her purse and tossed the strap over her shoulder. "You see my house keys anywhere?"

She always left them by the door. Wonder if her nurse sniped them. Now she had to change the frickin' locks and dig up her spare truck keys. What a pain!

"My spare key is under that big rock." She pointed in the general direction.

Miguel found the key, and she locked up, stuffing the spare in her back jeans pocket.

"Can you see much?" he asked.

"I think my sight is improving, but it's still pretty crappy."

Miguel gently grasped the back of her left arm. "This way, *mija*."

Settled in Miguel's twenty-year-old Toyota, they set off for the rental unit Jane used as her headquarters and tool storage.

"Señor Selkirk is a good man," Miguel said as they took the on-ramp to Highway 11. "He was so worried when you were hurt."

"He's been a huge help." Jane felt around and depressed the button to roll down the passenger window for a little air. Miguel's air conditioning had crapped out years ago.

A hefty chuckle erupted from her foreman. "I might be getting old, but I know love when I see it, *mija*. He called me many times while you were in the hospital. Did you know that?"

"No. Why did he call?"

"To reassure us that you were improving and not to worry. He said that if the worst happened, he'd make sure everyone had a job. When you had to have the operation, I heard fear in his voice."

Jane clasped her hands in her lap. The more she learned about Nathan, the deeper her feelings grew. She was trying to keep a level head and not just march off the deep end with a man who seemed too good to be true.

"But I'm concerned. My wife tells me that he is married."

"Almost divorced. Apparently, his wife is a well-known actress."

"Sí. Rosa loves to watch movies. So do the children, but Bonita William's movies aren't for the little ones."

Miguel had five kids. Three boys, ranging from seventeen to five years old, and two daughters, eleven and thirteen. "I don't have time to watch movies. I prefer reading if I have time, which isn't often."

The vehicle swayed to the right, taking the next off-ramp, which meant they were two minutes from the storage unit.

"Rosa is concerned that Señor Selkirk's intentions may not be honest. She reads those Hollywood magazines. They're not like us. Money and fame buys them everything. They can be dangerous if crossed. My wife is worried about your safety."

"Give Rosa a hug for me. And thank her. I can't be certain of anything, but I think Nathan is genuine. He said his divorce is imminent." She grinned. "He admitted he'd had a crush on me for two years but didn't introduce himself because he was married. Unhappily, but still married. Even after he and Bonita separated, he kept his distance."

The vehicle slowed, and Jane squinted, able to see a smudgy chain-link fence surrounding the storage facility.

Miguel shifted the car into park. Before getting out to unlock the gate, he said, "He sounds like a man with honor. You are my boss, but I see you like a daughter, Jane. I don't want you to get hurt."

Jane reached across the console and squeezed his arm. "You mean the world to me, too, Miguel. Now let's figure out how I can run this business without my eyesight."

CHAPTER NINE

Nathan slung his suit jacket over his office chair, transferred the images he'd taken on his phone to his laptop, and then printed copies.

In the security operations center on the second level of the resort's admin wing, he found his chief of security, Liam Peters, speaking with two of the monitoring team.

"A word, Mr. Peters."

"Yes, sir."

Nathan walked to the east corner, farthest away from any workstations.

"What is it, sir?" Peters asked.

"I'd like you to do a background search on these individuals," he said, handing over the copies he'd printed. "The woman's name is Lanna Freeson. She works for a temp nursing agency, providing home care. I want her history, criminal and otherwise. Use our facial recognition databases to see if you get a hit on the guy. Check the plates on that van, too. Registered owner, etc. If our databases don't return an identity on the guy, call Detective James Read at LVMPD and send him the images."

Peters accepted the high-res pictures. "Yes, sir. Is this time-sensitive? Are they in the resort?"

"It is, but they're not at the resort. I think they're drumming up a blackmail scheme. Lanna and this man took pictures of my guest and I last night."

"I see. I'll get right on it. Umm—"

Peters' hesitant expression set off alarm bells. "What is it?"

"Your wife, sir. Last night, Bonita repeatedly called several departments in the resort, looking for you. Somehow, she got a hold of your personal assistant's number. Called her incessantly and was verbally abusive on the phone. Barb contacted me, but there really wasn't anything I could do except suggest she take the morning off to cool down."

"I spoke with Bonita this morning." That fucking woman had zero boundaries. "I'll talk with Barb."

"Mr. Laker was also looking for you."

"Thanks. I'm headed there next. I'll check in later to see what you've found."

Nathan used a card pass in the elevator to access the seventh floor, where Vince's private office was located. He had a senior assistant, but she worked on a different level. Vince was in and out of the resort because he owned several locations.

He knocked on the nondescript, wood-grained door.

"Come on in, Nathan," Vince said through a speaker next to the doorframe.

Opening the door revealed two men. Vince Laker and a familiar face. "Steven. Nice to see you."

Steven Porter filled a business suit like few men did. Big guy. Not only in physique but in wealth. Steven owned and operated an extremely lucrative film production company in LA, but he also owned two top-tier resorts on the strip. Bonita had done everything under the sun to get herself in one of Porter's films but failed every time.

"Nathan. Good to see you." Steven extended a hand for a shake.

Both Laker and Porter surpassed the term ultra-wealthy. Nathan accepted the handshake from Vince's longtime friend.

"Have a seat, Nathan," Vince said.

He joined the two men near the twenty-foot-tall windows overlooking the strip, where four comfortable chairs surrounded a low-profile glass coffee table.

Steven took a seat as well. "Vince tells me Bonita and you are going separate ways. Are congratulations in order?"

Nathan chuckled. "Definitely. Been five years coming." He eyed Vince, the man responsible for his marital incarceration.

"Hey, it was a good idea in theory," Vince said.

Nathan settled on a leather-clad chair. "It was a shit idea

from the start, and I should have gone with my gut instinct."

Vince shrugged. "Worth a shot."

"Bullet in the head would have been better." He shifted his gaze to Steven. "Bonita turned herself inside out to star in one of your films. Why did you always shoot her down?"

Porter lifted a hefty black lacquered coffee cup from the table and took a sip. "My wife, Moira. I trust her instincts, and she never liked Bonita. Besides, I hate sleeping in the spare room if I piss her off."

Laker chortled at the man's confession. "Does that happen often?"

"Mm. Not often. She's got me trained."

Vince's clean-shaven jaw tightened with a grin. "I always liked Moira. Classy lady, and she doesn't take your bullshit."

"How's the twins?" Nathan asked Steven.

"Growing like goddamn weeds. They've almost finished kindergarten. With the twins in school, it gave Moira a little more free time. But on the weekends, I've got half a dozen ankle-biters running around my place because the kids have sleepovers and playdates. It's chaos, but a helluva lot of fun."

Nathan admired Steven Porter. The man ran an empire, but he prioritized his family above all else. He'd literally pulled the red carpet from under Hollywood's feet when he accumulated the biggest studios and brought them under one business name called Palm Productions.

"Am I interrupting a meeting?" Nathan asked. "I can come back later."

Laker rose and wandered to the wood-paneled bar. He filled his coffee cup from a silver carafe, sitting next to vintage bottles of hard liquor. "Nope. You're the meeting."

Nathan eyed Steven. "I am?"

Porter nodded. "You are." He shifted forward in the chair and adjusted his blue silk tie. "Vince wants to kick your ass out of the Jade. He thinks it's time you stopped pissing around as operations director. I agree. We're both prepared to back you if you're ready to wade into deep water. As a retired SEAL, I know you're used to taking risks."

Porter had a gift for backing promising start-up companies. Nathan's situation confirmed the theory that seven degrees of separation or less connected any two people in the world.

Two SEALs he'd served with, but not on the same team, Tony Bale and Mace Callahan, left the Forces a few years back and became private military contractors. Porter fronted the money to start the business because his and Moira's goddaughter married Tony Bale. Porter rarely failed when he invested in a business. The guy was willing to back Nathan. That in itself was one hell of a compliment.

"I appreciate the vote of confidence." He sighed and gazed at the wood-paneled ceiling, about to harpoon his future. "Two weeks ago, I would have launched into action."

Laker leaned forward. "What's the problem, Nathan?"

"It's not a problem, Vince. It's a temporary course correction."

Steven's eyes narrowed. "It's a woman."

Nathan blinked with shock. "Listen, you two are on cruise control at this stage of your lives." He swept a hand across his jaw and stared at the eclectic imprint on the beige carpet. "I want a clean slate before I dive into this endeavor. There won't be much time for anything after I do."

Laker said, "You talking about Bonita?"

"Yes, and no. She hasn't signed the divorce papers yet, but she will. That's not what I'm concerned about." He glanced at Steven, who wore a slip of a grin.

"Don't think I won't understand," Steven said. "The world stopped revolving when I met Moira. I royally screwed things up in the beginning. I was a goddamn mess until I cleaned it up. Who is she?"

Nathan cleared his throat. "Someone I've cared about for two years but didn't dare go near."

"Wait a second," Vince said. "You've been back and forth from the hospital to check on that landscape contractor who got run over."

He nodded. "Her name's Jane St. Eval, and yes, it's her. She's still blind from the accident."

"Huh, sorry to hear that," Vince murmured. "Anything we can do?"

"No. The doctor said her sight will return in time. I'm trying to protect Jane until the ink is dry on the divorce papers. Bonita is fucking psycho, Vince. Jane has nothing to do with my divorce, but Bonita will use her as the reason for our failed marriage. I also had the misfortune of hiring a nursing aide for Jane, who looks like she's hooked up with some scumbag that wants to blackmail me."

Both men's eyebrows rose.

"I just need time to square away all this shit. Divorce Bonita. Sell the house. Buy a new place, but most importantly, get to know the woman I'd fucking walk over hot coals for. She has dreams too, and I want to help her seed those dreams."

"Desert isn't going anywhere." Porter crossed his muscled arms over his chest and tossed a glance at Vince. "I'd already acquired a vast enterprise before I met Moira. That posed problems for me because she was an ordinary working woman when I dragged her into my life. My mistake was initially keeping something from her." He lifted his left hand to indicate he had a reason. "I didn't want her to misinterpret my intentions. But she found out from another source. I thought I'd lost her for good. It took time for her to trust me again, but eventually she did. Moira's the kind of woman who can bring any man down a couple notches. I needed that. I needed her."

Vince had a family, too. He and his wife had been married for thirty years. A gracious woman who had her own interests, but they made it work.

Nathan wanted Vince to understand that his priorities had changed to some degree. "Vince, you gave me an opportunity no one else would when I started at the Jade."

"And you paid me back tenfold," he responded. "You've made a name for yourself, Nathan, but you're on the bottom floor. If this woman is willing to ride the roller coaster with you, then you've got a partner and a solid foundation. Take the time to let that relationship cure."

There was his segue. "That's what I want, but it means I can't devote late-night hours to the Jade anymore."

Vince's lean shoulders shook as he chuckled. "I understand what you're trying to tell me without stepping on my toes. I trust you'll still have Jade's operation running smoothly, but you want time with Jane. If that's the case, then delegate some of your responsibilities. If you're going to take a step into the realm of owning your own resort, I'll eventually need a new director of operations. You might as well start searching for the right candidate now."

Nathan figured he'd blow a hole the size of Bagdad in his opportunity to keep Steven and Vince's support. But that wasn't the case.

Steven stood up and said, "I assume you've got ideas. We don't have to break ground tomorrow, but I want to hear your thoughts. How about we meet next week? Wednesday. Around six. My place for dinner. Bring Jane, I'm sure Moira would like to meet her. You and Lacey, too," he said to Vince.

Nathan knew that was code for a stress test. If Moira got good vibes, Steven would put the issue to bed.

Nathan rose and extended his hand toward Steven, who gave it a solid shake. "If nothing goes sideways with Jane's injury, I'll try to convince her to come. She's a little self-conscious because the doctors had to shave her head to save her life."

Vince gave him a fatherly pat on the back. "What happened?"

"Because of inflammation from the accident, a main artery cut off oxygen to her brain. They had to relieve the pressure."

"You didn't tell me that."

"Vince, no offense, but the last time you got involved in my personal life, you hooked me up with a fucking piranha."

"Jesus, I said I was sorry. You ever gonna forgive me for that?"

"Hell, no! If you gentlemen will excuse me, I need to beg my admin assistant not to quit because Bonita launched an attack on her last night before inviting her boy-toy actor to spend the night at my house. This morning, when I walked past her bedroom, she was giving the guy a blowjob loud enough for the neighbors to hear. And before I left, she headed me off at the pass and had the fucking balls to question me about where I'd spent the night."

Vince winced. "Sounds like she needs a little time in a round room."

"I don't give a shit what she does, as long as she signs the divorce papers and stays the hell away from me."

Vince escorted him and opened the door. "If I'd had any idea that she was that far off the rails, I'd never have nudged you into marrying her. Wish it had turned out differently."

He wasn't angry with his benefactor. "I don't. There's no one like Jane."

His cell dinged with an incoming message. Nathan expected a text from Liam Peters, but Barb sent the message. Guess she'd cooled off enough to come back to work.

Sir, a courier arrived with a package. You need to see this immediately.

He quickly responded. *Is it a letter demanding cash?*
Yes.

He nodded. "Looks like I was right about the blackmail. Time to put out another fire."

Steven followed them to the door. "I get at least three a week."

Vince shrugged. "I do, too. It's part of the package. Get used to it."

Nathan stepped into the empty, dark-paneled hallway. "Normally, I wouldn't worry, but these people took pictures of me and Jane last night. If they get to Bonita, all hell is going to break loose."

Steven Porter lifted his square jaw. "You need any help, just ask. I have the best legal team at my disposal."

"Thank you, but so does Bonita. The only thing she cares about is her image and career."

Porter stifled a grin. "Then you've got your *out* already, Mr.

Selkirk."

"I do?" He certainly didn't see it.

Without clarifying, he said, "Call me if she backs you into a corner."

"All right, I'll do that."

A couple of minutes later, Nathan launched into his office. Barb sat behind her tidy desk. She immediately stood up. "Before you give me that envelope, I want to apologize for Bonita's actions last night. Change your number. If there's a cost involved, send me the bill."

Barb Staggit was in her early thirties. Single. Competent. Pretty, with a nice body and deep chestnut-colored hair. And he was certain she had a thing for him. But the age-old trope of screwin' around with his secretary never crossed his mind.

Wearing a wide red belt and knee-length black dress that sat snugly against her curves, she rounded the desk. "I took a couple hours off this morning and did just that," she said. "Bonita accused me of keeping your secrets. She sounded totally drunk."

"She won't remember a damn thing. You didn't deserve to get caught in the crossfire. How can I make it up to you?"

"I appreciate the sentiment, but I'm fine." She picked up a large manila envelope. "This is what just arrived."

He slid the contents onto the desk. As expected, ten photographs of him and Jane at dinner scattered across the surface. Nathan unfolded the letter.

Mr. Selkirk, it appears that monogamee is not your stile. If you'd like to keep your secret then put fifty grand in a bag and deposit it in the garbage can across the street from the coffee shop on the corner of Smythe and Gibson by 5 tonight. If not, I'm sure your wife wud be interested.

Blackmail by someone with fourth-grade English skills. This shouldn't be too hard to handle. Nathan stuffed the photos and note back into the envelope while Barb's forehead creased with concern.

"Who is she?" Barb blurted, apparently not caring if it was her business or not.

"I know I can count on your discretion. She's important to me and someone I'm trying to protect."

His admin assistant's cheeks reddened. "From the pictures, she looks more than important."

Lanna's friend had taken several shots of Nathan when he'd kissed Jane.

"So…so, the rumors are true. Your marriage is over."

"Bonita and I separated over a year ago."

She clasped her hands and sighed with relief. "To be honest, I hate that bitch, and I'm glad you're divorcing her."

He grinned at Barb's honest comment. "There seems to be a consensus about that around here."

"That woman is horrible. You should have heard what she said to me last night."

His brow knit together with empathy. "Sorry. She's abrasive. I know that."

Barb pointed at the envelope. "The woman wearing the scarf in those pictures looks like she's hiding something. Does she have cancer?"

"No. She was in an accident. Head injury."

Barb's mouth gaped. "Accident? I thought I recognized her. She's a contractor here at the Jade, isn't she?" She tsked. "And here I thought I could convince you to fall in love with me."

Wow, straight from the hip. He palmed her slender shoulder. "You're a sweetheart, Barb. I couldn't do what I do around here without you. Wouldn't want to screw that up."

Barb rolled her eyes and smiled. "Yeah, I know, but a girl can dream."

He'd hired her around the time he'd married Bonita. Barb vetted the mounds of reports he received daily, prioritizing each request. He trusted her, and they had a good working relationship.

The outer door to his office *whooshed* open, and Jake Murphy, from marketing, stepped inside. A sharp-looking guy with dark cropped hair in his thirties came to a halt. Jake often dropped by the office instead of using in-house email, like the rest of the staff. Nathan's sixth sense told him Jake had worked up the nerve to ask Barb out and used resort business as an opportunity to make his pitch.

"Whatever the issue, Mr. Murphy, give Barb the details. She'll handle it."

"I will?" she said in a higher octave than normal. "But—"

He didn't have time for *buts;* he needed to find out what Mr. Peters had uncovered about Lanna, especially now that she and her accomplice had demanded money. Vince gave him the go-ahead to delegate. That's what he intended to do.

Jake looked just as surprised. "Sir, I wanted to discuss some new marketing ideas."

"Then *discuss* them with Barb over lunch."

The guy swallowed thickly. "Lunch? Um, yeah, okay."

"If she likes what she hears, she'll let me know." He whistled past Jake, leaving him to make his play. If he couldn't convince Barb to accept a date with him, he didn't deserve her. "Barb, I'm headed down to the security control room. If anything else arises as to what we just discussed, text me."

"Yes, sir."

He shut the door and rushed to the stairs.

Halfway down the staircase, a text popped up from Mr. Peters.

Urgent information

That's all Nathan needed to take the steps two at a time. He swiped his keycard against the reader outside of security operations and shoved open the reinforced metal door.

Mr. Peters stood in front of a desktop computer. The new hire, Mr. Crocker, who'd checked Jane after the accident, sat at the terminal.

"What have you found?"

Peters nodded at the trainee. "Mr. Crocker, if you will."

Crocker quickly opened a directory and clicked on one of the multiple files. A picture of Lanna and her friend appeared on the monitor. Classic unflattering police snapshots taken at the time of arrest.

Mr. Peters explained. "The man is Dirk Morgan. Twenty-five years of age."

"Let me guess, high school dropout."

"Yes. Last known address is Lovelock, Nevada. Both have done time for fraud, theft, and other assorted crimes. They're like a budding Bonnie and Clyde. Possession, armed robbery. Quite the couple. She's not with Jane now, is she?"

"I didn't say she was with Jane."

Mr. Peters fingered his tie. "Uh, yes. Of course. My apologies."

"Relax, Mr. Peters. Don't apologize for good instincts. You're chief of security for a reason. Good work."

"Thank you, sir. We had Dirk on file in our in-house database. We apprehended him after he stole a guest's purse. The police arrested him, and he was charged. Lanna is not in our files, but she has several convictions. I've sent all the information to your personal email."

Nathan had expected something, but he didn't expect this. He scrolled through the contacts on his cell, then dialed.

"Las Vegas PD. James Read."

"James, it's Nathan Selkirk. I need a favor and a few minutes of your time."

It didn't take long for an undercover Las Vegas PD unit to be sent to Jane's place, and Nathan headed to Read's office.

CHAPTER TEN

The Royal Jade worked with local law enforcement daily. James Read, detective in charge of fraud and its associated crimes, had served at the LVMPD for twenty years. He'd also spent ten years as a Marine.

In an eight-by-eight cubicle, James sat behind his desk in a high-back chair on casters. His dark hair, cut short at the sides, had silver streaks. Deep wrinkles near his eyes meant retirement wasn't far off. The contents of the envelope Nathan received, including the letter and the pictures he'd taken this morning, lay on the detective's desk.

"I'm familiar with Dirk Morgan," James said, perching his elbows on the armrests and steepling his fingertips. "He's not the brightest bulb in the box. I'll set up my guys to take him down after you drop off the bag."

"Need the money?" Nathan asked.

James grinned. "Nah. We'll give you a bag stuffed with paper. In case Dirk is lucky enough to evade my team, it's got a GPS tracker."

"Appreciate the help on this, but I need the original photographs destroyed. He used a camera. You'll probably find it in his van or the dump he's staying at in West Las Vegas."

James sat forward in his seat. "I can't promise that, but we'll search the van when we arrest him." The detective clasped his hands on the desk. "I'm guessing it's this woman," he pointed to a picture, "you're concerned about. Because that's not Bonita."

"Bonita and I separated. That woman's name is Jane. She's got a landscaping business and works her ass off."

"I didn't know you separated, but I've seen the tabloids. Bonita doesn't seem shy about flaunting her relationships. Why do you care if she sees these photos?"

"Apparently, her affairs aren't trending well. Bonita needs a scapegoat. She'll use Jane to garner sympathy, even if she has nothing to do with the divorce. Cancel culture is all the rage these days. I'm concerned Bonita will mention Jane's business, hoping folks will boycott her."

"Yeah, my kids are in college, but they're glued to their damn phones. The Internet and its associated crimes have opened a whole new era for law enforcement." He flattened his palms on the desk and stood. "Anyway, follow me. We'll get the bag, and you can drop it off at the location Dirk indicated. We'll be waiting in the wings."

"Lead the way."

At two o'clock, Nathan dropped by the Royal Jade's revenue accounting department. Albert McKenzie managed the highly trained staff. A redheaded woman looked up from her computer and smiled in greeting.

Nathan nudged his head toward the closed door to McKenzie's office. "He in?"

"I think so. One second, Mr. Selkirk." She quickly punched a three-digit code into the phone on her desk.

"Hello!" a brisk voice answered.

"Mr. Selkirk is here."

"Be right out."

A second later, Albert opened the door and lumbered out of his lair. "Nathan. What can I do for you?"

"I was wondering if you could do me a favor. A friend of mine runs her own business. She recently had a serious accident and lost her sight. Some accountants here do side jobs. Think you can send out a brief email asking if anyone would care to make a few bucks helping my friend until her sight returns?"

The redhead raised her hand as if waiting for the teacher to call on her. "Perfect timing, Mr. Selkirk. I'm available. My son is a senior, and college is expensive."

That was easy. He dug into his suit's jacket pocket and gave her his card. "Jane was in the hospital for two weeks, so there's some catch-up involved. But after that, it should be routine.

That's my personal number. Call me this weekend, and I'll put you and Jane together to work out the details."

She plucked the card from his fingers, opened the bottom drawer of her desk, and shoved it in the outer pocket of a black purse. "I will definitely do that. My name's Nora Hamilton. I also prepare personal and business tax returns. I'm happy to help." She winked at him and turned her gaze back to the computer.

Albert grinned. "Okay. Guess that takes care of that. Anything else, Mr. Selkirk?"

"Nope. As always, your department keeps a tight ship. Thanks for your time."

A few minutes later, he reached his office. Barb sat at her desk with her eyes glued to the monitor. "How did lunch go with Jake Murphy?" He kept walking and strolled into his roomy office, taking a seat behind his mahogany desk.

Barb followed and sat in the suede guest chair. She shrugged. "I don't know if I'm the best judge of new marketing ideas."

He leaned back in his chair. "Let's hear it."

After twenty minutes, Barb finished explaining Jake's ideas. "Personally, I like option number two. We already offer free hotel rooms and perks to all our customers, but linking up with an airline to give deep discounts on airfare allows customers more money to spend in the casino and less on getting here. Jake has already contacted the biggest carriers. He's a good salesman. Three main airlines are open to talk."

"And?"

She blinked. "And what?"

"Have you not noticed Mr. Murphy is in and out of this office like Superman uses a telephone booth?"

She straightened her shoulders. "I might have noticed."

He laughed. "Well, did he finally gather enough balls to ask you out or not?"

She fluttered her lashes. "Possibly."

Nathan nodded. "Good. I was giving up on the guy. Maybe he'll use fucking email for a change. As for his idea, I like option number two as well. Have him send me a summary report with the three contenders."

"Yes, sir. Also, Bonita called three times while you were out. Does she know about this blackmail scheme?"

"No. And I want it to stay that way."

Barb stood. "Got it. I forwarded you a few issues that need your attention today."

"Thank you."

She left his office and closed the door. Nathan swiveled in his chair and looked out over the bustling strip. Vehicles interspersed with taxis traveled bumper-to-bumper. Visitors moseyed down the wide sidewalks. He slid his cell from his pocket and selected Jane's number.

When she answered, he heard wind and traffic noise in the background.

"Hello."

"Hey, sweetheart. Just checking in. Where are you?"

"Boulder Summit Drive."

"What are you doing there?"

"I'm with Miguel and one of my teams."

"You're working?" he asked, amazed, but then again, not.

She laughed. "Can't sit around on my pretty duff all day. I think my sight is improving. A little."

"Hey, that's great."

"Well, yes and no. I got a little too cocky and tripped four times." She laughed at herself. "I can't really see anything clearly, but I see color and lumpy stuff."

"Don't push it, sweetheart."

"Yes, Dad. Anyway, I'm finished around five o'clock. Do we still have a date?"

"Do Texans like big hats? But I'll be late. Lanna and her boyfriend sent me a package with the photos they took last night."

"Shit. Those bastards. I fired Lanna this morning. I told her we had broken up. She tried to commiserate by telling me you were married. I burst her bubble when I said you weren't, but it wasn't common knowledge."

"I'm going through with the drop-off."

"How much did they ask for?"

"Fifty grand. Law enforcement will arrest him after the drop. Lanna's boyfriend's name is Dirk Morgan. Both of them have a substantial record of petty and not-so-petty crimes. I have to drop off—" Barb's raised voice came from the other side of the door, and then it flung open. He swiveled his chair. Well, fuck! "I have to call you back."

"Sure. Talk later."

He disconnected and stared as Bonita strode into his office, decked out in a designer dress, perfect hair, and that yappy mutt stuffed in her bag. Barb followed and discretely closed the door.

Maybe he should have stayed with the SEAL teams. He'd rather have bullets flying past his brainpan than deal with Bonita.

She pulled the terrier from her bag and dumped the dog on the carpet to run around. If that mutt pissed on his desk, he wouldn't drop-kick it out the window, but he'd love to watch Bonita tumble a few stories.

"What can I do for you, Bonita?"

She strolled toward the guest bar in his office and poured herself a drink. "I'd like to have a civilized conversation for a change."

That depended on how many ounces of gin she'd already downed today. "About what? Thought you were on your way to Malibu."

Her bony shoulders rose with a deep sigh, then she actioned a melodramatic turn on the toes of her spiked shoes. "When's your flight to Atlanta?"

"Later."

He watched her stroll across the carpet and slide into the guest chair. The slit in her skin-tight red dress parted up to her thighs when she crossed her legs. "Why don't we talk over dinner?"

"Talk about what?"

"Reconciliation. Nathan, I've never been a big believer

in psychologists, but I'm not opposed to seeing a marriage counselor."

He'd spoken to his lawyer yesterday. The guy had couriered the divorce papers to her legal team weeks ago. "Did you get the divorce papers yet?"

Her bright blue gaze darted toward his built-in shelves on the right side of the room. "No. Maybe they got lost."

"They're not lost. Your legal team has them."

"Why don't you have any pictures of me in here?" She sipped her drink, then set it on the edge of his desk.

Nathan forked his fingers and rested them on his stomach. "Did you send the boyfriend packing, or will I find he moved in when I get home?"

Her sleek, pale eyebrows flattened. "I didn't mean to hurt you."

"You didn't. We're separated, Bonita, and divorced once you sign those papers, which I want you to do on Monday. Preferably today."

"You don't mean that."

"Oh, I do."

"But why?" she said, using her high-pitched, keening tone. "I've been thinking about us a lot."

"Before or after you gave the boy toy a blowjob this morning?"

She stiffened. "Don't you see I'm just trying to get your attention? I think it's a cry for help."

"Then get some," he said, glaring at her.

"We didn't give things an honest try. Can't we start over?"

Nathan leaned forward and rested his forearms on the desk. "I don't know what's going on in that messed-up head of yours, but the marriage is over. It ended a few minutes after we said, 'I do'. I'm not going out to dinner with you, so some fan or paparazzi can snap a picture of us. You'll have to try something else other than spinning a story that we're fine and all the rumors of your infidelity are just rumors."

Her eyes narrowed. "That's not true."

"Sure, it is. Why don't you put on your big-girl panties, deal with the fallout like a grown-up, and move on? In a few months, you'll be on the junket for your latest film. No one is going to give a shit that you're divorced."

A well-crafted tear leached from her eye and rolled down her cheek. "But I will," she squeaked. "I feel lost without you. I don't know who to trust anymore." She sniffed and swiped away the tear. "I have just about everything I've ever wanted, except your love. I had so many good-looking men chasing me when we met. But I didn't see anyone except you. When you asked me out, I was so excited. You made me feel special."

Was she trying out a new script on him or what? Bonita's actions left so much shrapnel scattered through their marriage that he barely remembered what their early days had been like. Sure, she was exceptionally willing to please him in bed, but they'd never connected on any level. Not like Jane, who made his pulse thump with impatience.

The mutt came sniffing around his chair, then yapped with a shrill bark.

"Bonita, there are plenty of decent guys out there, but if you keep hooking up with men in the entertainment industry, you'll never trust their intentions."

"Did you ever love me?" she asked in a weighted tone. "Honestly. Did you care at all?"

Fond of her—yes, until everything went to hell. "Too many tides have washed in and out since then for me to answer that. When it comes to us, there's nothing to fix. Do us both a favor and sign the papers. Soon."

Bonita's brow wrinkled, and tears flowed from her eyes. She nodded jerkily, then stood. "You're in love with someone else, aren't you?" When he didn't answer, she inhaled sharply. "I noticed you're not wearing your ring anymore. You're not going to Atlanta this weekend. You're going to her."

He crossed his arms over his chest. "I told you this before. If you want to tell reporters you're divorced and I'm the bad guy, then do it. Sympathy for you will come rolling in, and you can hold those shoulders high and tell the world you're a strong, independent woman who doesn't need a man to complete you."

Her gaze landed on the liquor in the glass. She swept the tumbler into her hand and downed the contents. "And what if reporters ask you what happened?"

He shrugged. "That the marriage didn't work. Full stop."

Bonita's sharp chin jutted upward. "You'd do that for me?"

Wasn't any skin off his ass. He'd do just about anything to get rid of Bonita and her ilk. "I don't need to play the blame game or make you look bad." She'd done that all on her own.

A bittersweet smile coated his ex's expression. "I know I screwed up our marriage. I wish you'd give me another chance, but I can see you hate me."

"We're incompatible. That's different than hate."

"There's no going back, is there?" she asked with whispery longing.

He slowly shook his head. Even if Jane never existed, he'd be in the same spot he was now.

She called the pint-sized dog, who quickly ran into Bonita's arms. Lifting the mutt, she tucked it to her chest and picked up her purse. "What's she like, Nathan? Seriously, no judgment. I'm just curious."

He wouldn't be surprised if she recorded the entire conversation. "There's no one to blame, Bonita. You have no competition." Wasn't that the truth? There was no comparison between the way Jane approached life and Bonita's self-serving ideologies.

Bonita offered him a syrupy, weak smile. "It breaks my heart, but I'll sign the papers."

He wanted to do an end-run jump for joy but sedately said, "Thank you. Is your bodyguard waiting outside?"

She shook her head and slipped on a pair of obscenely large sunglasses.

"Wait a second." He selected Mr. Peters' number on his cell. When the chief of security answered, Nathan said, "Liam, it's Nathan. Bonita Williams needs a security escort from my office to her car."

"Right away, sir."

The edges of Bonita's ruby-red lips quirked when he placed his cell on the desk.

"I know I broke your trust, Nathan. But my affairs didn't mean anything. I didn't know how to love you or make you happy."

There might have been some truth to that. "Take care of yourself, Bonita."

"I'll meet security at the elevator. I don't want to say goodbye, but I guess it is."

For a change, she departed without a tantrum. He blew out a long, cleansing breath. Barb appeared and gripped the doorknob, quietly shutting the door his ex had left open.

He glanced at his watch. Two hours before he headed to the drop-off point to give Dirk a bag of blank paper cut into the same size as dollar bills.

No point in texting Jane. She couldn't see the message. She knew he'd be late. Once the sting operation went down and Dirk was in custody, hopefully James would confiscate the camera. He'd want the photos as evidence. Nathan didn't care if they existed in some police evidence lockup, as long as they stayed there.

****

Once Jade's security team deposited Bonita next to her car, she thanked them and slid inside. Smidge jumped out of her purse and stood on his back legs, then barked out the window at someone.

"Shut-up!" she shouted.

The dog whimpered and curled in a ball on the passenger's seat. Bonita inhaled a few deep breaths to stop from screaming. She smashed the steering wheel with her fist.

"Fuck!"

Digging her phone out of her purse, she stopped the

recording. He hadn't said shit to incriminate himself. She popped the cell in the bracket attached to the dash.

"Call, Andrea."

Two rings later, her personal assistant answered. "How'd it go?" she asked, sympathy dripping in her voice.

"Fucking horrible. I thought for sure inviting Bryce over last night would send Nathan off the deep end. I pushed his buttons, hoping he'd smack me, but that bastard didn't even flinch."

"Sorry, Bonita, but I didn't think that would work. Those Navy SEALs are trained to keep calm in any situation. What about my idea?"

"Nope. I tried everything. Tears. Flirting. Begging. Told him I wanted another chance. A total line of bullshit, but I'm an actress, after all. An Oscar-worthy performance."

"Guess that means he wouldn't go out to dinner with you."

"No!" She crossed her arms in a huff. "Asshole figured out exactly what I was trying to do. Not your fault, Andrea. It was a good idea."

"Least you tried. I've been tweeting and posting all day. You've got thousands of die-hard fans who stick up for you."

She sneered. "Yeah. And thousands who're calling me a slut and unfaithful. My image is everything."

"All people really care about is your next movie. The trailer is coming out tomorrow."

"No, they don't. I need to save face. The rumors about me and Bryce are everywhere."

Andrea sighed. "They're not exactly rumors, are they?"

"Doesn't matter! I need a reason once word gets out about Nathan and my divorce. One that will cast me in a good light."

The sound of fingertips on a keyboard meant Andrea was multitasking.

"Didn't Nathan say you could put the blame on him?"

"Nathan *Holier Than Thou* Selkirk is wearing a halo in all of this. He's been different lately. I know he's seeing someone. He didn't come home last night, and he wasn't at the Jade."

"Then hire an investigator to follow him. Get the evidence

and leak it. Your fans will lap it up, and you can play the poor dejected wife with a cheating husband, and that's why you fell into another man's arms."

"Nathan sees everything when he enters a room. He'll figure out he's being followed. Dammit!" She slapped the steering wheel again, and Smidge yipped. "Shut up, you stupid mutt. God, I hate this fucking dog."

"People love Smidge when you post pics of you and him. They think he's so adorable."

"I want to drop the little shit off at the pound. Damn thing pisses all over my bedroom."

Andrea sighed. "Anyway—let me find you a private investigator. Someone discrete."

"Go ahead," she snapped, still fuming that Nathan refused to have dinner with her. "Find out who he's fucking. I'll bury her with bad press. If she's in the entertainment industry, I'll pull in some favors to have her canceled. But she's probably some rich bitch who seduced him at the resort. I don't give a shit if their affair started after we were separated. I'll just tell people it happened before the separation. At least it will give me an out."

"Yeah. Yeah, for sure. And what about the other issue? Have you decided?"

Bonita tapped her fingertip against the wheel. "Not yet."

"It's a hard decision, I know." Andrea's voice dipped with meaning.

"Pfft. Not hard at all. If I can use it to my advantage, I will. Nathan is champing at the bit for me to sign the divorce papers. I don't think I'm quite ready to do that."

"Whatever you think is best. And remember, you have an interview here in LA tomorrow afternoon at three with Keisha Toppins' Everything Hollywood show."

"I'm leaving for LA now. I'll be there."

"Okay, great! The show has a limo scheduled to pick you up in Malibu around one thirty."

"Make sure they don't ask about my marriage."

"Of course, but you could use it to your advantage."

"How?"

The typing in the background ceased. "You're convinced Nathan is seeing someone."

She laughed. "Of course. Why else would he push so hard for the divorce? I'm Bonita Williams. Men fantasize about fucking me when they screw their pathetic wives. What's your point?"

"My point is a private investigator is one person. Instead of hiring a PI, why not use your devoted fans? If Nathan is with another woman, someone will see them and post a pic. You have warriors on your side, Bonita. Use that. Drop a hint during the show. One set of eyes will turn into thousands."

"Hmm." Not a bad idea. "Every dumped or discarded woman would relate. If I can spin this, the attention will shift to Nathan and away from me."

"Absolutely," Andrea said. "Think about it. Oh—and I saw a few rumors on the boards I monitor that Palm Productions is looking for a new lead actress in an upcoming rom-con adventure planned for next year."

"Usually my agent is all over that. Beckett hasn't called me."

"The rumor dropped fresh an hour ago."

She'd been trying to get into one of Steven Porter's films for years. Fucker never cast her. Not even an audition call. She'd even debased herself and tried to get close to his wife, Moira. That bitch never returned her calls. Palm production actresses cleaned up at the Oscars. She didn't have one of those sitting on her mantle yet. A rom-con wouldn't win the coveted award, but she'd have a foot in the door.

"Do some more digging. I want a shot."

"I'm all over it. Talk later. And hey, don't worry about the divorce. Everything's going to be fine."

Bonita disconnected the call.

"Everything isn't fine, you stupid bitch." The long whiskers above the terrier's eyes twitched. "What are you lookin' at?"

She started the Porsche, then tore out of the VIP parking area, nearly hitting a couple of senior citizens walking to their vehicle and hanging onto each other for support. Once she found the woman screwing Nathan, she'd destroy the bitch.

CHAPTER ELEVEN

Nathan pulled up next to the garbage can at the corner of Smythe and Gibson a minute before seventeen hundred hours. He left the BMW running, rounded the front of the vehicle, and scanned the area. Plenty of people walked along the sidewalk that fronted small shops in this area of town. Light traffic motored down the street, but he didn't see the blue van or Dirk. Opening his passenger door, he retrieved the police-issued bag and stuffed it in the garbage, then buried it under empty cardboard cups and other trash.

About to get in his car, Nathan spotted his target. Dirk stood next to the coffee shop with his back turned. *Hey, asshole. Hope you like prison food.*

Nathan got behind the wheel and drove down the street. Taking the first left, Lady Luck made an appearance. He spotted Dirk's crappy blue van. Passing at the posted speed, he didn't see anyone in the vehicle.

He kept driving, turned left at the next street, and parked. Ditching his suit jacket and tie in the backseat, he double-backed on foot to the van. Nathan crouched behind a black pickup across the street and called Detective Read.

"Drop's been made. I spotted Dirk next to the coffee shop."

"Yeah, we got him in sight. Waiting for him to make his move."

"I found his van. It's on Smythe. Half a block south of the corner."

"Thanks, Nathan. I'll send two of my guys over there to cover the van." He ended the call.

From his position, Nathan saw the garbage can where he'd stuffed the money. His cell rang. Jane's name appeared on the caller ID.

"Hey, darlin', your sight improving?"

"Just lucky. I took a chance and selected the last number in my history."

"Ready for our date?" He watched a woman jog down the opposite side of the street with a Labrador.

"Just got home. I need a shower."

Instantly, he wanted to be with her and grinned at the X-rated image in his mind. "I shouldn't be too long."

"Are you at work?"

"Nope, I'm squatting behind a truck, waiting for Lanna's boyfriend to take the bait."

"Say what?"

"PD is ready to pounce. I'm covering Dirk's van."

"You can take the SEAL out of the Navy, but not the risk-taker out of Nathan Selkirk."

He chuckled. "Something like that."

"You sound like you're having fun."

"I want to watch his ass get busted, but I don't see Lanna."

"Don't get shot, okay?"

"Don't plan on it. I'll be there soon. Jump in the shower. Unless you want to wait for me, I don't mind helping you out in that department."

Jane's good-natured laugh made him smile. "You are a tease, Mr. Selkirk."

"And hey, we have a dinner invitation for next Wednesday."

"Sounds interesting. See you soon, Dick Tracey."

He disconnected the call and shook his head, shoving the phone in his back pants pocket. "All right, shithead. Go get that bag."

It didn't take long before Dirk darted for the money and dug his arm into the trash can. Read's officers converged on foot and with ghost cars. Dirk couldn't write worth shit, but the little bastard sure could run.

He dodged and leaped, evading Read's men like a running back. As if sprinting for the goal line, the guy's sneakers slapped on the ground. He darted between both officers on Smythe, the bag of fake money tucked tightly under his arm.

The kid wore a grin until Nathan tackled him to the ground, pinned his face to the pavement, and wound his arms behind his back. Dirk yelped and wiggled, but Nathan dug his knee into the middle of the dirtbag's back.

"Relax, you little shit. It's over."

The scuffle of several feet came to a stop and surrounded Nathan.

Nathan released his grip once law enforcement snapped cuffs around Dirk's wrists, and the cop yarded the punk to his feet.

Detective Read wore a broad grin when Nathan stood up. "That was some takedown, Selkirk."

"Thought I'd lend a hand," Nathan said.

A plain-clothed cop patted Dirk down and pulled a set of keys from his front pocket, then tossed them to Detective Read.

Read glared at the grimy-looking young man. "Where's Lanna?"

"Lanna who?" The grungy little bastard jerked his head to shift greasy bangs from his eyes.

"Read him his rights," the detective instructed.

"False arrest. I found that bag." Dirk tried to yank himself from the cop's grip—unsuccessfully.

As the officer dragged Dirk toward the patrol car parked on the street twenty feet away, Read said, "Let's see what's inside the van."

Twisting, Dirk shouted. "Stay the fuck outta my private property, asshole."

Nathan stood back and let the cops conduct their search. An officer opened the back doors to reveal a van stuffed to the roof with crap. Obviously, Lanna and Dirk lived in this thing. Food wrappers. Cans of food. Blankets. A hodgepodge of junk.

After twenty minutes of searching, Read jumped out the back end of the cramped home on wheels and shook his head. "Sorry, Nathan. There's no camera in there."

"Fuck." He ran a hand through his hair. "Lanna must have it."

Read's cell rang and he held up a hand, signaling Nathan to wait, then answered the call. "Yeah, I got it. Thanks." He stashed his cell. "I had a unit head over to the motel you told me about. The room's been cleaned out. Looks like Lanna's on the run."

"And probably has the camera. Shit!"

"I'll put out an APB for her, but she's gonna stay low. They probably had a prearranged meeting spot."

Nathan scanned the street. "Lanna probably watched the whole thing go down. She knows Dirk's busted."

Read nodded. "Possible. We'll have the van towed to impound. I'll have my guys take a second look. I'll let you know if we find anything."

Nathan shook James's hand. "Think he'll be released on bail?"

"These days, probably. We bust 'em, but they're usually back on the street in a week. He'll see a judge seventy-two hours after we file charges. Extortion is a Category B felony. If convicted, he faces one to ten years' imprisonment. Dirk has a long record. Not all of them are misdemeanors. If the judge deems him a flight risk, they'll deny bail. That's the best-case scenario. If not, he'll bolt and go into hiding. Might leave the state."

"The justice system might do fuck all, but I can. Any chance you can give me a head's up if the judge sets bail?"

"I can't, but I'll put you in touch with someone who can. What's your plan?"

"Hire someone to trail him. Some team guys I know started a military contracting service. They can track Dirk, and he'll lead me to Lanna and that camera."

Read lifted a hand to stop Nathan from explaining more. "Don't think I need to hear the rest of that plan, but I wish you luck."

"Thanks for your help, James. I owe you and the wife a getaway weekend, all-inclusive, at the Jade. Just text me when, and I'll make the arrangements."

"I'll take you up on that. I've been working a lot of overtime. I need to earn some brownie points with Sandy."

Nathan thanked the other officers in the vicinity and strode past the patrol car, where Dirk sat cuffed in the back seat. The guy banged the window with his head, leaving a greasy smudge. Read noticed and ordered the officer in the patrol car to roll down the window.

"Got something to say?" Nathan asked.

"I know what you want. Drop the charges and I'll tell you where it is."

Read's jowls cinched tight. "Kid, you're being charged with extortion. I have all the evidence the DA needs. There're no deals here unless you want to turn over the camera now. If so, the judge might take it into consideration."

Dirk's nostrils flared, and his beady, dark eyes narrowed.

"Where's Lanna?" Nathan asked.

"If I don't show in an hour, she's gone, and so is the camera. So get me the fuck out of these cuffs, asshole."

Nathan figured the little prick had already made a deal with some rag to sell the photos. "So you're willing to rot in prison while Lanna sells the pictures and takes off to California? Hope she sends you a postcard."

"Fuck you, man."

Detective Read circled his finger in the air at the officer behind the wheel, and the window rolled up. "I'll text you my contact at the DA's office. They'll tell you if he makes bail."

"Thanks."

Nathan crossed the road and headed for his car. Until Dirk's initial hearing, Lanna would stick around. Which meant he had seventy-two hours or less to find her. Nathan reached his vehicle and stood under the balmy evening sun.

With the temperature in the 80s, it was the ideal weather for his date with Jane. He called Barb, asking her to dig up the number for Mace and Tony's military contracting business.

Two minutes later, she texted him the number in San Diego. He turned his wrist. Eighteen hundred hours. He dialed the number and a recording instructed him to call another number for emergencies.

Within three rings, someone answered. He recognized the

voice.

"Tony Bale, you probably don't remember me, but this is Nathan Selkirk."

"Lieutenant! Course I remember. How the hell have you been?"

Two young children interrupted the ambient background noise with their squabbling. A woman with a sweet tone hushed the boys. "Can't complain. Sounds like you have your hands full."

Tony chuckled. "That's Troy and Cash, my two monsters in the making. They're twins. Double the trouble. Lumin, babe, I'm going in the office." After a few seconds, a door closed. "What's up, Frog?"

Nathan dove in and summarized why he'd called. Dirk wouldn't see a judge until Monday at the earliest, so they had time. "We're in standby mode, but I'll send you a retainer. If Dirk makes bail, then we initiate the plan."

"I got a better idea. Lumin hasn't seen her godparents, Steven and Moira Porter, for a while. I'll pack up the family and bring two contractors with me. We'll head to Vegas tonight. It shouldn't be difficult to pin down Lanna's location. If the dirtbag doesn't get bail on Monday, we'll find that camera, regardless."

"Good plan. Let me know where to deposit the funds."

A ruckus ensued, starting with the bang of a door hitting a wall and Tony's kids shouting. In Dad Mode, Tony yelled, "Boys! Kitchen. Now!" The door closed again. "Sorry about that. They have a lot of energy. And don't listen to a damn thing I say."

Nathan grinned. "I saw Steven Porter this morning. Apparently, his twins are a handful, too. Anyway, let me know what the retainer costs and I'll have the funds transferred."

"What funds?"

"For your services, Tinman. I'll arrange rooms for your contractors at the Royal Jade."

"Listen up, Rider; you cover the food and bunks, and the rest is on us."

Nathan dipped his head, smiling at the use of his team name, surprised Tinman remembered. "Okay, T-man, but I owe you one."

"Anything for a brother. I'll text you the names of my contractors so you can make arrangements. Let's rendezvous tomorrow morning."

"I'm taking Jane on our first *official* date tonight. It's been two years in the making. Meet you at the Royal Jade. My office. Noon."

"You got it, LT."

****

"Ahhh, that warm wind feels so good." Jane stretched out her arms and tipped her head back. The purr of Nathan's motorcycle shut off. Begrudgingly, she dismounted. He loosened the strap under her chin, and she removed the helmet. "Where are we?"

They'd spent a half hour on the bike, and Jane loved the ride with her arms wrapped around Nathan's taut waist.

"Ready for our first date?" he asked.

"Sure, but what are we doing?"

"Even without your sight, I wanted this to be something you remembered."

Jane squinted, seeing someone stride toward them. Probably a man, by his long-legged gait.

"Mr. Selkirk, everything is prepared. Are you ready to suit up?"

"We are. Thanks, Dillon."

"Suit up?" she asked, suddenly nervous. "Suit up for what?"

He grasped her hand, gently tugging for her to follow. "I'm taking you somewhere you've never been. Least, I don't think you've ever done this before."

He led her toward a truck parked to their right. She grinned. "You're being very mysterious."

She heard a *swoosh*, then the sound of a zipper.

"Hold out your arms," he instructed.

Going along with the surprise, she did as he asked. Nathan slid her arms through something and cinched it tight around her upper body. She ran her fingers across the smooth fabric. "A

134

vest?"

"Exactly."

Continuing to prep her, he strapped something around both her knees and placed a helmet on her head, securing the chin strap. The clues collided. She squinted at a large object next to them. A white blur with red, blue, and green strips.

"Is that—? Are we going hang gliding?"

His deep chuckle resonated with warmth through her cells.

"Ever been?"

"No. The girls and I did a tandem sky dive once when we were in college. I've always wanted to try this. Is it you and I? Or am I going with someone else?"

Nathan placed his mouth next to her ear. "Just you and me, sweetheart. Soaring with the thermals."

Her body shifted as he tugged on the lines attached to the back of her vest. "You've done this before, right?"

"One of my favorite hobbies when I get a rare day off. This is my equipment."

"What do I do?"

Nathan gave her a few pointers, and they practiced running in tandem to prepare for the launch. The sun dipped on the horizon, but there was still plenty of light.

Butterflies of excitement fluttered in her stomach. "I was exhausted when you picked me up, but I'm wide awake now."

"Yeah, I had one helluva day, too. But we're leaving that all behind."

Nathan connected their belts and straps to the hang glider. She'd ride next to him, and he'd do all the steering.

He lifted the glider. "You ready?"

She squeaked with excitement. "Oh, my God. Okay. Okay. Ready!"

They took a few running steps and soared off the launch pad. The glider dipped and then rose, sailing into the thermals. Quiet. So quiet.

Nathan's body shifted, his arms outstretched, and he steered the glider with the metal bar he grasped. No clouds marred the sky, and the desert floor fell away as they climbed. The setting sun intensified the ground's rich, rustic palette.

"How high are we?" she asked as they soared far above the ground.

"We'll climb to a thousand feet. We're at three hundred right now."

Jane and her friends had experienced a lot of fun adventures, but this topped them all. The glider's sail didn't make a sound. Her stomach rolled as Nathan changed their direction, sweeping to the right.

"I love this!"

"Feels good, doesn't it?"

"Will you teach me how to do this?"

He laughed. "Just say the word, sweetheart!"

"Word!"

Nathan kept them in the air for an hour. He even let her grasp the bar and take control for a few minutes, giving her a few pointers.

"The sun's setting. I'm taking us down," he announced.

She could have stayed here all night. "If we have to."

"Hang on. This technique is called a spiral landing."

Using quick, tight loops, they descended in a circle, but what a ride!

They approached the ground at a dizzying speed. Strong winds buffeted their bodies, creating a bumpy ride.

As they landed, the wheels attached to the control bar made it easy. She expected a prolonged drag, yet they quickly came to a halt.

With her palms on the ground, she grinned. "I am in love." She shimmied to her knees, then stood.

Nathan detached her vest harness from the sail. "Feelings are mutual, sweetheart."

"I'm talking about gliding. Just to be clear."

He coughed and replied, "Yeah, sure. Of course."

She'd put her life in this man's competent hands, and she never once doubted he'd get her back to the ground in one piece.

Nathan Selkirk had a captivating charisma that weakened her normally independent disposition. She craved his nearness. If honest, in her current condition, she only felt safe when he was close.

Someone sauntered toward them and she assumed it was the same guy who'd been there at the launch.

"Good flight?" Dillon asked.

Nathan chuckled. "I think she's impressed. Sounds like I'm buying another glider."

Once free of all the equipment, Jane waited as Nathan gave the man a hand breaking down the glider and storing it on the back of a truck. Dillon dropped them off where Nathan had left the motorcycle.

Even without clear vision, the experience had been incredible. "I'm speechless," she said, standing next to the bike.

Nathan's thick arms wrapped around her waist. "Once your sight is back, we'll do it again."

"I can't wait." Jane slid her hands over the leather jacket that covered his broad shoulders and twined her fingers around his neck. "There's something else I want to do again."

He tipped his forehead to rest against hers. "Yeah," he said in a low timbre. "I want to make love to you all night, but we can't."

Deep in her core, an intense ache took issue with his "no sex" policy. "Are we going home?"

He backed away and placed a helmet in her hands. "Thirty-minute ride to our destination."

She tugged the helmet onto her head, then propped her hands on her hips. "Good, because at the end of the road, we're having hot, steamy sex. You read me loud and clear, sailor?"

Nathan gave her a quick kiss. "If I have to."

She laughed. "That's an order."

"Against my better judgement and severe lack of patience, my answer is—yes, ma'am." He tightened the strap under her chin. Before dropping the visor on her helmet, he said, "Truth is, I can't keep my fucking hands off you."

He planted a punishing kiss on her lips, then closed her visor.

As promised, within an hour, they stood inside a luxury suite somewhere near Red Rock Canyon.

He took his sweet time removing her clothes while kissing the sensitive spots on her neck. She tried to get things moving, but he stayed her hand. Seduction was an art form, and Nathan Selkirk had perfected his technique.

She loved the way he touched and teased her. For Jane, his body was a roadmap of muscled hills, rigid angles, and warm skin. With each caress, he drew her closer, taunting her with the promise of ecstasy.

Jane's past experiences with men were a rush to the finish line. Nathan's lovemaking was a lesson in patience as he slowly tightened the screws in the sexiest way possible.

Entangled in each other's arms, he laid her on a giant bed of crisp, cool sheets. Wrapping her hand around his thick erection, she squeezed. His breath hitched, but he didn't cave to temptation. The aching need between her thighs tingled from his fingers and mouth, but he resisted giving her what she wanted.

Was he stalling? "Nathan, I'm fine."

"Don't lie to me."

She cupped his jaw. "I'm not." Jane pressed a deep kiss on his mouth. "I love how you touch me. But I need more, and I want you now."

With her reassurance, he rolled her onto all fours.

From behind, two strong fingers eased into her channel, and a sigh erupted from her mouth.

Nathan planted a kiss on her spine. "Fuck, you're so wet. You have no idea what that does to me."

Panting, losing her mind, she sunk her fingers into the plump pillow under her head.

Every nerve ending in her body sung when his wide crown dipped into her core.

Jane bit her lip, her pulse thumping. Nathan gripped her hips and pistoned his stiff shaft with an agonizingly slow tempo.

His moans of pleasure set fire to her lust. Plunge after

delicious plunge, he struck her G-spot.

Her mind whirled, and her heart soared.

"Aww, Jane." His right hand slid around her hip and thumbed her bud.

Like leaving the ground in the glider, she lifted off and hurtled over the edge. Nathan followed her off the ridge as her inner muscles spasmed around his cock.

Minutes later, they lay together in comfortable silence. Nathan curled his arm around her shoulders. Night had fallen and with her decreased vision, the room became pitch dark. She couldn't see a thing, but she didn't need to see anything cuddled next to his warmth.

She must have fallen asleep. When she woke, Nathan caressed her thigh, which she'd slung over his hip at some point.

"What time is it?"

"Don't really care," he said.

She nuzzled closer. "Me either." He probably didn't like being tangled up with her long leg restraining him, but when she tried to move, he palmed her ass.

"We're perfect just like this." He kissed the top of her head.

She ran her palm over his molded, smooth shoulder. Jane didn't need her sight to know Nathan ate a clean diet and kept himself extremely fit.

"Are you hungry?" When his stomach grumbled almost on cue, she grinned. "Guess that's my answer."

"Any headaches?"

"I'm fine. I love your concern, but don't worry."

"That's not how I'm made, babe. I'm always concerned about you."

Since they'd met, he'd always put her well-being first. His parents were still married, and he'd learned traditional values from them. During his time in the SEALs, Nathan had probably filled his downtime with pretty women. But he hadn't married until he was thirty-four. She wondered why Bonita would ruin the marriage in such a short time with a handsome man who obviously had committed himself to her.

Jane propped herself on one elbow. "I know most people are on their best behavior when they first meet. There's lust and infatuation, but you seem so put-together. Confident. A man with ethics and charisma. Why didn't your marriage work?"

Nathan swept a stray hair from her cheek. "You're asking me to admit what I did wrong?"

"You have a famous wife. A beautiful home. An important position. Opportunity from here to the horizon. You started a marriage without so many stressors that break a relationship."

"All of that is true, but the most important element was missing."

"Are you going to tell me you didn't love her?"

"When Bonita had her first affair, I didn't really care. Suppose that explains a lot. When she filmed a movie, I didn't miss her. Maybe if I had, things would have worked out differently."

To Jane, it sounded as if Nathan had regrets. "Couples don't always have a passionate start, but they find a comfortable tempo—a partnership—and love grows."

Nathan palmed her cheek. "That's exactly what I expected when I proposed. Bonita wanted things from me that I wasn't ready to handle. She lives her life like there's a camera rolling in the background. Constant drama. Over-the-top emotional scenes. Drove me fucking nuts."

"But you hung in there for five years."

"When I left the SEAL teams, I had plenty of motivation to find a new direction. I made the most of my opportunities. But I wasn't hatched in a golden nest like Bonita. She pretended otherwise. When I didn't jump into the role she expected, everything crumbled."

"Sorry."

Nathan shimmied up the bed and leaned against his pillow. "I'm not. Not anymore."

"Are you worried about Lanna and the photographs?" Nathan had told her he'd hired an old friend from the SEALs to help locate the camera. Apparently, they were on their way to Las Vegas.

"I'm concerned about you, not me."

"Why?" She perched on her hip.

"Bonita is a spiteful bitch. It doesn't matter that we're separated or how many guys she fucked during our marriage. If she gets ahold of those photos, she'll come after you. There's no reasoning with her."

Bonita had dropped by his office today, but Nathan seemed to think she finally accepted their marriage was over.

"Not much she can do," Jane said. "I don't run in her circles."

"No, but she'll knit together a sob story. She has a huge following and there's a chance it will affect your business. That's why I need to destroy those photographs."

She hadn't thought of that. "I hope not. Twenty people rely on me for a paycheck."

Nathan skimmed her shoulder with a comforting touch. "If the worst happens, you can lean on me."

Shit! Jane had quite a few contracts with the wealthier class. Would they cancel because of Bonita?

"That's not me, Nathan. I would never allow you to bail me out."

"I'm not surprised you'd say that. It's your business, and you feel responsible for its success or failure." He paused and placed his warm hand over hers. "I'll do my best to make sure your crew finds employment. That's not a big deal. It's whether you'll blame me for my ex's actions."

She'd worked so damn hard to build her business. Jane nibbled on her bottom lip. It came down to whether a relationship with Nathan was worth the risk.

"If I hadn't been hit by the cab, would we be here? Now. Together," she asked.

"Probably not," he answered honestly. "But that doesn't mean I would have stayed clear of you forever. There wasn't any hope of that. The accident shortened the timeline. That's all."

How many ways did she love this man's no-bullshit way of dealing with issues? "By the sound of Bonita, she wants vindication, whether it's now or later. No matter who you get close to, she'll use her connections to mess with that person."

"I wish it wasn't the case, but most likely."

Jane trailed her hand up his firm bicep. "As cliché as this sounds, I don't see myself tossing my responsibilities aside and diving for cover behind you. I've always taken care of myself."

"Now that I know you better, I see that," he said, his tone sullen. "I just want you to know that you can. And on the other side of whatever happens, I want us to make a lifetime of memories. I want *you*, Jane."

Nathan offered her a safety net. A future. Someone to grow old with. "You have one heck of a sale's pitch, Mr. Selkirk."

There was the off chance that she'd read him completely wrong and he'd abandon ship somewhere down the road. A danger all couples faced.

"In college, I had a steady boyfriend. We went our separate ways when we graduated. I've dated but never really clicked with anyone. I'm thirty-two and, with my business responsibilities, got out of the dating scene. You literally dropped out of the sky and I don't really know what to do with you."

"Hmm. I think you need to talk with someone, and I know exactly who that is."

He always had a solution. "Is that so?"

The nurses described him as gorgeous, but Nathan definitely had intelligence and, as a SEAL, a vast reserve of endurance.

"Yup. Just so happens, we're having dinner with Steven and Moira Porter."

"Oh, yeah. You mentioned something about dinner on Wednesday. Who are they?"

"That's a long story, but Steven is one of the most powerful men in LA, not to mention Vegas. He's fifty-one years old, but the guy became a billionaire in his thirties. He met Moira long after he'd established himself. She was like you—a single woman committed to her profession. Steven never lacked for female company, but as I understand it, the second he laid eyes on Moira, his priorities changed. They had their share of issues. Big ones."

"What happened?"

"Apparently, he convinced her, like I'm trying to convince you, that they had a future together. Moira and Steven are married and have two children. They're happy."

Jane loved happy endings in romance novels. She'd hoped one day she'd find her forever guy, too. Was Nathan that man?

"So you think she has some words of wisdom for me?"

"Not sure, but she faced the same issues as you. Steven literally dominated the film industry and associated with the upper echelon of society. Moira didn't care about his wealth. In fact, it worked against him. I've met her and she's a nice lady. Steven didn't give a shit about her pedigree. He just knew he loved her. I'm nowhere in his league, but Vince and Steven are willing to back me as a resort owner. If I go for it, things will change."

Wow. Okay. "Are you saying that I'll have to turf my work boots and dirty gloves for sequined dresses and shoulder-rubbing parties?" No way was she doing that. "If so, you can stop there. Sorry, that's not me." She shuffled her butt a few inches away, but he gripped her hand.

"I'm saying I don't expect you to change at all. Just like Moira refused to change for Steven, they found a balance. They're stronger together. When I met Porter and Laker this morning, I put the brakes on."

Befuddled, she asked, "On what and why?"

"On going forward with a plan for me to build a resort with their backing. I told them everything that was happening with Bonita. With you. And that I needed some time."

"Time for what?"

Nathan's thumb slowly traced her lip. "Time for us to build a foundation. I'm not working around the clock anymore, Jane. No more entertaining the VIPs' wives. You're my priority."

Her heart did a double flip. "I hope you didn't tank your dreams because of me."

"Initially, I thought I had. But I really didn't give a shit. That's how much you mean to me. Steven understood, and he wants to meet you. Vince and his wife Lacey are coming to dinner as well."

"Damn. Does that mean I have to buy a wig?"

He burst out laughing. "Not at all. They know about the accident. They just want to meet you."

"I can hear doubt in your voice."

"Only because of what Bonita is capable of." Nathan withdrew his hand from her arm. "If I were smart, I'd leave you alone. Let the dust settle, but that's not what I want."

And if she were smart, she'd tell him to keep his distance, but it's not what she wanted either.

"There are tons of entitled egomaniacs like Bonita." She tapped his firm pec, then kissed it. "And plenty of people who aren't intimidated by assholes like her. Such as me."

He spit out a laugh. "Jesus, babe." Nathan leaned forward and planted a lingering kiss on her mouth. "You're my kind of beautiful." He eased her back onto the mattress. "I fucking love you so much, it's making me crazy. Is there a chance in hell you'll fall in love with me?"

Holy shit! He loved her. Jane's pulse roared with elation. "You just used the L-word."

"First time for me, sweetheart. What I feel can't be anything else but love. And you didn't answer my question."

"Mm." She pretended to think about it, then said, "Percentage is about as good as you feeding me within the next hour."

"Get your ass out of bed," he ordered playfully.

She stretched her arms above her head and yawned, in no hurry to get moving. His deep chuckle sent shivers of excitement through her blood.

Nathan's large palm slid down her stomach, then cupped her sex. "On second thought—" His warm tongue lapped her nipple. "Let's order in."

CHAPTER TWELVE

Nathan arrived at the Jade a few minutes before noon. Nora Hamilton from accounting had called this morning. He'd given her Jane's number and the women arranged a meeting this afternoon. He'd deposited Jane at home, checked the townhouse to make sure Lanna wasn't lurking in some corner, and broke the speed limit to meet up with Tinman.

Bursting into his office, Tony Bale and his two contractors, a buff guy with a military cut and a lean female with brunette hair in a ponytail, stood in his outer office.

"T-man."

They shook hands, then Tony introduced his crew. "This is Sheila Craig and Merle Robinson."

"Nice to meet you." They both nodded. "Let's head into my office." Nathan ordered lunch for Tony and his contractors before he sat down.

Settled at the oval table where he conducted management meetings, he gave a briefing of the situation for Sheila and Merle's benefit. Sheila had spent seven years in the Marines, and Merle retired from the US Rangers. Nathan retrieved a folder from his file cabinet and tossed the pictures of Dirk and Lanna on the rosewood table.

"Lanna's lying low. Cops don't have a clue where she is."

"Does she have family close by?" Sheila asked.

"She grew up in Lovelock, but no family connections. Looks like Dirk and Lanna lived in the van when they were low on cash. Police impounded the vehicle. I followed Dirk to a shithole motel in West Las Vegas. Cops confirmed Lanna cleared out before I made the drop."

Merle put a finger on her photograph and dragged it across the table. "You said she was a nurse."

"For a temp agency, home care."

Merle narrowed his eyes at the photo. "Don't think we need to chase our tails. If they were living in a dive motel and trying to embezzle money from you, she probably doesn't have a lot of funds. Why don't we approach the agency and see if they'll call her out on a job? They won't want their reputation tarnished when we explain that this chick is bad news."

Nathan glanced at Tony, who grinned and said, "Hired him for a reason."

Sheila crossed her arms and nodded. "Turns out I've been in a serious accident and need a little home care. We just need a home."

Nathan gathered the photos and shoved 'em back in the folder. "I'm officially impressed." Obviously, these two were at the top of their game. "Not a problem. I'll rent a place this afternoon."

A knock on the office door prompted Nathan to answer. He stepped back to allow four trollies pushed by hospitality servers to enter. The staff quickly laid out an array of Michelin-grade dishes and left a silver bucket filled with ice, soft drinks, and beer on one trolley.

The senior server stood with his hands loosely clasped in front of him. "Anything else, Mr. Selkirk?"

"No, thank you, gentlemen. Looks great."

The staff departed the office, closing the door behind them.

Tinman chuckled. "Now, I'm impressed. What the fuck, Rider? You went from slogging through South American swamps and dodging bullets to tailored suits and staff at your beck and call."

He chuckled. "Believe me, it's just a different kind of swamp."

"Uh-huh." Tony plucked a beer from the pail and twisted off the top.

"Help yourselves," Nathan said. "I'm going to make a call to rent a house."

When everyone finished lunch, Sheila and Merle headed out to visit the temp agency in person.

"We'll report in once we get feedback from the agency," Merle stated.

Tinman lifted one finger and gave a half-assed salute.

"How long are you staying?" Nathan asked once they were alone.

T-man sat forward in the office chair. "Till we reel in your trouble. Lumin and the boys are with Moira and her kids. I thought I had a Gong Show at my place. It's louder than a firefight at the Porters' place. You have any kids?"

"Not yet." He grinned. "Maybe one day. How's Mace? You two were still green behind the ears when I left."

Tony shoved the plate aside, with only crumbs left. "He's solid. I guess you retired before Nina arrived. That's his wife. She works at Base Command."

"Huh! Fraternizing with the staff. She enlisted?"

"Civilian hire. How long ago did you leave the teams? I can't remember."

"Been eight years. Seems like a lifetime."

"Miss it?" Tony asked.

"Sometimes. I retired after twelve years of service. Why'd *you* get out?"

Tony eyed him. "For Lumin. I don't go into the field like I used to. It depends on the contract. Neither does Mace. Nina had a daughter already when she arrived in San Diego, but she and Mace had a son once they married." Tony paused, and his gaze dropped to the table. "They named him Patrick." Tony's shoulders straightened, and he nodded. "After Patrick Cobbs."

Nathan saw Cobbs' death still sat heavy on T-man. Changing the subject, he asked, "Your wife is Steven Porter's goddaughter."

"Yeah, that's how we met. I almost lost her during the plague."

A near miss for America and what could have been a devastating end. And not that long ago. "I hated being an outsider during that time. I watched the news like a hawk." Nathan heard Captain Patrick Cobbs had died on that mission to stop the terrorist. Fucking total tragedy. Nathan didn't bring it up because the guys still serving in Delta Squad told him T-man had been with Cobbs when he'd died. "The guys told me that Thane Austen got promoted to admiral."

Tony set aside the empty beer bottle. "Sure did. Commander of the West Coast Chain. He's in Hawaii with his wife, Kayla. He has two kids now."

"Now there's a guy I never thought would give up on bachelorhood."

Tony laughed outright. "Well, you haven't met Kayla."

"Imagine she's something else."

"Not what you'd expect, but holy fuck, does she have him reined in. When you see Ghost with her and the kids, you wouldn't believe it."

When Austen worked in the teams, they'd called him Ghost. The most lethal warrior Special Operations had ever seen. Nathan rarely drank during business hours, but he joined Tony and twisted the cap off a brew.

"Ghost and I used to terrorize a few bars back in the day. I figured the guy was a fucking magician because of the way women flocked to him. Made things simple for me. I just stood by and got the ones he didn't go home with."

Tony cracked up. "I remember. Mace and I had deep respect for you two. Not only what we learned from you during missions, but your skills with women. Wasn't it Ghost who gave you your team name?"

Nathan swept a palm across his jaw. "Yup. It turned into Rider, but it was initially Ride Her. Fucking guy."

A broad grin eclipsed Tony's angular features. "Dare I ask?"

"As long as it stays in this room. I was no different from any other twenty-year-old. When I finished my Quals, I landed in Team One, Alpha Squad, for two years."

"That's rare," Tony said.

"Yeah, I know. Austen was a CPO back then. He hadn't been commissioned yet. One night we were partying at Breakers. I'd just finished my first deployment. This woman, who wasn't exactly beautiful, kept coming on to me. You know how guys toss shit at each other. If women knew what we said, they'd never come near us with a ten-foot pole. Anyway, being a twenty-something dickhead, I was hoping something better would come around. Ghost, who noticed everything and wanted to yank my chain, wandered over. He leaned in and said, if you don't like what you see, then turn her around and ride her."

Tony barked with laughter. "And that's what you did."

"Yup. From then on, Austen called me Rider. Name stuck."

T-man's cell dinged. He took a quick look at the message, typed a response, and set his phone aside. "When it came to the fairer sex, Ghost didn't change until Base Command hired Kayla."

"Her too?"

"Both her and Nina are Canadian."

"You're shitting me."

"No lie. It was when the Blood Shark was hunting his victims."

"The serial killer?"

"The same. Dumb fucker only made one fatal mistake."

"Which was?"

"He put his sights on Snow White. That's what we called Kayla."

"Buddies from Delta Squad told me Ghost caught the guy," Nathan said.

"Caught him. Killed him and fed him to a shark. Justice and irony served up in a few bites."

"Good. The son of a bitch deserved to be fish bait."

T-man leaned back in the chair and crossed an ankle over his thigh. "Lumin and I are staying with the Porters. Steven mentioned you married the actress Bonita Williams. I caught Moira rolling her eyes. You haven't met my wife, Lumin, yet, but she doesn't cast shade on anyone, and I'm pretty sure I heard her mumble 'bitch'."

"I mentioned my career was a swamp. She was the alligator that tried to chew my ass off."

"So this woman, Jane, who you're protecting and who's in

those pictures with you is…"

Nathan considered his words before answering. Putting it into terms any SEAL would understand, he said, "She's the fast response craft at an extraction point that saved my ass."

T-man eyed him. "In other words, she's like Ghost's Kayla, Steven's Moira, and my Lumin."

"Yeah," he said, toying with the label on his beer. "Yeah, she's the one. I fucked up marrying Bonita. Now I have to fix that mistake. I just don't want Jane to have to pay for it. Even if Bonita doesn't get a hold of those photos of Jane and I, I'm just delaying the inevitable."

Tony cleared his throat, rested his forearms on the table, and then clasped his hands. "Am I wrong in guessing you've already considered stepping back, but can't?"

Even when T-man joined the teams, he had good instincts. "Several times. If it's my only option to protect Jane, I will. We talked about this last night. She's aware of the risk and willing to take it. But I'm not prepared to let her do that. Bonita knows how to work her fans and the media. A scandal, whether real or not, keeps her trending."

Gnawing on his right cheek, Tony nodded. "So Lanna Freeson is holding all the cards while she's in possession of the camera."

"My guess is she's already contacted the tabloids, trying to sell the photos. Even if I get the camera back, the damage is probably already done."

"Not necessarily. Negotiations with a tabloid take time. If Merle and Sheila draw her out within the next forty-eight hours, do you want a shot at talking to Lanna, or do we take the camera and scram? As I recall, you were a pretty damn good negotiator."

Tony posed an interesting option. Dirk and Lanna's extortion scheme was over, which left selling the photos.

"If your team finds Lanna before Dirk's hearing, I might convince her that Dirk won't get bail and handing over the camera will keep her out of jail. She'll withhold the photos from the tabloids until she's got the money in hand. Which means I've got a shot at cutting that off at the pass before it happens." He met Tony's gaze. "Yeah, corner Lanna and I'll talk with her."

T-man checked his watch. "I'll call you once Merle and Sheila confirm the op is a go."

They parted ways. Tony headed back to Porter's place, and Nathan seated himself behind his laptop. About to open his email and take care of Jade business, he paused, his index finger on the mouse.

What the fuck was he doing?

He signed off and shut the laptop cover. It was Saturday. Jane, not the Jade, needed his attention.

****

Nathan parked his car along the sidewalk near Jane's townhouse. He opened the driver's door, then closed it again, seeing Nora Hamilton, the accountant, exit the unit. Once she climbed into her Nissan Pathfinder and drove off, he scanned the area, then got out. He hated this game of hiding in the shadows.

With the coast clear, he strode up the walkway and knocked on the white door, where a green floral wreath hung centered a foot lower than eye level.

"Hello?"

"Hey, sweetheart." A sense of relief washed over him when he heard the lock retract before the door opened.

"Hi, yourself." Jane stepped back to let him in.

"Just saw Nora leave. How'd it go?"

"She's great." Jane closed the door after he stepped inside. "Nora's going to drop by for a couple of hours after work each night until we're caught up. She knows her stuff. I like her."

"Good to hear." He followed her into the living room and they sat on the couch. "I got a good vibe from her, too. She seems like an amiable woman."

"She is. In fact, I might consider keeping her instead of doing all the accounting myself. It certainly would free up my time. We briefly discussed her hourly rate. Instead of hiring five new guys and adding another crew, maybe I'll wait and keep Nora."

"Great idea. Why don't you hire five new guys, and I'll cover Nora's costs?"

Jane laughed and shook her head. "Ya know, wealthy men usually rent a loveshack for their girlfriends. I never heard of paying for an accountant before."

Nathan leaned over, grazed his thumb across her cheek, then placed a sweet kiss on her lips. "Okay, so you want me to keep my nose out of your business and my wallet shut?"

She grinned. "You catch on quick, Mr. Selkirk."

"Let's call it a temporary restraining order until we..." How should he put this? "Until we agree to more permanent arrangements."

Jane wrinkled her pert nose. "You're not fooling anyone, Nathan. You want to marry me, don't you?"

"Close," he said, playing along. "I don't *want* to marry you. I *will* marry you." There it was. He loved Jane. No second-guessing required.

"Hmm, that sounds kinda permanent."

He thumbed her perfect bottom lip. "Sweetheart, I'm laying my cards on the table."

She sat back and cocked her head a little. "And—I suppose you want a family."

His pulse ticked faster. They'd never ventured into this territory. "You're thirty-two, and I'm seven years older." Nathan had made the mistake of avoiding this convo before hitching up with Bonita. He clasped Jane's hand. He couldn't miss Steven Porter's pride while talking about his kids. According to Tony, none of their old teammates regretted tying the knot and having children. "I do, Jane. I always wanted to be a father."

Jane straddled his thighs and draped her arms over his shoulders. "I've never seen you. All I have to go on is your character." She popped her eyebrows. "And maybe a couple other things you're good at."

He grinned at her verbal checkmark in the bedroom. Satisfied woman, happy wife. He planned to make her extremely satisfied.

"But I know how you make me feel," she said in a serious tone, tipping her forehead to his. "I'm pretty certain I love you, and I definitely want a family. Probably more so than you, because I was abandoned as a baby and never had one of my own."

Abandoned as a baby? He knew she'd been in foster care. Why wasn't she adopted? It was a conversation for another time. Nathan ran his hands down her sides and squeezed her firm hips.

"Aw, sweetheart, I never thought about that. But you're going to have a huge family once you meet mine. They're gonna love you."

Jane's lips twitched with a smile and tears glistened in her eyes that he didn't expect.

She swallowed thickly. "I'd like that."

His heart melted, seeing for the first time that the strong, spicy woman he adored had an empty, bittersweet hole she'd camouflaged. Warmth seeped into every corner of his soul. Loving someone was far more than attraction and chemistry. It was the frayed ends of two lives, choosing one enduring future. Committed not just in a vow but in actions. Until this second, he had no comprehension of that depth, and the epiphany struck home.

"First chance we get, Jane." He traced his fingertip across her sweet chin. "We're going to knock Texas off your bucket list."

"Sounds good," she whispered.

Nathan wrapped her in a crushing embrace and kissed the ever-lovin'-shit out of the woman who made him see the world from a whole new perspective.

Jane finally nudged him back and grasped his shoulders. "So, how did the meeting go with Tony?"

"Think I need a shot of caffeine. How about I make us a cup of coffee and fill you in?"

"Sounds like a plan, but let's sit outside and enjoy the sunshine."

"Meet you out there."

Jane shifted off his lap and stretched her hand out, as she often did when navigating by herself. He watched to make sure she didn't stumble and beat her to the patio door, sliding it open. On Tuesday, she had an appointment with the neurologist. Nathan would go with her to hear the doctor's explanation as to why her sight hadn't returned yet.

If her vision didn't return to normal, they'd have more hurdles and adjustments to make, but whether or not she had her eyesight, it didn't make a difference to him.

CHAPTER THIRTEEN

T he sun beat down on Jane's cheeks as she closed her eyes and wallowed in the beautiful afternoon.

"You look awfully content," Nathan said, sitting in the spare lawn chair she'd picked up at a garage sale for three bucks.

"I have a knack for masking guilt while appearing relaxed. Before the accident, I usually worked on Saturdays. My customers expect results. The only thing they care about is that the job is done. The who or the how means nothing to them."

Nathan raised her hand and placed a kiss on her knuckle. "Then enjoy your compulsory vacation. Are your crews working today?"

"I alternate my staff to give them every second weekend off but still cover the contracts."

Jane mulled over Nathan's offer to pay for Nora's accounting fees. Obviously, although they'd never spoken about wealth, Nathan's far exceeded hers. She wanted to maintain her independence and her business. Her mystery man, slash significant other, seemed all too willing to help her achieve success.

"Owning a garden nursery has always been a dream for you, hasn't it?"

"Pretty much. In college, I majored in plant biology because it offered so many options. Botany grabbed my attention and never let go."

"And after college, you cut your teeth by working in a garden nursery?"

"Two nurseries. I took every opportunity to learn more about ornamental horticulture, cultivation, and plant care. Three years later, I worked for two large landscape companies in Colorado. Then the accident happened, and I lost Celia and Kate.

When I came here to Nevada, I didn't have the capital to start a nursery and opted to start my own landscaping business."

A few birds sang from a tree in her neighbor's backyard, but the steady drum of vehicles on the highway, less than a quarter mile away, nearly drowned them out.

"I'm guessing you have a five-year plan."

"More like ten," she answered. "With enough contracts, eventually I want to buy some land and specialize in the plant life native to Nevada. The Royal Jade contract helped a lot and brought more business from residential clients. Realistically, I need another team to handle the workload."

"Then hire them, Jane. When we buy a new place to live—"

"You mean when *you* buy a place—"

"No. I mean us. I'll be back in a second."

Nathan slipped inside and returned with the coffee, settling a mug in her hand. She nodded her thanks. "Even though you watched me for a couple of years, we've only known each other a little over two weeks. You're still technically married. The last thing a guy wants is to jump into another relationship. I'm suspicious."

"Don't be. I didn't have a relationship with Bonita. More like a battleground. From day one. We never sat around like this, talking about our dreams over coffee."

"Did you have a healthy sex life?"

He chuckled, obviously amused by her question. "I thought you majored in botany, not psychology."

Talking with Nathan was always easy, but she admittedly pushed the boundaries to see if he'd shut her down. Other than initially withholding his position at the Jade and watching her for so long, Nathan had been honest.

"You know what I mean, Nathan!"

He cleared his throat. "Yeah, I do. What can I say? We did what most married couples do, but after her first affair, things cooled off. I moved into a different bedroom six months after we married. When I sleep, it's usually because I'm bone-tired. Bonita would come home after a night of partying with her friends and, well—it was like living with a teenager."

"I'm kinda surprised you didn't break your vows, since she did."

"Hmm, plenty of opportunities. No question. But declining those offers really wasn't all that hard."

"But *you* must have been."

He choked, then laughed. "Sweet Jesus, woman. You're going to fit like a glove with the other SEAL spouses."

She grinned and sipped her coffee. "You and Bonita must have had some common interests."

"Now you're sounding like a marriage counselor."

She hummed. "Just making conversation."

Jane heard Peony and Piper meowing at the sliding glass door. She hated keeping them inside, but there was just too much traffic in the area, and her cats weren't streetwise.

"Well then," Nathan said. "Explain to me how someone as beautiful as you isn't married yet."

"Beautiful?" Now it was her turn to snort. "Celia and Kate tried to hook me up a few dozen times." She shrugged. "Since coming to Nevada, I don't have spare time. I go for a walk after work sometimes just to clear my head. There's a park not far from here."

He cleared his throat again. "Meet anyone there?"

"Think I mentioned it's been three years since I've...you know."

"Mm-hmm," he said, his tone tight. "That's where you met him?"

She'd seen a few nice-looking men at Rafael Park, but only one really stuck in her mind. She'd thought about him so often. Riveting green eyes. She didn't like polished, pretty boys. The guy made her girly-bits stand up and pay attention with his rugged, stunning features. The kind of man you only see once in a lifetime. They'd talked for only a second, but she couldn't forget his face.

"Jane?"

"Huh? Oh yeah. Um, we stopped to talk, and he asked me out.

We dated for a month. Guess I wasn't available enough for him, and I never heard from him again."

"By that smile on your face, you have fond memories," he said gruffly.

"What? No." She laughed nervously. "No. Not him."

"Someone else?" he asked sharply.

"Do I detect a tone of jealousy, Mr. Selkirk?"

"Depends."

She kind of liked that Nathan seemed irked by her fantasy guy. "Oh, go on. You can't tell me you haven't seen someone you instantly lusted over."

"I have. You!" She heard Nathan exhale. "Sure wish I would have seen you five years ago. You would have saved me a lot of aggravation."

"Getting hit by a taxi once is enough, thanks."

A shadow blocked out the sun, then Nathan's lips brushed against her mouth. She traced his streamlined jaw and couldn't help but smile.

"So, do I need to worry about this guy you have the hots for?"

He kissed her hard, then kissed her again.

Jane wrapped her arms around his neck. "No, I'm pretty sure I wasn't his type."

"What does that mean?"

She didn't know exactly how to describe the man she'd seen that day. Her fantasy guy was so extraordinarily handsome. She knew she didn't have what it took to keep someone like him. Jane remembered that brief meeting with clarity. The intensity in his eyes made her quake all over. He vibrated with an aura of extreme confidence and super-charged sexuality. Jane had never run across anyone like him in her life—before or since. She didn't even bother checking him out when they went in separate directions because she knew he'd never turn around for a second look at her.

"Means I kinda like you better," she said.

Nathan nibbled on her neck. "Good answer."

His cell rang, and he backed away. "It's T-man," he said. "Hey

Tony, I'm here with Jane. I'm putting you on speaker."

"Hi Jane. I'm Tony Bale."

"Hi there. Thanks for making the trip out to Las Vegas."

"It's no trouble. Unless something goes sideways, we should wrap this up by five. I've got orders from Moira that you're both coming to dinner tonight. She and my wife, Lumin, want to meet you."

"Um. I think we have an invite for Wednesday," Jane said.

"Looks like it's tonight *and* Wednesday."

She shrugged. "What do you think, Nathan?"

"Up to you, sweetheart. You feeling up to it?"

She had no clue what to expect, but Tony was part of Nathan's past in the SEAL teams, and Steven Porter wanted to back Nathan's vision of owning his own resort. Considering the lengths Nathan had gone to protect her, she certainly had no problem supporting him.

"Sure, that sounds good."

"Great. Okay, L.T., Sheila and Merle didn't have to do much convincing to get the temp agency to call Lanna in. She accepted the job. We'll throw some bandages on Sheila. Lanna's scheduled to arrive at four o'clock. I'll text you when I have the situation under control, and you can infil after that."

"That gives me an hour. I'll be there," Nathan replied.

"No worries, Rider. We'll have this cleaned up shortly."

Tony hung up.

The constant hum of traffic from Highway 11, three blocks away, invaded the tiny, fenced backyard. The next place she intended to live would be located miles from a busy road.

"You really think she's going to hand over the camera?" Jane asked.

"I just need the card in the camera. One way or the other, I'll get it," Nathan said sternly.

"No one's getting hurt, right?"

"Not unless she hurts herself. It'll take about an hour to get to Providence from here. You need anything before I go?"

"Nothing. But I noticed Tony called you LT and Rider. I'm

guessing Rider was your team name, but what's LT?"

"My rank when I left the teams. I retired from Delta Squad as a lieutenant."

Jane didn't know anyone in the military and wasn't familiar with the hierarchy. "Isn't a lieutenant an officer?"

"It is. I started off as enlisted. A few years down the road, I gained a degree in cyber operations. I received a direct commission, then attended officer training school."

Now things made sense. "Those were the skills you talked about that got you in the door at the Royal Jade. Huh! So you're an officer and a gentleman."

Nathan's deep chuckle did more to warm her than the sun overhead.

"I better get moving, but I'll get you a refill before I go."

"Don't worry about it. I'm sorry you have to go through all this trouble. I know you're doing it to protect me from Bonita."

Nathan crouched in front of her. "Sweetheart, this isn't your fault. Not mine either. I'll get this squared away, and we can concentrate on other plans."

"See ya soon."

Nathan planted a quick kiss on her lips. "Very soon."

****

Tony's text appeared on Nathan's cell. *It's a go!*

Nathan stashed the cell in his suit's inner jacket pocket and headed for the front entry of the furnished rancher he'd rented. Situated in a middle-class neighborhood with manicured lawns and far removed from the strip, it afforded them privacy. The paved driveway sat empty. Without the van, Lanna must have taken the bus or hired a cab. Approaching the front door equipped with a touch keypad, he noticed the closed blinds on the windows facing the street.

When he stepped inside the entry, he saw what he expected.

Lanna sat on a dining room chair in the middle of a moderately sized living room. Sheila stood behind the chair with her arms crossed. A bandage covered her head and both arms. They'd even gone the distance to apply fake blood under the bandages. Merle leaned against the wall next to the TV, wearing shades, and checked his cell. T-man retrieved another dining room chair and planted it in front of Lanna. She wasn't going anywhere with her wrists and ankles zipped-tied.

Her eyes widened, and she mumbled something like "Ooh, ucking astard!" around the cloth gag across her mouth when she saw him.

He'd let her talk, but first he'd calm her down.

T-man gave them space, then nudged his head at Merle to vacate the room, but Sheila remained in place.

Lanna yanked at her bindings. She wasn't going anywhere and eventually grilled him with a hateful glare. A bluff, because she gripped the armrests, turning her knuckles white.

"Et me oh!" she said, her forehead creased tight.

"I have no intention of burying you out in the desert. So relax."

Nathan saw Lanna's closed backpack on the coffee table. T-man would have told him if the camera was in there or not, which meant he hadn't searched the contents, leaving it to Nathan to decide how this would play out.

Lanna's nostrils flared. Nathan waited. After a minute of just staring at the nursing assistant, her thin shoulders drooped.

"This is your shot, Lanna," he said. "You're only going to get one chance. Looks like you and Dirk have been together since you were kids."

Her dark, blue-eyed gaze shot to the front window, covered by white horizontal blinds.

"At some point, you need to choose between loyalty to a guy who isn't the best choice for you and starting again without him. Dirk won't make bail. The judge will look at his record and consider him a flight risk. With his past, he'll probably get a ten-year sentence." Nathan paused for effect. "And I'll make sure he does."

Her gaze darted back to him, fear radiating in her eyes.

"You both cooked up this plan to extort money from me and sell the photos to a tabloid. I'm going to let you in on a secret." He leaned forward, resting his elbows on his thighs. "Bonita and I separated over a year ago. Divorce papers are signed, and she's got a new man in her life. Selling those photos to a tabloid might get you a few bucks but that's about it."

"Ooh rand," she muffled.

"Two grand, eh? You're not much of a negotiator." Shit. So one or more of the tabloids knew they existed. There was no way she'd gotten the cash yet.

"Nuff," she said and shrugged.

"Dirk told you to sell them for bail, but he isn't getting bail. Ten years is a long time to wait, Lanna. I don't want those photos to protect myself or Bonita. Neither of us gives a shit what's in some Hollywood rag."

"Ane," Lanna said.

"That's right. Jane. She's the one who will get hurt. She's just like you, trying to scratch out a life. I don't want her involved."

"Oke upf wid you."

Jane had told Lanna she'd dumped him. "Yeah, she did. That doesn't mean those photos won't cause a problem. So here's your choice." Her eyes narrowed, but he had her attention. "You give me the camera card and I give you five grand, and you can stay in this place for one week to figure out your next steps. Or—I call LVPD, and they'll be here to arrest you in fifteen minutes. Instead of wearing blue scrubs, you can enjoy the comfort of an orange jumper. Simple decision."

Lanna's eyes darted around the comfortable, modern home, and her brows arched. Nathan got up and walked to the glass-topped coffee table, then picked up the black bag with shoulder straps. She didn't say anything when he released the zipper and opened the pack to look inside. A keychain he recognized with a metal cactus hung from the ring. Jane's keys. He pocketed those, then retrieved a Canon digital camera they'd probably stolen from a tourist.

"T-man?"

Tony strode to his side and Nathan handed the camera over for him to check the images.

"What's your decision, Lanna?" he asked as Tony checked the camera's contents. "Take my deal, or I hand you and the camera over to PD? Either way, you're *never* gonna collect on those photos." While Tony checked the camera, Nathan pulled a manila envelope from the bag. He slid the images onto his palm. Three copies of each photo they'd taken at the restaurant.

Tony held the camera at arm's length so Nathan could see the small screen and clicked through the pics. The card was still in the camera.

Lanna worked her jaw to remove the cloth. With a nod at Sheila, Tony's contractor loosened the gag.

The blonde, with beady eyes and a pug nose, inhaled a deep breath before she said, "You're full of shit. Dirk will make bail, but thanks for the tip that I should get more for the photos."

"Is that your final answer?"

She glared, her jaw cinched tight.

He panned a look toward T-man. "Call PD."

"Wait!" Lanna shouted. When Nathan lifted his hand, Tony paused with his thumb hovering over the cell. Lanna shut her eyes for a long moment. "You're trying to tell me you'd give me five grand for what's on the camera. And I can stay here for a week."

"That's the deal. I'll take these copies as well. After two weeks, if the photos haven't appeared in some tabloid or a story that mentions Jane's name, you'll get the money." He had to make sure Lanna hadn't squirreled away extra copies. Even if Dirk made bail, they wouldn't have anything to dicker with the unscrupulous Hollywood rags.

"Give me half the money now!"

Nathan refrained from exposing any expression. Lanna planned to run. She'd take half to make her escape. The only wildcard was if Dirk made bail on Monday. His first call would be to Lanna.

He handed Tony the envelope with the copies, then nodded

at Sheila to release the woman.

"Wise decision, Miss Freeson," he said, reaching into his inner pocket and dumping twenty-five one-hundred-dollar bills on the coffee table.

Lanna stared hungrily at the money. "If Jane dumped you, why do you care what happens to her?"

Tony, Sheila, and Merle waited by the front door.

Nathan eyed the woman's pale features and the dark circles under her eyes, contemplating his answer. "Because, like you, she's a victim of circumstance." When Lanna's forehead creased, he explained a version of the truth that wasn't far off the mark. "She doesn't have any family. She scratches out a meager living with her landscaping. Her accident brought us together. Because of me, she was drawn into a situation she never asked for and will take the fall."

Lanna rubbed her wrists where the ties had left indentations. "Jane said you came on to her to save the resort from an injury lawsuit. Didn't look that way to me. I think you got the hots for her."

"I'm good at my job and responsible for her trouble. The accident left her blind. That's bad enough. It's why I'm taking the camera and giving you the money in exchange."

"So you're some kind of asshole executive with a conscience?"

"Take this opportunity to start over, Lanna."

She hurried to the table and swiped the bills into her hand. "No skin off my back. I've wanted to dump Dirk for a long time. You just made it possible. Are you serious about me crashing here for a week?"

"It's all yours. The code to the house is 8945."

Nathan turned and headed for the front door Tony had left open when he and his team departed. For a small price, he'd tamped out the fire and cut off a potential storm of trouble. He met up with Tony and his contractors on the sidewalk.

"Thank you." He shook Sheila and Merle's hands.

Sheila grinned, creases forming around her mouth. "No.

Thank you. That suite at the Jade rocks."

"Enjoy the amenities. Charge everything to the room. I'll take care of it."

Merle's carved features broke into a grin. "We will. I'm guessing we're on standby for Monday when you find out whether or not the dickhead boyfriend gets bail."

"I'd appreciate that," Nathan said. "He might hook up with Lanna. If not, he might scram."

"Or payback," Merle said, his biceps flexing as if ready for a fight.

"We're on it," Sheila answered. "Merle and I are heading back to the Jade." She turned her attention to T-man. "See ya, boss."

Tony tipped two fingers to his head in a loose salute. Merle and Sheila headed down the sidewalk. Once they were fifty feet away, Merle slung his arm over Sheila's shoulders.

"Well-well."

"Yeah," Tony said. "It's new. Mace and I have been discussing whether we should do anything about it."

"Are you worried their feelings will compromise a mission?"

"Maybe yes, maybe no. They're both talented and professional." He shrugged his straight shoulders. "Anyway—" He handed over the camera and envelope.

Nathan pulled a lighter from his pocket and torched the envelope right there, then extracted the camera's card, crushed it under his heel, and pocketed the remains to toss in the trash later.

"Moira said dinner's on when we're done."

He gripped Tony's shoulder and gave it a shake. "Bravo Zulu, Tinman. I couldn't have done this without you."

Tony shook his head. "Bullshit. But since you're wearing thousand-dollar suits these days instead of holding position in the trenches, I'm happy to help. I'm gonna head back to Porter's place." Tony walked backwards and said, "Hope your gal doesn't mind a few war stories, cuz I have plenty to share, L.T."

"Aw, man. Come on. She thinks I wear a halo. You gonna fuck that up?"

"Hell, yeah! See you soon."

CHAPTER FOURTEEN

Near dusk, with their stomachs full, Jane rested her hand on Moira Porter's forearm as they strolled through her vast backyard. Lumin walked ahead of them, keeping up with her two-year-old twins. Moira's twins, a girl and a boy, were somewhere close by. They'd left the men inside, swilling alcohol and telling war stories.

Even without clear vision, Jane saw the angles and curves of the manicured garden and smelled the fragrant scent of fresh flowers.

"Is that bougainvillea?" she asked.

"It is," Moira said. "I spend a lot of time out here. Like you, I enjoy digging in the dirt."

"Do you employ a full-time gardener?"

"I do," she said. "But when I need to clear my head, I'm out here."

Jane heard the whispering burble of a water feature. "I'd love to see it someday. I mean—hopefully."

"Nathan told us your blindness is only temporary."

"That's what the doctor said, but he also thought my vision should have returned by now. I'm trying to stay positive."

Moira slowed her steps, then stopped. "I gotta tell you, Jane, you're worlds away from Nathan's ex. In a good way. I never got the feeling he was happy with Bonita. Personally, I never liked her. A shallow, vain brat with the morals of a barracuda."

So Moira knew Bonita.

"Tell me what you really think," she teased.

Moira chuckled. "Little harsh, eh? I've seen all sorts of women hooked on the arms of wealthy men since I married Steven. There's very few I consider friends."

"Dog-eat-dog world in the higher food chain, huh?"

Lumin returned with her twins, one in each arm. "I'm going to put these two to bed. Don't leave, Jane. I'll be back soon."

"You got it."

Nathan had described Lumin and Moira to her because she couldn't see their facial features clearly. He said Lumin was in her mid-to-late twenties, with platinum blonde hair and a slender, tall physique. She was a defense attorney in San Diego. He described Moira as a petite brunette in her forties with a big heart and commonsense values.

Moira picked up the conversation where they'd left off.

"It took me a while to fit into Steven's lifestyle. I absolutely hate rubbing shoulders when we attend events, which is a lot. But I adjusted. If Nathan builds a resort, he'll face all sorts of added responsibilities."

"Like fending off loose women?"

"By the bucket loads," she admitted. "Vegas is one thing, but my husband's film production company adds another layer of temptation. The number of women willing to spread their legs to get into one of his films is absolutely astounding. That's why I had to be a thousand percent sure that whatever Steven wanted from me wasn't just a phase."

Jane liked Steven Porter. There was an air about him. A competent man, but not brash. She sensed the same dignified and capable essence in Nathan.

"Do you think Steven sees himself in Nathan?"

"Without a doubt," Moira responded, taking a step to indicate they continue to walk. "Steven told me that Nathan wants a pause before initiating a plan to build a new resort."

"I know. It shocked me when he said it was because of me. And, of course, to complete his divorce with Bonita."

"I think my husband understands. He didn't become the largest production company in the world because he's impatient."

"You're not what I expected," Jane admitted. "I mean, dinner was a family affair with lots of laughter and easy conversation. When your cook served dinner on the table, instead of serving everyone individually like they were royalty, I relaxed a little, but I was still shit scared I'd end up wearing my food and embarrassing Nathan."

They rounded a curve, following the edge of the gardens on either side. "Steven tries his best to be home every evening, and we eat together as a family. It's easy now because the twins are so young, but once they reach their teens and realize they're more privileged than others, I'm hoping we've raised them to be humble, not entitled."

"I was raised by a foster family. Nice people."

Moira hesitated, then said, "So was I."

"You're kidding." That surprised Jane.

"I lost my parents and brother when I was ten. They all died in a car accident."

"I never knew mine. I was given up at birth."

"And you weren't adopted?" Moira sounded surprised.

"No. My foster parents didn't know much about my mother. She was young, and her name was Clea."

"That's odd. Most people who want to adopt love the idea of getting a newborn."

"Not in my case. There's a stigma attached to kids like me."

"Like you?"

The subject wasn't something Jane purposely hid from people. Just not a topic she usually led with when meeting new friends. "I was a crack baby."

"I see."

Moira's voice didn't have a judgmental tone, so Jane explained. "No one wants to adopt children like me because the prevalent belief is that we're destined for physical and mental disabilities. The myth is that we're addicted to drugs all our lives. It's not true. I've never even smoked pot. Not a single desire. I was always an A-student in school. There are a few groups that are finally challenging the narrative. Slowly, the data is disproving those initial beliefs, but the idea still scares away most prospective parents who want to adopt. Professionals warn people that we'll have aggressive tendencies, ADD, and other detrimental issues."

Moira cupped Jane's hand. "That is so sad. Does Nathan know?"

"No. But we both want children. I just don't know how to table the conversation."

"Are you worried the issue might make him see you differently?"

Jane nodded. "Honestly, I think so. I mean, I've only known Nathan existed for a little over two weeks, and I'm already head over heels in love with the guy." She laughed. "I don't even know what he looks like. The nurses at the hospital all fell in love with him."

"You're falling for the man based on who he is, not what he looks like."

"Nathan stayed away from me for two years because of Bonita and his commitment to the Royal Jade. To him, it's been a long waiting game, and he wants to make things permanent."

"You mean marriage."

Moira's twins ran up like two little whirlwinds. "Mom, can we have some ice cream? Pleeeez," they said in unison.

"No, but you can have some toothpaste. Go get ready for bed."

"Moooom!"

The age-old cry made Jane grin. The kids stomped towards the luxurious rear patio.

"Just a second, Jane. I have to text Steven, or he'll cave. I hate cell phones but they come in handy."

A second later, Jane heard the phone ring, then Steven's voice. "Aw, babe. Come on. It's the weekend. They're having fun."

"They'll be jacked up until midnight. No ice cream."

In the background, Jane heard the twins make their second appeal for dessert. "Daaaad, can we have ice cream?" Emily asked.

With the Porter's billions of dollars, they could afford popsicles with diamond-encrusted sticks, but all Emily and Evan cared about was a sweet treat.

"Steven!" Moira warned.

He sighed. "Sorry, babies. Ice cream will be there tomorrow. Go brush your teeth. I'll come up and tuck you in." There was a pause, then Steven said, "We're going to head out to the patio, babe. You finished your stroll?"

"Just about. Would you put on some hot water for tea? You want a cup, Jane?"

She nodded.

"Make that two cups. And if Nathan's still drinking, cut him off. Jane can't drive home."

Steven laughed. "Jesus, you're sexy when you're bossy."

Moira tsked. "See you shortly."

She waited until Moira placed Jane's hand on her arm, and they headed toward the blurry lights on the patio behind the immense residence.

"So, what were we talking about? Right, Nathan. You never met before your accident?"

"No. I'd like to think my heart won't change when my vision returns, but—"

"But you're worried you won't like what you see. That's perfectly understandable. Before I met Steven, I was married. Once I divorced, I didn't run across many men who made my heart flutter. None, in fact. Steven was the exception. Women literally threw themselves into his path. He has those timeless, alluring features most women stop in their tracks to get a second look at. Firm jaw, piercing eyes, broad shoulders, and an incredibly intoxicating aura."

Jane smiled. "I'll take your word for it."

"Well, that's my point. There are a lot of similarities between Nathan and Steven. The same characteristics and charisma. That's probably what the nurses thought, too. There's just something magnetic about men like them. For me, I couldn't believe Steven wanted anything but a roll in the hay. Our relationship started when I came to Vegas for a vacation. I never expected to meet a man like him or that he'd fall in love with someone like me."

"That's so romantic."

"Pain in the ass, actually, but that's a story for another day. Everyone has different tastes. I don't think you'll be disappointed when your sight returns."

Jane's feelings for Nathan grew because of his care and concern. He maintained he'd never cheated on Bonita. That had to take some serious moral fortitude in his profession. "We're worlds apart. I mean, I'm a woman with a pint-sized business. I'm not a famous actress."

"There's plenty of obstacles when women like us join men like Nathan or Steven. You can't see it yet, literally, but when Nathan looks at you, it's obvious that he loves you. And if you love him, everything will eventually fall into place."

Nathan wasn't the issue, but his ex might be. "It sounds like Bonita will make trouble, no matter what."

They reached the patio. Jane heard the men talking and saw the smudgy flicker of flames in a grand outdoor fireplace.

"Wouldn't surprise me," Moira said. "She's nothing but a narcissistic piece of crap. Women like her have a false sense of superiority and a fan base that sucks up to get attention. She uses her sexuality to lure men and gives young women an unrealistic image of what they should look like and expect from the male population. Once Nathan gets the divorce settled, you can put that bitch in your rearview mirror. Eventually, she'll pop and wither like the overinflated windbag she is."

Jane cracked up. Moira certainly didn't curb her thoughts. "I hope you're right, but Nathan's worried she'll try to ruin my business. I've worked my ass off for five years to earn loyal customers." Sacrificing herself was one thing, but she had twenty people who relied on a paycheck.

Moira sighed. "Cancel culture is a pestilence in our society. It disgusts me. Hollywood is chock-full of that nonsense. It's unavoidable, but you're a landscaper. If you lose a few customers who want to kiss her ass, then so be it. There are plenty of people with money and backyards in this part of Nevada. Not everyone waits with bated breath to hear what that slut thinks."

Nathan had been right. She felt better after talking with

Moira, who didn't have an entitled bone in her body. "Thanks. I'll try to remember that."

Moira guided her up the four steps to the patio. "Hey, call me anytime if you need to vent. Seriously. In fact, you, me, and Mandy should have lunch this week."

"Who's Mandy?"

"My best friend and sister-in-law. She married Steven's brother. He owns Digital Yank."

"The computer company?"

"The same. Steven is a triplet. Identical triplets. Mandy rowed the same boat as you and me before she finally allowed herself to believe Dane's intentions were something other than getting into her pants. I think you'll like her. She's a laugh a minute."

"I'd love to meet her."

They reached the men sitting around the fireplace. "How about we come and get you on Thursday at noon?"

"Sounds good."

Nathan stood up. "One second, sweetheart."

He placed a chair behind her so she could sit without falling on her ass. With no light left in the sky, the fire was a wavering, blurry image. Jane rubbed her upper arms against the chilly air.

"I'll get your sweater," Nathan said. He returned and draped the sweater around her shoulders.

"Thanks."

From behind, he leaned over and kissed her cheek. "You okay?" he asked quietly next to her ear.

"More than okay."

He sat in the cushioned chair next to her and held her hand.

Lumin joined them. "Boys are asleep." She took a seat next to her husband. "Those two are like lightning. They crackle and pop until they fizzle out, then they don't budge."

Tony chuckled. "Something like their old man."

"No," she said in a sweet voice. "You snore."

Steven and Moira laughed at their goddaughter's comment.

Sipping on a steaming mug of tea, Jane listened to Nathan's

friends' lighthearted banter. Lulled by the warm fire, her eyes grew heavy.

"Nathan." Steven's gravelly voice drifted in the background. "We have plenty of guest rooms. Why don't you take Jane upstairs?"

Jane blinked, realizing she'd nearly fallen asleep. "Sorry." She shook her head to wake up. "Since the accident, I keep falling asleep." She sat forward and realized she wasn't even holding onto the mug anymore. Someone had taken it from her hands.

"Thanks," he said, standing. "Come on, sweetheart. Time to retire."

"No. No. I'm fine."

"Please," Moira said, touching her hand. "Nathan shouldn't drive, anyway. There's everything you need upstairs. Third room on the right."

"She's right, darlin'. I'm probably over the limit."

Jane squinted. "Okay. Moira, Steven, thank you. Night everyone."

A round of *sleep well* and *night* from Tony, Lumin, and their hosts followed them as Nathan led her inside and to the stairs.

"Aren't we overstaying our welcome?" she asked.

"Not at all," he said, remaining behind her as she mounted the stairs to the second floor.

"They're nice people. I didn't get a lot of time with Lumin, but she seems sweet."

"T-man mentioned that's her superpower. Opposing attorneys underestimate her until she's standing in front of a jury, crushing the other team under her heel. Apparently, she wins ninety-five percent of her cases. As a defense lawyer, that's damn good."

The suite seemed spacious, with vaulted ceilings and its own bathroom with guest toiletries, like a hotel. Exhausted, Jane brushed her teeth quickly, washed her face, and joined Nathan under the heavy comforter in the king-sized bed within minutes. She snuggled against his warmth as he wrapped an arm around her waist and kissed her forehead.

She drifted off in his protective embrace and the words. "I love you, Jane."

CHAPTER FIFTEEN

Nathan woke to the squeals of kids and their feet thundering up and down the hallway outside of the bedroom. The minor ache in his temples confirmed he'd downed too many thirty-year-old Scotches from Steven's impressive collection last night.

Jane slept soundly, facing away from him, the bedsheet draped across the deep curve of her waist. At some point in the night, they'd reached for each other, and he'd made love to her, not completely waking up. Erotic. Sensual. The memory made his dick thicken just thinking about it. He traced his fingertip along her slender arm and down to her hip.

"Ten more minutes," she mumbled into the pillow.

Tucking his chest against her back, he kissed her warm shoulder. "It's Sunday. Sleep as long as you want, sweetheart.

She tilted her head back. "This bed is like a cloud."

"Go back to sleep."

Nathan took a shower, washing the fogginess from his brain. When he strode back into the bedroom, towel-drying his hair, Jane breathed deeply, sleeping peacefully. She needed the rest. He dressed and headed downstairs.

In the kitchen, Moira and Steven stood next to the huge marble-topped island. A laptop sat in front of them. Steven slapped the cover shut the second he saw Nathan.

"Morning," Steven greeted. "Sleep well?"

"Extremely," he said, eyeing Moira, who plastered an odd smile on her lips. "Appreciate you letting us spend the night. Where are the kids?"

The billionaire, wearing a gray t-shirt and washed-out jeans, leaned against the counter. "They're glued to the TV. The hardass here," he jerked his head toward Moira, "lets them watch a couple hours of cartoons on the weekend."

"Coffee?" Moira asked brightly.

"Love some. Thank you."

Nathan crossed the spacious kitchen, decorated in a high-end colonial style. A chunky, rustic pine kitchen table sat next to a line of floor-to-ceiling windows that brought the morning light blasting into the heart of the mansion. He joined Steven at the island and looked at the closed laptop.

"As soon as Jane wakes up, we'll head home."

"Nonsense." Moira poured him a cup of coffee and shoved it across the island. "You're staying for Sunday breakfast. Let Jane sleep."

"The day after getting out of the hospital, she went back to work. The woman thinks she's invincible. I can't convince her to slow down."

Steven grinned and glanced at his wife. "I know someone else like that."

Nathan felt tension in the room. Maybe it was just his imagination, but he asked anyway. "Something wrong?"

Porter stretched his wide shoulders and again glanced at his wife.

She tossed an apron strap over her head and secured the belt around her waist. "You might as well show him. He's gonna see it sooner or later."

"See what?" Nathan asked. His thoughts zoomed to the photographs. Had Lanna screwed him over already?

Porter grimaced and opened the laptop. "Fair warning. You won't like this." He clicked on a link to a popular Hollywood show with a live studio audience. The host, Keisha Toppins, interviewed celebrities.

Nathan strode closer to see the screen. The video was paused, but he saw Bonita sitting in the guest chair.

"Fuck," he muttered. "What has she done now?"

Porter clicked on the mouse, starting the video from the beginning.

Keisha, an attractive African American woman with high

177

cheekbones, wore a colorful yellow dress. She greeted Bonita and thanked her for coming on the show. Bonita promoted her new action movie, releasing next year. Keisha played the trailer for the audience and Nathan's ex received a round of polite applause.

Keisha crossed her long, elegant legs. "Bonita, your marriage to Nathan Selkirk has come under scrutiny lately. Your fans want to know if the rumors are true, especially the ones that you're involved with your co-star, Bryce Steele. Care to set the story straight?"

Bonita slathered her features in a practiced expression of doubt, then subtle anguish. Her shoulders slumped, and she sighed. "I love my husband." She flattened her palm over her heart and looked straight into the camera. "I know women out there can identify with the unforgettable moment when you look into a man's eyes and know he's the one. Our love affair was like a fairytale."

Nathan spit out a sarcastic laugh. "Not so much."

Keisha smiled warmly at her guest. "So the rumors aren't true?"

Bonita swept her curled blonde hair over one shoulder and batted her obscenely long false eyelashes. "I'm always hounded by paparazzi. They circulate rumors to sell tabloids. It's just something popular actresses like myself have to endure."

The host nodded. "But the pictures of you and Bryce have been circulating for a while now. Especially of you kissing him."

"That's the thing," Bonita said, lifting her hands in the air, palms up. "Someone snaps a shot from a scene in the movie and sells it to a tabloid. Suddenly, I'm unfaithful to Nathan."

Keisha's brows knit together in sympathy. "That's terrible."

"Bryce and I are dear friends. He's a sweet guy, and he's been a shoulder to lean on."

Nathan crossed his arms and exhaled. "You lying bitch."

Moira spit out a laugh.

The camera zoomed in on Keisha. "Why do you need a shoulder to lean on?"

Bonita twisted her clasped hands as if tortured by some

truth she didn't want to expose. "Nathan used to support my career, and I supported him. In his executive position, he takes care of the VIPs, especially the wives of VIPs. It means dinners and shows, but it's completely innocent. In turn, he understands I interact with my co-stars occasionally to promote our films."

"Sounds like a strong marriage," Keisha said.

"It was." Her voice dropped to a weak, breathy tone. "But I noticed a difference in Nathan recently. I mean, he doesn't seem as attentive or loving. He doesn't come home at night. Women know in their hearts when something's gone wrong." She cleared her throat, and her forehead creased into tight lines. "I love him so much, but I think there's someone else, and it's breaking my heart."

Nathan slammed his eyes closed. *You deceitful bitch!*

Porter stopped the video. Nathan took a long swig of coffee and set the mug on the counter.

Moira rounded the island and slid an arm around her husband's hips. She was literally five foot nothing next to Steven's six-foot-four frame.

"Bonita just prompted thousands of her fans to keep their eyes open for you. I don't know how you put up with that woman without lashing back."

"Because he doesn't want to stoop to her level," Steven said.

Nathan yanked out a chair at the kitchen table and sat. "This might be a ploy for her to look blameless after she signs the divorce papers. She hasn't yet."

Moira joined him at the table, bringing his cup and topping it up with coffee. "Photographers and reporters will be on your tail nonstop because of this interview. If you're seen with Jane, Bonita will point a finger, saying, '*See,* he *was* cheating on me!'"

"I don't care what some crap tabloid says about me. Two weeks ago, I parachuted into Jane's life, and I brought all my baggage. The accident caused enough disruption. She built her business from the ground up. I don't want to see it fail because of me."

Steven poured himself a cup of coffee and sat at the table.

"Listen, it's not because of you. It's Bonita. Until you settle your divorce, our home is a safe place."

"Absolutely," Moira said. "Jane and I have a lunch date this week. I'll make sure we're seen together. As a friend, her comings and goings from here won't lift an eyebrow. If the paparazzi follow *you* here, they won't think anything of it."

Jane rounded the wall separating the kitchen from the stairs. With her hand outstretched, she carefully walked to the table. "I appreciate your help, Moira." She placed her fingertips on the rustic wood tabletop. "Nathan, this is a game to Bonita. She'll keep playing it until she can't suck any more sap from the social media tree. That could take months. If we end this now, the paparazzi and Bonita's fans will follow you, but there'll be nothing to see."

Nathan turned the white mug in his hand around and around. The room remained absolutely silent. Finally, he set the mug down with a *thunk*. "No. No fucking way. That psychotic bitch doesn't get to manipulate your or my life. I played it straight, as Steven said. And I'll continue to do so, but this goddamn nonsense ends now."

Jane's eyebrows lifted. "You mean well, but this isn't about me. This is about the lives of twenty people who work for me. Moira. Steven. Thank you." She placed her fingertips on the table. "It was nice to meet you both."

His pulse quickened, sensing Jane's retreat. "I will fix this."

She plastered a polite smile on her expression. "If it's all right with you, I'd like to go home."

Jane had showered and covered the bandage on her head with the scarf. He straightened the silk cloth, then palmed her cheeks and kissed her, even though he felt an axe severing their relationship. "Whatever you want, darlin'."

Neither of them said a word on the twenty-minute drive home.

"We're here," he said, coming to a stop in front of her townhouse.

Jane felt her way to the latch and opened the passenger door.

"Take care of yourself, Nathan."

He slammed his eyes shut. "Why Jane?"

She got out of the vehicle, and whether she wanted him to or not, he escorted her up the short, paved walkway. The townhouse looked like all the others in the complex, except hers had potted plants with brilliant pink flowers and lush green leaves on either side of the stoop.

After digging the keys he'd found in Lanna's pack out of her purse, she paused. "You've done so much for me, and I'm grateful."

"Sweetheart, you've got the appointment with the doc on Tuesday. I'm taking you."

"No, you're not. Don't make this harder than it has to be."

He held her hands to stop her from putting the key in the lock. "Listen, when I was deployed, I watched the married guys handle being thousands of miles away from the women they loved. Depending on the operation, sometimes they'd go weeks without making contact. I have to clean up my mess, but that doesn't mean we can't talk every day."

Jane's forehead creased. "To what end?"

"The future we talked about—it's not gone. Promise me you'll pick up when I call."

She shrugged. "Nathan, you probably think this is about Bonita. It's not. At least not entirely."

Fuck, he knew what was coming. Too much. Too fast. The accident. Her injury. Him coming onto her the way team guys entered a building; kicking in doors and mowing down anything in their way to reach an HVT.

"Then what?"

She paused, her gaze lowering. "I'm off-grid, and you're palatial mansions."

"Jesus Christ, Jane. I have enough goddamn money. I'd live in a fucking igloo if it meant spending the rest of my life with you."

"You have big dreams, and I think you should grab them by the throat and go for it. It's not about money. It's about the challenge. I can't even begin to comprehend the conviction it took to become a Navy SEAL, but I know that very few graduate. You did."

"Glad you realize that, because I'm not backing down for a reason that doesn't make any sense."

"Then I'll explain so it makes sense. I don't fit into the paradigm of a socialite, Nathan. I didn't understand the vast differences between our lives until I caught the end of Bonita's interview. You're both huge personalities. A famous actress mentioned *you* on TV."

"Bonita dug a pit and threw me in it. I told her to blame the divorce on me, but instead, she concocts a line of bullshit and uses her followers to dog me and find you. She's playing a high stakes game. I don't give a shit what happens to me because I'm all in with you. She made a blind bet with her interview and she will lose."

"I hope she loses—for your sake. As paltry as my life is, it's uncomplicated. And I want to keep it that way."

She smiled and raised her head, looking at him but her eyes didn't focus. How could she see anything clearly with all the drama she had to endure? "You and I belong together, Jane. I don't expect or want you to change anything."

"Kiss me goodbye and walk away," she said, her words choked with emotion.

She had the strength to do what he couldn't. He'd ridden in on a wave of hope, and she'd been pounded by the weight of his baggage.

He took the keys from her hand and unlocked the door. "I'm sorry, Jane. I can't kiss you if it means goodbye."

****

Monday morning, Nathan strode into his office, and Barb jumped to her feet. "I've had fifty calls already from reporters wanting an interview. And that doesn't include the women who have called and left threatening messages. What's going on?"

"Bonita declared war. Who's the most reputable of the

publications or shows that called this morning?" he asked, heading to his desk.

Barb followed him into his air-conditioned office. "Umm, I'd have to double-check, but I think it's Hollywood Bytes. It's a primetime half-hour show that covers the film industry. Paige Landry's assistant called, asking if you'd be willing to conduct an interview. They're pretty reputable."

"Excellent. Call her back. Get her in here by three!"

"Mr. Selkirk, are you sure? I mean—"

"Yes, I'm sure." He glared at Barb unintentionally—his temper still in overdrive.

Her eyes widened. "Okay. On it."

Nathan shunted his suit jacket off his shoulders, then called his lawyer.

When his lawyer's admin assistant put him through, he said, "Jack, it's Nathan Selkirk."

"Nathan, hi. Sorry, nothing back from Bonita's legal team."

He wasn't surprised. "Time to kick this up a notch. Bonita has no intention of signing those papers. Where do we go from here?"

"I'll file with the courts. We'll get a trial date. If Bonita was smart, she'd sign the documents. She's getting off easy, considering what she's worth and what you're willing to accept. A judge could toss the premarital agreement."

Fuck. Bonita would love a trial. More press, more opportunity to perform in front of a judge. He hoped an interview with Hollywood Bytes would start enough fires under Bonita's ass that she'd change course. "Hold off on that for a week. I'll get back to you."

"Sure. If I hear otherwise, I'll let you know immediately."

Barb stuck her head in the doorway. "Paige will be here at three o'clock unless you want to meet somewhere else."

"Here is fine."

"You've got the Monday morning meeting with department heads in fifteen minutes. Usual place. The agenda is in your Inbox."

"Thanks, Barb."

The rest of his day whistled by, dealing with Royal Jade business. At two o'clock, he called the courthouse contact provided by Detective James Read. The clerk's response was short and sweet. The judge denied Dirk's bail. At least that was one issue kicked to the curb. He texted T-man and told him the news, and received a thumbs-up.

By three o'clock, he was back in his office.

Paige Landry arrived with a cameraman in tow. The woman with a brunette bob and pearl earrings had hosted the primetime Hollywood media show for years. She had a friendly character and an enormous fan base that valued professional reporting rather than sensationalized gossip.

"Thank you for agreeing to an interview, Mr. Selkirk," she said, shaking his hand when he greeted her at the door. "I'm sure you were inundated with requests after Bonita's appearance on Keisha's show."

"I was." He offered her a guest chair to the left of his desk and sat across from her. "You're the only interview I will give regarding Bonita."

A genuine smile lifted her coral-colored lips. "I'll do my best."

The cameraman set up his equipment and nodded at Paige. "Ready." He held up three fingers and counted down. "Three, two —" He pointed to indicate the camera was rolling.

She introduced Nathan and summarized his background, mentioning his time on the SEAL teams and his current position.

Paige sat with her legs primly crossed and a pad of paper pinched between her fingers. "On Friday, your wife, Bonita Williams, gave an interview to Keisha Toppins. Within an hour, Bonita's accusations were trending on social media. As we've seen, when there are issues in a marriage for high-profile figures, the public instantly takes sides. You and Bonita married five years ago."

"We did."

"Instead of beating around the bush, I'll come straight out

with the question. Are you cheating on your wife?"

Nathan retrieved a wad of folded papers from his inside pocket and laid them on the coffee table. Paige leaned closer to see the title sheet. Her eyes widened, and she quickly motioned for her cameraman to zoom in.

"You're legally separated from Bonita!"

"For over a year now. Bonita agreed to a divorce settlement months ago. The papers are at her attorney's office. She neglected to mention that on Keisha's show. I don't hold any ill will toward Bonita. Legally, she's still my wife, but she's moved on."

Paige blinked and clasped her fingers around one knee. "Are you referring to the rumors about Bryce Steele, by any chance? Bonita addressed this in her interview and intimated the photos were taken during the filming of a movie."

"As far as I know, there's no movie being filmed in my house. But the other day, I heard him moaning in my wife's bedroom. I didn't meet him until he walked barefoot into my kitchen, wearing a smile and a pair of jeans."

"Oh, dear. Uncomfortable situation."

"It was for him. He didn't expect to see me. Bonita's been unfaithful throughout our marriage. She'd apologize for an affair, and I'd accept the apology. If the public wants the truth, they should know the entire truth. I'm not interested in playing out a dramatic role to keep her in the headlines. A separation agreement means we're still legally married, but the marriage is over, and she's free to be with whomever she wants. I just didn't expect to find him in my house."

Paige ignored her notes with the bombshell he'd dropped. "It looks to me like Bonita's act on Keisha's show was to draw sympathy and cause trouble. This separation agreement is the smoking gun that just shot Bonita's ruse in the foot. She's denied the rumors about a separation, but it's actually true."

Nathan rested his elbows on his thighs and clasped his hands. "Movies create superstars, but Bonita and I are like any other couple. Sometimes marriages don't work, especially when adultery is involved. I never cheated on my wife. Bonita's image is important to her. People might judge her actions, but I don't. I wasn't the right man for her. She's free to find that guy and move on."

The camera turned to Paige. "Mr. Selkirk, we've never met before, but you're exactly what I expected. You served this country by giving twelve years of your life to the Special Forces. I have the utmost respect for that. It's obvious that you're a man who upholds traditional values. I appreciate you taking the time to set the story straight." She faced the camera. "Thank you for joining Hollywood Bytes for this eye-opening interview. Reporting live from the Royal Jade Resort in Las Vegas. Until next time—good evening."

The cameraman stepped away from his equipment and shut off the mobile light stand behind Paige.

"Nathan," Paige stood up. "I think when we air this tonight, shit is going to hit the fan."

He laughed. "Probably, but I've endured enough of Bonita's dramatic bullshit. It's time to move on. For both of us."

She narrowed an eye. "Now that the camera isn't rolling, were you faithful?"

He stood as well. "One hundred percent. Bonita screwed around on me in the first year of our marriage."

"You don't seem too broken up about it. Does that mean since your separation, you've found someone else?"

"My folks have been married for nearly fifty years. I know what a healthy marriage looks like. The next woman I marry will be for life."

She grinned. "In other words, no comment."

"In other words," he responded. "Bonita won't take this interview well. The truth is detrimental to her career. Backed into a corner, she'll use her claws when she comes out swinging."

The cameraman gathered his equipment. "I'll be down in the van, Paige."

She waved. "Be down there shortly, Don." She turned and extended her hand. "Well, if that's the case, call me. When I saw

Bonita's pathetic soap opera performance on Friday, I had a gut feeling there was something else going on. I've dealt with just about everyone in Hollywood. I've seen actresses like her wither and die time and time again. Only the most talented stars shine for a lifetime. She was reared in the privileged belly of Beverly Hills. Her mother can act, Bonita—can't."

Nathan shook her hand. "Thanks for your time."

She winked at him. "Hey, I did a little research before I came out here. Is there any truth to building your own resort?"

"The idea has been tabled. We'll see."

"Thanks, Nathan. It was nice to meet you." She picked up her Gucci leather clutch and left his office.

Nathan sat in the leather-bound chair behind his desk and clasped his hands, resting them on his stomach. Hollywood Bytes had literally millions of viewers. He'd tossed the grenade. It was up to Bonita whether she'd pull the pin and blow herself to bits.

He picked up his cell and thumbed his way to Jane's number. So far, she hadn't answered his calls today. Even a strong woman like her had a tipping point. She'd reached it yesterday.

If Jane thought of herself as off-grid, then he'd order a hundred yards of soil and dump it in the backyard of wherever they ended up living, and she could grow carrots and tomatoes to her heart's content.

But there was no fucking way on earth he was giving up on Jane St. Eval.

CHAPTER SIXTEEN

W hen Nathan left the Jade around six p.m., he ran into a group of reporters. They were easy to spot with microphones clutched in their hands and milling around the casino exit to the parking garage.

"Mr. Selkirk!" A woman with sleek, dark hair in her twenties shouted and intercepted him.

The other reporters swarmed.

The woman shoved a microphone in his face. "What do you have to say about your wife's claim that you're unfaithful? Is it true you cheated on Bonita Williams?"

He raised his hand when the other reporters lobbed questions at him. "Earlier this afternoon, I gave an interview to Hollywood Bytes. If you want an answer, then watch the show."

Nathan shoved his way past the reporters, still barking questions. When they tried to swarm him again, security stepped in and stopped their progress.

Nathan arrived home, relieved Bonita wasn't around, but two photographers blocked the driveway. He opened the wrought-iron gate remotely and the men moved aside, but closed in on the car when he drove past, snapping pictures. Nathan kept his gaze straight ahead, and the gate closed behind him, leaving the paps outside.

After entering the kitchen, Nathan checked the fridge, but nothing appealed. He cracked open a beer and headed to his bedroom. After tossing his jacket and tie on the bed and toeing off his shoes, he opened the pivot glass door to let the fresh evening wind circulate through the room. He scanned the twenty-foot-tall brick privacy wall that surrounded the property. There weren't any reporters hunkered at the top of the enormous palm trees that lined the backyard.

188

The swimming pool glittered with invitation. Maybe he'd swim off his frustration later.

Loosening the top two buttons on his cotton shirt, he sat in a lounge chair in his bedroom and called Jane. She might spit fire but as long as he kept her talking, the line she'd drawn in the sand would inch closer in his favor. Although he'd be going solo to the business dinner on Wednesday at the Porters, he remained optimistic.

"Hello?"

"Hey, sweetheart. How was your day?" he asked, reaching for the TV remote. Nathan thumbed the button, switching to the channel where Hollywood Bytes would start in fifteen minutes, then muted the TV.

She tsked. "Nathan."

"Jane," he responded, teasing her and using the same serious tone. He grinned. "Hey, I'm just a friend, checking up on a friend."

"Like hell you are!"

If she didn't hang up in one second, he was good to go. "Busy?"

She sighed. "Tired. But I picked up two new contracts in Ascaya."

"Nice neighborhood. Congratulations. Monthly contract?"

"They committed to a year. Just came out of the blue."

He chuckled. "I'm guessing that might not be the case."

"What do you mean?"

"I mean, Moira Porter has been busy."

"Oh gosh, I never thought of that. I asked where they'd seen my work. They said a friend recommended me. I never thought of Moira. I need to call and thank her."

"Thank her when you two go out to lunch this week."

She paused and cleared her throat. "That's not happening. I'm calling her tonight to cancel."

"Hey, you two got along like a house on fire. Don't let me fuck that up as well."

"I like her, but..."

"Moira liked you, too. She's the most sincere woman you'll ever meet." In the meantime, he'd call Moira and thank her himself. This was the woman's trademark. She'd go the distance for a friend. "Any noticeable improvement with the vision?" A lengthy pause followed. "Jane? What is it?"

"Nothing. I've got the specialist appointment tomorrow."

He didn't like her evasive answer. "Tell me the truth. Is it worse?"

"Kind of."

"What do you mean, kind of?"

"I used to see light at the outer edge of my plane of vision, but this morning when I woke up, the light was gone."

Nathan palmed his neck. "Might be a minor setback. The doctor will send you for more tests. Don't give him a hard time."

"There's some good news."

He'd noticed Jane didn't linger on an issue, especially if it had a negative connotation. "Tell me." He propped his feet on the burl wood coffee table.

"I've got an inch and a half of hair already. I consider myself at the punk rock stage. Not enough to cover the incision on my head, but soon."

The physicians had accessed her brain just above the hairline on her forehead. "Sweetheart, I love you with or without hair. Is Nora there?"

"Nathan, stop saying that!"

"What? You want me to lie? Okay, um, how about this? Is Nora there, you ornery wench?"

Jane spit out a laugh, and it sounded as if she covered the phone with her hand for a few seconds. "Yeah, much better. No. It's her daughter's birthday, so her family is going out to dinner. Nora said she'll be by later. I told her not to worry and come tomorrow, but she insisted."

"Sounds good, and hey, I don't want you to get pissed at me, but I have something to confess."

"Like what?" she asked warily.

He heard one of the cats meow in the background. "I know

we talked about this, but—"

"But what?" she said, her voice tightening.

"Your business is expanding. You need more help."

"Nathan! What the hell did you do?"

He winced. "I dropped by Nora's office today and told her to bill me instead of you."

"Seriously? Did you listen to a damn thing I said yesterday?"

"I listened, and I'm making amends. You can hire the new staff you need."

"The accounting fees are a write-off. You're not doing me a favor, and you're not fooling anyone, Nathan. This is your attempt at keeping us connected."

Did she actually think he'd silently pack up his heart and walk away? "No, I'm helping out a friend."

"Can't you just let me wallow in a broken heart for a few weeks?"

Three minutes to go before Hollywood Bytes started. "No, because a broken heart means someone stopped loving you or you stopped loving someone. That isn't the case, Jane. Not with us. You wanna try to deny that?" She huffed, but to him it was a flicker of hope. Jane needed time to figure things out. "We've never lied to each other. You want to start now?"

"I want you to leave me alone so I can cry my eyes out and get over you."

"I don't want you to cry or get over me." He watched the muted commercial for underarm deodorant flash by on the TV. "I want you on me, not over me. I'll call you back later."

"I'm not indulging in phone sex," she said abruptly.

He grinned. "You sure about that?" He liked the idea. So did his swelling cock. "It's part of a healthy sex life. Guys in the teams did it all the time with their wives and girlfriends."

"You're an irritating friend."

She didn't sound ticked off. More—frustrated. Sexually frustrated. "I can make a house call and relieve that tension I hear in your voice."

"I'm *fine*. I've gotta go."

Was she talking through a clenched jaw? It certainly sounded like it. "Love you, sweetheart."

He disconnected the call and turned up the TV volume. Paige prepped the audience with a short monologue on Bonita, including a clip from Keisha's show where Bonita had lied her face off. With that planted in the audience's mind, she rolled the interview with him from this afternoon.

Slam dunk.

Within fifteen minutes, Nathan's cell rang. He answered after the third ring. Show time!

"What's up, Bonita?"

"You fucking asshole," she screeched. "You fucking bastard!"

"What's the problem?" he asked calmly.

"You son of a bitch. People are freaking out over your stupid interview. You've made me look like a fool in front of all my fans."

"It's Monday," he said. "I asked you to have the divorce papers signed and returned to my attorney."

"You can bet I'm going to sign them, and you can shove them up your ass."

Typical Bonita response. He imagined her personal assistant, Andrea, would be actively involved in damage control at this point.

"This isn't the end of the world. Just the end of our marriage," he said, relaxing in the chair. For months, he'd waited patiently while she'd boned a long list of men. All she had to do was pick up a pen and sign the documents. "You want this divorce as much as I do. Finish it."

"You don't know the damage you've caused, and you can bet your fucking ass I'm going to get even."

"I'd strongly suggest you don't lie about Bryce's visit."

"You can't prove a thing. My devout followers will believe me over you."

He chuckled. "I'm sure they will, but if you do anything other than sign those papers and have them in my lawyer's office by tomorrow noon, I'll release the video."

"What *fucking* video?"

"Did you forget I specialize in cyber operations? I wired our house for twenty-four-hour surveillance. The video of me talking to Bryce in the kitchen is extremely clear."

"You cocksucker! I hate you."

He'd backed her into a corner, and she had no other options. "I'll expect a call from my attorney tomorrow."

Bonita's terrier barked with a frenzy in the background.

"You can have your goddamn divorce, Nathan. Thanks for ruining my life."

"Have a good night, Bonita."

He disconnected the call.

Nathan picked up his beer and strolled outside to the edge of the pool. The backyard was a multi-million-dollar oasis with water fountains, private sitting areas, and extensive greenery. Soft sandstone tiles surrounded the pool and in-ground hot tub.

Teak lounge chairs sat around the deck to catch a few rays. He rarely took the time to chill, except for enjoying a morning cup of coffee outside. A stained cedar gazebo covered the outdoor kitchen and bar for entertaining.

He and Bonita had bought the place just before they married. They'd held their reception in the backyard. An upscale affair with a who's who of Hollywood attending. His parents and family had come, but it had been obvious to him that they'd felt out of place. Bonita's parents had barely acknowledged his family.

That night, his new wife chiseled the first crack into their marriage. Half-cut, she'd staggered out of their master bathroom wearing a black and red negligee. Because she'd downed so many drinks, it loosened her lips. She'd leaned against the bedpost and said, *"I didn't realize your family were such hicks. I mean, where did your sisters buy those awful dresses? A second-hand shop? It was embarrassing."*

She had acted as if his family lived below the poverty line, which they weren't.

"You'll probably hate me for this, but please tell me I don't have

to associate with those people very often. I'll have my assistant take care of birthdays and whatnot."

She'd crawled across the massive king bed, straddled his lap, and lifted the negligee over her head, flinging it to the floor. Most guys would have looked at Bonita's enhanced breasts, blonde hair, and inflated lips and considered themselves lucky. She'd leaned forward to kiss him, and he'd jerked his head back.

"My family aren't hicks, Bonita. They're honest, hardworking people."

She balanced on her knees, swept the bedsheet aside, and revealed his deflated cock. "Of course they are, honey. Now, fuck me."

Until the day they married, Bonita had stuck to a script. He'd had his doubts about the thirteen-year age gap, but she'd acted patient, mature, and sweet. The wedding and months leading up to the big day had been nothing but a publicity stunt to keep the media focused on her. Everything she did had a reason, and that reason was Bonita's fame. She'd started her acting career at age six. By twenty-six, she was a seasoned, celebrated commodity to the movie industry. Between films, she'd fall into a depression, thinking her career was over, and drank more and more. As soon as her agent dropped a new script in front of her, she was on top of the world again.

Unlike her mother, whose Emmys and Oscars lined the mantle, Bonita hadn't garnered that type of recognition. Nathan doubted she ever would.

He finished his beer and sighed. Starting tomorrow, reporters would dog every move he made until the buzz settled down. Once the divorce papers were signed, he'd change the security codes on the property and contact a realtor.

He and Jane might have to play it low-key for a while, but life was about to get a whole lot better.

****

Jane delayed her lunch date with Moira two weeks in a row.

Instead of dumping the idea, Steven's wife kept calling for short, friendly chats. Within a couple of days, her new friend asked, point blank, what was going on with her and Nathan.

She spilled her guts. Twenty minutes later, Moira showed up at Jane's door and sat on her ratty couch, listening to the laundry list of fears that she'd never admit to Nathan. Things like, she brought nothing to the relationship. He had everything. The little she owned meant independence, which she was terrified of losing. Nathan's popularity would grow, and she didn't want to play the part of a socialite.

Jane gushed her unfiltered insecurities all over the living room carpet. Nathan saw her as something she wasn't. He'd eventually figure it out, and the heartbreak would be so much worse.

Moira had consoled her, counseled her, and then told her the big news: Bonita signed the divorce.

Jane refused to see Nathan, but he called after dinner every night, asking her how her day had gone. He shared what happened during his work at the Jade. Sometimes the stories were funny and she'd laugh. Other times, they were sad, like when he told her of an older gentleman who had a cardiac arrest and died instantly. His wife of sixty years held his hand and said, *"I'll be with you soon, darling."*

At first, she was angry that Nathan kept playing *the friend card*. Still, they ended every call the same way: *"I love you, sweetheart. Have a good sleep."* To which she'd reply, *"I'd sleep better if you'd stop calling."*

Tonight, he called her bluff.

"You sound tired, Jane. I'll let you go. Get some sleep. I love you."

She replied like she always did. A long, long pause ensued.

He exhaled as if he'd run out of his endless enthusiasm. "Then tell me you don't love me and block my number."

It took her by surprise and tears welled in her eyes. At that second, she wasn't sure who was stringing who along. Instead of getting pissed, her heart squeezed into a tiny knot. She thought she didn't have any tears left. She'd cried them all out as a kid who no one wanted and as an adult when Celia and Kate died in her arms.

Nathan had inched his way into her heart. Without him, there'd be an enormous gaping hole because she'd never met anyone like him. He'd gone all in and staked his claim in her life.

She folded.

"Jane?"

Sitting on her bed with her knees tucked to her chest, tears rained down her face. An excruciating ache filled her chest. Did she honestly want a Nathan-free life?

She sniffled and wiped the back of her hand across her cheek. "I can't. You have to do it. And you should," she answered, because they'd always been honest with each other. He owned more of her heart now than on the day she'd told him to stay away.

"Then you're shit out of luck, babe. Hey, I know you needed time to figure that out, but I've been climbing the walls without you." His comforting timbre crept across the airwaves and embraced her in an invisible hug. "We're okay, sweetheart."

"I feel foolish."

"That makes two of us."

"Why do you say that?" She slid under the soft comforter and laid her head on the pillow.

"Because, like an asshole, I ambushed you. I expected you to fall in love with me; no questions asked. Impatient as all hell, I dragged you into my foxhole with Bonita's live fire raining down and hemming you into a battle you had nothing to do with. A car hit you, for fuck's sake. You lost your sight, and I took advantage of that situation. All because I couldn't wait to hold you in my arms. I'm so sorry, Jane."

"Are you sure you want us to be okay? If you're not, I'm sort of used to walking by myself. You went through a lot too, Nathan."

"When it comes to you, I've never had a single doubt. The question is whether you can forgive me for being an insensitive dick."

Insensitive? "You've done nothing but protect me during the most challenging time of my life. I don't like feeling weak. It scares the crap out of me."

"You're not weak. Not in my eyes."

"You have literally hundreds of beautiful women at your doorstep and endless opportunities to find someone with equal status. I don't understand what you see when you look at me."

"Before I wore Armani suits, I was raised in a Texas dust bowl with five siblings fighting over Mom's last oatmeal cookie. In the Forces, I crawled through dense jungles, sweltering hot deserts, and laid in swamp water up to my chin for days while insects chewed the ever-lovin shit out of my ass. I earned my *status* by cutting a swath through life with hard work. And I fell in love with a woman who is exactly the same as me."

She'd literally never looked at Nathan's life as a whole. How he'd *earned* his position. She'd blindly viewed him from where he was when she'd met him. Like water swirling down a drain, her fears about not being good enough disappeared.

"Well, why didn't you tell me that to begin with?"

He broke into a chuckle. "What can I say? I led with the wrong foot trying to impress you. I should have known better."

She heard a door close on his side of the line. "Are you at home?"

"Yup. Just locking everything up. You in bed?"

"I am, but I can't sleep."

"Hmm, let me see." There was a rustle and then a sound as if he'd sat down, and a faint click in the background. "How about this one… *'It was the best of times, it was the worst of times…'*"

Jane smiled and closed her eyes, lulled by his comforting voice. "I love it when you read to me."

"And I love you with my whole heart." And he continued to read.

****

Jane waited by the front door of her townhouse for her lunch date with Moira and Mandy Porter. A mid-sized vehicle came to a stop in front of her townhouse.

"Hey, Jane! You hungry?" Moira asked, walking up the cement walkway.

"Starving."

A woman, several inches taller than Moira, with dark hair, joined them.

"This is my sister-in-law, Mandy."

Jane smiled at Moira's sister-in-law. "Heard lots about you. Thanks for the invitation."

"Ho," Mandy said. "You have a treat in store for you."

"I do?"

"Hell, yeah. You won't believe how everyone kisses Mrs. Porter's ass."

Moira tsked. "Seriously? Shut your pie hole, Mandy. Besides, you're Mrs. Porter, too. Don't listen to her, Jane. She's preggers again and a little crazy."

Jane laughed, recognizing the way the women teased each other. A memory of doing the same with Kate and Celia brought a bittersweet twinge to her heart. "Is this okay to wear? To be honest, I had to guess what I picked from the closet."

Mandy chuckled. "Jane, you could wear ballet slippers and a muumuu, and no one's gonna say shit if you're with Moira."

Moira groaned. "Oh, my God. Let's go."

The women flanked her, and Mandy hopped in the backseat. Once buckled up, Moira started the engine.

The car pulled onto the street, and Moira made a quick U-turn. "I thought for sure Bonita would stir more shit after signing the divorce."

Last night, Jane fell asleep while Nathan read to her. This morning, he called before heading to work. "The man is literally on Cloud Nine," she admitted. "I think he's having fun dodging all the photographers and reporters. But they're on his tail all the time."

"Meh," Mandy uttered from the backseat. "Give it a month and they'll be sniffing around for their next target. I noticed Bonita hasn't said squat about Nathan's interview, but I bet she's frothing at the mouth."

"That's because Nathan has a video of Bryce in his kitchen," Jane revealed. Nathan had played Bonita's and his interviews over the phone since she couldn't operate her laptop yet. "You're right, Mandy. She's seriously pissed off and threatened to get even. Nathan warned if she tried to lie about her affair, he'd release the video."

"Check and mate," Moira said, joining the traffic on Highway 11. "That guy isn't just another pretty face."

"Moira and I scouted the tabloids this morning over coffee," Mandy said. "Someone leaked the truth. The major rags are on fire with headlines like *Bonita Williams' Divorce Finalized*. But my favorite was the one that read *Five stars for Bonita Williams' role in her doomed marriage*."

Moira laughed and slapped the steering wheel. "She's totally in love with Nathan on Friday and divorced by Tuesday. Gotta be a world record."

Jane nodded. "You two seem to be loving this."

"Moira ever tell you about Grace?" Mandy asked.

"Ugh." Moira switched into the left lane. "No, I didn't tell her. When Steven and I first met, I had to face off with his ex. He dumped her before the wedding, and she never got over it. That woman is toxic. To this day, if we run into her at a party or event, she tries to stir up trouble."

Jane shifted her purse to the floor. "I hope I don't end up in the tabloids."

Moira took an off-ramp. "You might, but it'll probably say something like Bonita Williams' ex finds true love."

On the way to the restaurant, Jane learned Moira and Mandy hadn't only been friends before Mandy married Steven's brother, but they'd worked together. Mandy shifted from search and rescue communications to environmental response after her friend left Canada.

"Do you still work?" Jane asked.

"Not right now. I've got two sons," Mandy said. "A four-year-old and a three-year-old to chase around. Dane's girls from his first marriage, Charlotte and April, are twelve. Their mother is a ditch rat. She moved to Paris with her second husband, and we fought and won sole custody. And as Moira mentioned, I've got another bunlette in the oven, but eventually I'd like to go back to work."

"Fat chance on that," Moira said.

"Do you live in Las Vegas?"

"Wish I did, but no. Dane and I live in Malibu. My husband's headquarters are in LA. I have to snipe the corporate jet when I want to visit Moira, which I do a lot, to the chagrin of his top executives, I might add." She chuckled as if she liked to stir a little trouble.

"Moira mentioned your husband and Steven look identical."

Mandy lowered the window in the back seat. "Yeah, it's a little weird. They're nothing alike in personality, but they look the same. I've made the mistake of spanking my husband's ass, only to find it's Steven. The guys think it's hilarious."

Moira said Mandy's husband, Dane, owned Digital Yank, a global computer company. "And there's another brother. What does he own? Finland?"

Moira stopped at a red light. "Kyle had a bit of a rough start in life."

Great! She'd stuck her foot in her mouth within the first ten minutes. "Oh, I'm sorry."

"Don't be. He's been clean for twenty years. Kyle lives in Vegas. He's the senior executive manager at the Grand Palms. Runs the place like Nathan runs the Jade. By the way, the whole family is coming to our place on Saturday. We try to get together once every couple of months. You and Nathan are coming too."

"We are?"

"Absolutely. We're having a Texas-style barbeque."

Mandy chuckled. "You don't wanna miss that. It's complete chaos, but we have fun."

"But it's for family," Jane said.

The light changed, and Moira made a left, heading toward the heart of the Las Vegas strip. "Nathan talked up his mother's rib sauce recipe when he and Vince came over for dinner. I told him to put his money where his mouth is, and he accepted the challenge."

He told her this morning that Steven and Vince liked his idea about building a resort in Laughlin. Said it was risky, but thought focusing on outdoor events rather than gambling was innovative.

Moira made another left turn. "Nathan's worried about you. He said your neurologist isn't happy with your recovery."

"I'm scheduled for a battery of tests and another MRI next week. I hope they don't go digging in my brain again. My hair is finally growing back." Moira drove into the long, sweeping driveway of a resort. "Is this the Grand Palms?"

Jane couldn't see much, but remembered the lavish architecture of natural stone and tropical elements.

Moira slowed the vehicle, then came to a stop, shoving the gearshift into park. "It is."

"This is your resort, isn't it?" Jane asked.

"Yes, ma'am. It turns out the landscaping contract is up in two months. Interested?"

Nathan thought Moira had something to do with her newest contracts. "Moira, were you responsible for me getting those contracts in Ascaya?"

"Who, me?" she asked, her tone rising three octaves.

All three car doors swept open. A man's deep voice said, "Afternoon, Mrs. Porter."

They exited the vehicle and Moira placed Jane's hand on her forearm. "Ever been to the Grand Palms?"

"You mean to play? No. Never spent one red cent in a casino, but don't tell Steven that. I pour every cent I earn back into my landscaping business."

Mandy strolled on Jane's left side. "Girl, you're smart. The house always wins."

Roaming visitors filled the lobby and the casino floor. Slot machines sounded off with bells and cheerful tunes. The squeal of excitement from a lucky guest met Jane's ears as they strode along the colorful carpet. Moira navigated them through the maze of walkways, and they finally stopped outside a set of closed wooden doors with blurry gold lettering above the entry.

Jane squinted, but it didn't help. "Can't see the name."

"Oasis Secrète," Mandy said.

Jane hadn't been completely honest when she told Nathan that her vision had backpedaled. Not only had the outer circumference darkened, but what she could see had shrunk to a pinhole. Up until now, she'd been optimistic. Dr. Nelson said they'd know more once she had the MRI, but he suspected they'd missed something during the brain scans. Jane wasn't freaking out, but she was getting close.

Mandy opened the door and they strolled into a tropical oasis. Instead of dimly lit, natural light rained down from overhead. Lush plants that Jane smelled more than saw added a slight moisture to the air. When the door closed behind them, the sounds of the casino were completely mute.

"Mrs. Porter. It's so good to see you. Welcome," a woman greeted. "Right this way."

"Let the ass-kissing begin," Mandy muttered.

Jane snickered. "Better than an ass-kicking."

"True dat! It's a widely known secret that anyone who's anyone eats here. It's a status thing. Getting a reservation is nearly impossible, unless you're a *somebody*. Makes me wanna gag," Mandy whispered.

She liked Mandy. Like Moira, she didn't put on airs just because her husband had achieved great success. "I'm not a *somebody*, so why are we here?"

"Because the food is friggin' awesome!"

"I'm okay with that. I lost my eyesight, not my taste buds."

They came to a stop at a table next to a water feature. She heard the splash of water landing on rocks. A waterfall? Now, that was cool. Jane used one edge of the seat to get her bearings and eased herself onto the comfortable chair.

The hostess, standing on her right side, said, "Ma'am?"

Jane thought she was talking to Mandy or Moira.

"Ma'am, your menu."

She realized the woman addressed her and flattened her hand, palm up, for the menu.

"Oh! My sincere apologies. We have a brail menu. I'll be right back."

"No. That's fine," Jane said. "I'll let my friends decide."

Moira sat adjacent to Jane's left and placed a comforting hand on her forearm. "Is it just me, or has your vision worsened?"

She nibbled on her top lip for a second. "Don't tell Nathan. We haven't seen each other for two weeks." He'd wanted to come over this morning for coffee, but she suggested they see each other after he finished work. "Last night we worked things out, but I didn't tell him how bad my vision has gotten."

"Why? He cares about you."

"He's finally happy and so relieved Bonita signed the divorce. I can't ruin that for him. My condition might be temporary." She inhaled and shook her head. "Or—it might be permanent."

Mandy grasped her right hand. "Hey, girlfriend, don't go there. Besides, from what Moira told me about Nathan, he sounds like an awesome guy."

If these women were Celia or Kate, she wouldn't have felt so embarrassed when tears welled in her eyes. Jane didn't know if the tears were about her dead besties or her condition. "I still know what the handle of a shovel feels like in my hands. I can still dig." She clenched her jaw. "Fuck, who am I kidding? I'm the eyes and creativity for my business. Without my sight, I'm screwed."

Moira patted her arm. "Mandy's right. Don't go there, Jane. Not until you know for sure. Even if the worst happens, Nathan won't leave your side. In fact, this won't bother him one bit because he's a man. And men like him and Steven love taking care of their women."

"Hey," Mandy blurted. "You forgetting somebody?"

"Okay. Okay. Dane, too."

"Thank you."

Jane grinned at the women's swift exchange. "Nathan's overly protective. I don't want him shouldering my burden."

"Burden my ass," Mandy spouted. "It'll give him the excuse he needs to whisk you away like—fuck!"

Jane blinked at Mandy's quick stop and expletive. "What's wrong?"

"Incoming, Moira," Mandy said in a low voice. "Twelve o'clock. You have got to be shitting me."

Jane had no clue what Mandy was talking about.

A blast of nose-clogging perfume struck Jane before a woman said, "Moira. Oh my goodness, it's been so long. How are you?"

Moira gave Jane's hand a squeeze. "I'm good, Bonita."

CHAPTER SEVENTEEN

With Bonita's name uttered, Jane's blood vessels constricted.

Coincidence?

Not likely. Fate had arrived to punch her in the face again.

The customary sounds of a restaurant and the refreshing splash of the waterfall receded behind the loud drum of Jane's heart.

"How's Steven? I haven't seen him since the Oscars," Bonita asked.

"He's busy but well," Moira answered politely.

"I've been busy too, promoting my next film. I barely have time to breathe. There's so much excitement about the movie. My personal assistant can't keep up."

Jane listened to the woman's voice as it vaulted into high pitches and overly animated patterns.

Moira cleared her throat. "Congratulations. Good luck with the promotion."

"At this stage of my career, my movies always draw a crowd."

A swish of movement polluted the air with Bonita's perfume, reminding Jane of honeysuckle on steroids. Bonita seated herself without invitation, across from Jane.

"I'd love to have lunch with you sometime," Bonita said. "Or better yet, we could go on a shopping jag. When Cartier sees women like us coming, they're all smiles."

Jane could only imagine Moira's facial expression, probably frozen in a polite but patient frame.

"I'll keep that in mind, Bonita, but there aren't enough hours in the day with my volunteer work, my family, and friends."

"I don't believe I know your friends. Hey there, I'm Bonita Williams."

Jane sat with her hands in her lap. Mandy took the lead. "Mandy Porter. We've met."

"Oh! Sorry, I meet so many people," Bonita exclaimed. "Are you Steven's sister?"

"Sister-in-law," Mandy corrected, layering her words in ice cold enough to freeze the waterfall.

Bonita had tormented Nathan for five years. She screwed around on him and made a mockery of their marriage. Jane wished she could see the woman.

"And you are?" Bonita asked.

Moira interrupted. "Put your hand down, Bonita. She can't see it. This is our good friend, Jane."

"Oh, my bad. Are you blind? Shit, that sucks. Guess you've never seen any of my films."

Jane's nails dug into her thigh. Everything circled back to Bonita and her stardom. A sure sign of egomania. Jane couldn't imagine Nathan married to this dipshit.

"No, I don't watch TV."

The woman laughed as if Jane had said something silly. "I don't do TV. I'm a motion picture actress. Acting runs in my family. I don't think I've ever seen you before. Is your family in politics?"

Nathan had mentioned his ex was all about connections. Since this restaurant served the upper crust and Moira married a billionaire, Bonita assumed Jane ran in the right circles.

Tempted to say her family ruled a small kingdom in Bellostravia, which didn't exist, she answered, "No. Not politics."

In a deadpan tone, Moira asked, "How's Nathan? I always liked that man."

Jane pinned her lips to stop from laughing. Not only did Moira stick it to Bonita, but also made it clear she didn't follow the little narcissist's life story.

"I guess you didn't hear. It's been all over social media. He left me," she said, dramatic anguish dripping from her words. "I love him to death. I mean, Elizabeth Taylor married Richard Burton twice. So I'm not giving up on Nathan. He always wanted a family." She lowered her voice. "Very few people know this yet, but I'm pregnant. It's going to fix everything. He'll be so happy. I'm not sure when I'm going to tell the world, but soon."

All the blood drained from Jane's veins. Her teeth clenched, and she closed her eyes. She barely felt Moira's grip tighten on her hand.

"Congratulations. How pregnant are you?" Moira asked.

"Four months," she said brightly. "I didn't want children until I was thirty, but I'm so excited. Anyway, I'm here with my mother. I just thought I'd drop by and say hello. Oh, and my agent tells me that Steven is looking for a new lead in an action-adventure film at Palm Productions scheduled for next year. I'd do *anything* to have that role! Put in a good word for me, would you?"

Moira released Jane's hand. "By the time they start filming, you'll be very pregnant. Don't think that's what they're looking for."

The actress giggled like a teenager. "I'm sure we can work around that. Actresses do it all the time. It was nice to see you again, Moira. Bye!"

Jane felt numb. *Pregnant.* God!

"Hey," Mandy said, "I call bullshit. That Bryce guy probably knocked her up, but she's so fuckin' pissed that Nathan made her look like an idiot, she plans to bounce this bogus story to cause a flurry of speculation."

Jane forked her fingers together and placed them on the table. "Is this what you two have to deal with all the time, because I don't want any part of it?"

"Moira, more than me," Mandy answered. "Women have come out of the woodwork announcing they're carrying Steven's baby, hoping he'll settle out of court. The world is full of dirtbags. The worst are unfounded sexual allegations, but none have amounted to anything because they aren't true. Bonita is just another cheap tramp, looking for attention."

"But what if it is true? What if it is Nathan's child?"

The server stepped up to the table. "What can I get you ladies to drink?"

"Beer," Jane said, needing to dull the ache in her chest. "Don't care what kind. Just—beer."

Moira and Mandy ordered as well, then waited for the server to leave.

"Jane," Moira said sternly. "My gut tells me Nathan isn't going to sit idle. She said she's four months along. That means he can go to court and file for a prenatal paternity test right now. If she's lying about this, she'll wear the blame again. I don't think she wants that."

"I don't think she cares," Jane said. "How old is she?"

"Twenty-six," Moira answered.

"I didn't realize she was that much younger than Nathan."

Mandy tapped on Jane's hand. "I'm a stepmom. My girls, Charlotte and April, are frigging awesome. Even if it is Nathan's child, he won't go back to Bonita."

"Maybe not, but that means she'll always be in our lives. Nathan is gonna freak. I don't want to be the one to tell him."

Moira's fingernails drummed on the table. "We'll have lunch, even if you've lost your appetite, and then we'll drive over to the Jade and visit Nathan. Together."

"Hey, there's your husband," Mandy said. "And there's a guy with him."

"What?" Moira jumped to her feet. "Shit. Shit. Shit. That's Nathan!"

Jane's heart pounded in her chest. "Nathan's here?"

Moira left the table.

"What's happening? I need a play-by-play."

Mandy cleared her throat. "Yeah, okay. Um. Moira intercepted Nathan and Steven. Nathan's attention just snapped toward the table where Bonita's sitting. I don't think you have to worry about telling him the bad news if that scowl on his face is any indication. Ho, boy. Steven just dropped a massive paw on Nathan's shoulder."

When Mandy stopped talking, she asked, "And?"

"Ummm."

"What's, *um*, mean?"

"Jane."

Nathan's low timbre and familiar aftershave encompassed her. She swiveled in her seat, her pulse pounding madly. "Hey." She bit her bottom lip. They'd been so close to a fresh start.

Nathan's hands slid to her waist, and she stood. He drew her tight to his chest, his warm palm cupping her cheek. "Sweetheart, I missed you."

His powerful embrace lifted her spirits, and she hugged him, pressing her cheek against his firm chest. "Didn't Moira tell you?"

His deep chuckle made her tip her head back, even if she couldn't see his features. "I haven't touched Bonita since we separated. There's no way in hell that kid is mine."

"What? But she said—"

"Bonita can play all the games she wants, but there's no goddamn way I'm having a family unless it's with you."

"Nathan! Who is this?"

Bonita's volume was loud enough to attract attention from other guests. His ex must have bolted across the restaurant when she saw Nathan.

"Seriously, Nathan?" Bonita wailed. "I love you. How could you do this to me?"

Her demanding, high-pitched tone snapped the string on Jane's last fucking nerve.

"I'm pregnant, Nathan. With our child," Bonita shouted.

Jane's temper exploded. She fisted her hand, ready to deal with this slut the old-fashioned way. Nathan clasped her wrist and held it against his thigh. But he couldn't stop her from speaking her mind.

"Listen, you lying skank. I don't know who knocked you up, but it wasn't Nathan. Why don't you be a good girl and slither off and find your baby daddy? Or are there too many donors, and you can't figure out which one's responsible?" She took a step forward, with Nathan still gripping her hand. "If you try to involve Nathan in any more of your *bullshit*, I will make it my life's quest to prove to everyone what a cheap, lying piece of trash you are!"

Mandy laughed and then cackled. "Friggin' eh, Jane. You heard it here first, folks!" she shouted. "Hey, Bonita! Take your serious case of psycho and piss off."

Moira laughed at Mandy's not-so-discrete suggestion. Steven spit out a laugh.

Nathan found the situation humorous, too. "Jesus, I have never seen Bonita that shade of red before."

The entire restaurant erupted with mutters, witnessing the saga unfold. Some guests laughed, and one person shouted. "No wonder your movies suck. You can't act worth shit."

"What's happening?" Jane asked.

Nathan laid a passionate kiss on her mouth, then said, "She stomped out of here. Her mother's in hot pursuit."

"Let's get a bigger table and eat! I'm starving," Mandy said.

Servers pushed another table next to theirs, and everyone sat down. While Steven ordered a drink, Nathan slung his arm across her shoulders and kissed her again...and again.

She placed her hands on Nathan's firm thigh. "I'm sorry. I lost my patience." Still shaking with adrenaline, she said, "This will cause more trouble, won't it?"

"Who fucking cares?" Mandy spouted. "She's not worth the time or energy. You dropped a house on that egomaniac. Ding dong, the wicked witch is dead."

"I second that," Moira said.

Jane used to think of herself as a woman with backbone. With the loss of her vision and all the chaos after meeting Nathan, she thought she'd lost her nerve. But Bonita had pushed all her buttons, like a major reset. She'd made two new friends. Women who'd married well but didn't wallow in self-importance. Status didn't influence Mandy and Moira. She liked them. Liked them a lot. Jane had spoken her mind and prepared for the fallout. Of course, she blindly put a thousand percent faith in Nathan and believed he was telling the truth.

She felt around the table, and Nathan placed the glass of beer in her hand. "Looking for this?" he asked.

She lifted the pint in the air. "Sticks and stones, ladies!"

Nathan placed his lips next to her right ear. "The second we're finished with lunch, I'm taking you home."

"The second I'm finished with lunch, I want you to take me home. No more hiding in the shadows, Mr. Selkirk."

"Hmm, yes, ma'am."

"Lordy, you two!" Mandy joked. "I wanna eat, ya know. Stop slobbering all over each other. By the way, I'm Mandy Porter."

He laughed. "Hey, Mandy, I'm Nathan Selkirk."

Lively topics that had nothing to do with the starlet filled their lunch conversation. Everyone enjoyed the delicious food. For a while, Jane forgot about her other issue. "Nathan, if you have time, we need to talk."

"That sounds ominous. Can I make love to you first?"

She placed a hand on his arm and smiled. "It's important, but it can wait."

"Kyle," Moira greeted. "Take a load off. Join us."

"I heard there was a disturbance in the restaurant. Came down to investigate. Should have known it was my family creating a ruckus."

"Shit," Nathan muttered. "They *are* identical. Fuck, it's uncanny."

"Who is it?" Jane asked.

Steven Porter introduced the new arrival. "Nathan, this is my brother Kyle. Kyle, this is Nathan Selkirk, Operations Director at the Royal Jade."

Nathan got to his feet and probably shook the man's hand.

Steven continued the introductions. "And this is Jane St. Eval, his—"

"Fiancée," Nathan finished.

Jane looked to her left in the general direction of Steven's brother. "Hi."

Silence returned.

And the pregnant pause lingered.

Then lingered some more.

"Um, problem?" Steven asked.

"Yeah. Sorry for staring," Kyle responded.

He sounded exactly like his brother Steven. She shrugged. "I'm blind. I wouldn't know if you're staring or not. Nice to meet you."

Moira said, "You look like you've seen a ghost, Kyle. What's going on?"

Maybe he was waiting to shake her hand, so she lifted hers. A large hand gripped her fingers. He didn't shake but held it warmly.

"Bizarre! You are the spitting image of a woman I once knew. Long time ago," Kyle said. "It's uncanny."

"They say everyone has a doppelgänger," Moira commented. "How long ago?"

"Hell, I don't know. I haven't seen Clea in over thirty years, for sure."

"Ohhhh, myyy, God," Moira whispered emphatically.

"Moira?" Steven asked with a questioning tone. "What's going on?"

Coincidence, Jane thought. Although Clea wasn't a common name.

"Jane! Stranger things have happened," Moira said.

Nathan sat next to Jane and said, "I'm not following."

"Neither am I," Steven added.

"Sweetheart, you want to clarify?" Nathan asked.

Jane sat back in her chair. "It's something I omitted telling you about myself. Not that I held back the information on purpose. I—just wanted to wait for the right time."

"Whatever it is, you can tell me," Nathan said, his timbre serious.

Could she? Or would Nathan suddenly see her differently? "When Moira and I talked the other night, I told her I was raised in a foster home, and so was she."

"Okay? Good so far," he said. "You told me that too."

"Moira lost her parents when she was ten." She gnawed on her inner cheek, stalling. Revealing the details of her birth in front of everyone, especially the Porters, was intimidating. "My parents gave me up at birth, but no one adopted me because... um. Because I'm what they call a crack baby. My mother was a user." She slid her tongue over her bottom lip. "The only thing I knew was her first name."

Kyle or Steven—she couldn't tell which—groaned. "Her name was Clea?"

Jane nodded.

"You have got to be kidding," Kyle or Steven said.

"Kyle, you look pale. Why don't you sit down?" Moira suggested.

"Holy craptastic miracles," Mandy said. "Is it possible Jane's part of our family?"

Jane heard the legs of a chair pulled across the floor and placed to her left. "Jane, do you know where you were born?"

She assumed it was Kyle. "Yes. Colorado. That's where I was raised."

"Jesus," the man uttered. "Denver."

"Yes. Denver." Her heart fluttered with unease. "Why?"

Steven sat on the other side of the table, and when he spoke, Jane could finally distinguish between the two. "My brother, Kyle, he—"

"I was an addict," Kyle admitted. "I lived on the streets for years. Clea and I met in LA. We, um, we hooked up and moved to Denver. We were young. Nineteen. Something like that. She —she got pregnant. We were both screwed up at the time. We couldn't raise—the baby was born January 1st," he stuttered.

Jane tensed like a board. All she could do was nod in utter shock. "That's my birthday."

"It can't be." Kyle jumped from the seat.

"Kyle, wait!" Steven shouted. "Stay here. I'll talk to him."

Nathan squeezed her shoulder. "Jane, say something."

She folded her hands and pressed them against her mouth. "I don't know what to say. Like any kid who's abandoned, you wonder who your parents are. I convinced myself they were dead. If they were addicts, they had to be dead."

"Jane," Moira shifted into the seat Kyle vacated. "Kyle stopped using in his thirties. He didn't rejoin the family until about six years ago. He's just like Steven. Extremely intelligent. A genius, actually. If Kyle is your father, it means you're not alone anymore."

"She's right, babe," Nathan said. "But maybe before jumping to conclusions, if he's willing, we should find out for sure. The odds are astronomical."

"Yeah." She nodded. "Yeah, that makes sense. How old is he?"

"Fifty-one," Moira answered.

Moira moved from the chair, and a mild scent of aftershave told her Kyle had returned.

"Jane." She felt a thumb under her chin, and she turned to look in his direction. "You are so beautiful. Just like Clea. My heart is racing with guilt and excitement. I don't want to give either of us a sense of false hope, but do you want to find out?"

Nathan squeezed her shoulder. "Sweetheart, if you need some time to think about this, then take the time. You've had one hell of a ride lately."

She weighed Nathan's suggestion.

"Jane's dealt with a lot since the accident," Nathan said, addressing Kyle.

"What happened?" he asked.

Jane sighed, her mind whirling as well. "Got hit by a cab. I lost my eyesight and fell in love. That's just this month."

Mandy spit out a laugh. "Don't forget that you forced Bonita to walk the plank and might have found your father. Girl, you got this!"

Jane straightened her shoulders, then nodded. "I do. Damn straight, I do. Take the good with the bad, right?"

Nathan chuckled and gave her shoulder a gentle shake. "There you go, taking on the world again. But you know, it would be kind of cool to have your dad walk you down the aisle when we tie the knot."

She raised her chin. "You haven't asked me yet."

Everyone at the table laughed.

When the laughter died down, Nathan said, "Challenge accepted, darlin'. Two years ago, when I saw you for the first time, somehow, some way, I knew I'd grow old with you." Nathan leaned forward to address Kyle. "Sir, I've only known you for five minutes. You may or may not be Jane's father, but if you are, I'd like to marry your daughter."

Kyle chuckled at Nathan's comment. "Um, this is about the strangest day of my life, but yes, if that's what she wants."

"Great! Jane St. Eval, will you marry me?"

In the same boat as her *maybe* father, this was the strangest day of her life. She tipped her head. "And what if I don't get my sight back? I wasn't completely honest about what Dr. Nelson told me. You have enough on your plate. I don't want you to worry."

Nathan kissed her temple. "Jane, the only thing that would make me worry is if you said no."

"Mandy. Moira. I'm counting on you ladies to tell me the God's honest truth. I've never seen Nathan. Is he hot, yes or no?"

The women cracked up, laughing. Someone slapped the table, then Mandy said, "Here's the God's honest truth. I used to think my husband, Dane, and his brothers were the hottest men on the strip. But I'm here to tell you, Nathan beats them hands down. Think *Thunder Down Under* with brains, brawn, and bravery. When those peepers of yours work again, you're going to drool."

Steven and Kyle snorted, and Nathan groaned at Mandy's description.

Jane wrinkled her nose. "Okay, I'll marry you."

The notion that she sat between the two most important men in her life, one of whom she never thought she'd ever meet, struck her as a blessing. Was Kyle actually her father? She turned to the left and reached out her hand. "Kyle."

Two warm hands cupped her fingers. "Right beside you, Jane."

"Do you feel like dropping by a clinic? I love mysteries, but I need to know the truth. No pressure. I mean—I—" She didn't expect anything from the man.

Kyle blew out an audible breath. "Steven. Do you know a place that will give us the results today?"

"Done," his brother said. "Mom and Dad are going to shit themselves."

"Is that a good thing?" Jane asked.

Moira's soft hand clasped Jane's arm. "It's a very good thing. Everyone's invited to our place tonight for dinner."

****

By seven o'clock, Nathan, Jane, and the Porters had finished dinner, and the dishes were cleared away in Steven and Moira's luxurious but comfortable kitchen. Nathan surveyed the Porter clan sitting around the rich, tawny-stained rustic table.

Dane, Kyle and Steven's brother, arrived just before dinner with his four children: two older twin girls and two much younger sons. The Porter brothers' parents, Daniel and Gail, both in their seventies, had hitched a ride with Dane from LA.

Mandy sat beside her husband, with her dark-haired son, around four years old, sitting on her knees, while Dane held the other son, slightly younger, on his lap. The two older girls, Charlotte and April, stood behind them and hooked their arms over their father's and stepmother's shoulders.

"So, what's this surprise?" Daniel Porter asked, directing the question toward Steven.

Nathan held Jane's hand. "I'm nervous," she said, leaning into his arm.

Nathan was nervous for her. From the get-go, Jane seemed to fit in with the family. It was bizarre, but as Moira had said, stranger things have happened.

Steven placed a laptop in front of Kyle. "You got the code?" he asked.

Kyle exhaled. "My fingers are shaking so bad." He laughed nervously. "Nathan, would you do the honors?"

"Sure, slide the laptop down here."

The laptop passed through three pairs of hands until it landed in front of him.

The brothers' mother had a dignified but friendly aura. Gail tipped her head in question. "My, this is quite the mystery."

Nathan entered the clinic's URL. Kyle retrieved the code from his jeans' pocket and handed Nathan the piece of paper. He typed the code they'd given Jane and Kyle after they'd visited the clinic, promising the results would be available after six.

"Kyle, do you want to give your parents a quick summary before I hit the enter button?" Nathan asked.

Daniel and Gail turned their attention to their son. "What's going on, Kyle?" his father asked.

Kyle stood and shifted down the table to stand behind Jane's chair. He placed a hand on her shoulder, and she smiled, her eyes staring straight ahead.

"I screwed up in inexcusable ways when I was younger. Six years ago, when you allowed me to make amends and join this family again, I had to earn your trust. Today, I learned there was someone I may have hurt even more. And if—" He choked up with tears, which caused everyone's foreheads to crush in sympathy and understanding. Kyle shook his head, seeming to steady himself. "If—this turns out to be a blessing I don't deserve —I'll spend the rest of my life making up for the biggest mistake I've ever made."

Daniel and Gail shared a quizzical look between them.

Kyle nodded at Nathan. With the flick of his thumb, Nathan hit the enter key, and the results rolled out on the screen. In the top right corner, the answer sat in a red square. Nathan's heart swelled. He took a deep breath and nodded, still mired in disbelief.

"99.9 percent. Kyle is Jane's father."

The uproar in the room must have woken the dead. Even the dogs barked with excitement and ran around the kitchen, wagging their tails. Kyle's parents' eyes grew to the size of owls.

Jane's hands covered her face. Her father urged his daughter out of the chair and strapped his arms around her shoulders.

Crying, she buried her face in his chest.

Tears streamed down Kyle's cheeks, and he slammed his eyes shut. "I'm so sorry I left you behind, baby."

Jane flung her slender arms around his neck. "I can't believe it. I have a family."

When everyone settled down, Daniel and Gail Porter strode toward Kyle and Jane.

Kyle stepped back, and his mother embraced Jane, tipping her head with a maternal smile and tears in her eyes. "My sweet girl. Welcome home."

Jane burst into tears again. Nathan clapped Kyle on the shoulder. "Incredible. Just fucking incredible."

Kyle swept the tears from his face with the back of his hand and gazed at his brothers, Dane and Steven. Nathan saw a silent message pass between the triplets. The type of message only brothers understood.

Moira and Mandy beamed with happiness. They had another niece, but it was the instant friendship between the three women that seemed so easy from the start.

Steven and Dane nudged their heads toward Nathan, and they rounded the long kitchen table. Nathan hadn't moved from his seat, allowing the family to celebrate the news. Jane was busy talking with her grandfather.

Nathan sensed there was something on Steven's and Dane's minds, and he stood up.

"So!" Dane said.

Fuck, Nathan couldn't get over how all three were spitting images of each other. It was hard on the eyes. It literally made him feel off balance, as if he'd knocked back half a dozen tequila shooters.

Dane stuck a tongue in his cheek. "I hear you want to marry our niece."

Steven grinned as Kyle stepped in line with his brothers.

"He asked me for permission," Kyle said. "I said yes, but at the time, I didn't know he'd just divorced his first wife on Tuesday."

Dane clasped his hands behind his back and tilted his head.

"From Bonita Williams? Really? Steven said you were in the Special Forces. It begs the question as to how you survived that experience as a single-celled wonder."

Oh crap. Nathan recognized a hazing on the horizon. In the SEAL teams, the new guy always had to ride the gauntlet of gears until the next new guy assigned to a team relieved him of duty.

Playing along, he said, "In my defense, *Uncle* Dane, I made a mistake, and I'm big enough to admit that."

"Are ya now?" Steven said with a half-cocked smile on his face.

He lifted his hands in peace. "Steven—"

Steven poked a finger in the air directed at him. "That's *Uncle* Steven to you."

"Emm, that's just weird. Isn't it weird?" he asked.

Dane laughed. "Weird," he thrust his thumb at Kyle, "is having to call him Dad."

Mandy sauntered over with her lanky gait and plopped their two youngest children in Dane's arms. "Stop screwin' with the new guy and put your hobbits to bed."

"Babe," he whined. "You're being a killjoy."

Mandy rolled her eyes. "Are you about to argue with a pregnant woman?"

The older girls, Charlotte and April, draped themselves against their stepmother. "So this means Jane is our cousin."

Mandy swept her lithe arms around the girl's slender shoulders. "Exactly. Why?"

The girls' bright red hair led Nathan to believe it came from their biological mother. Charlotte grinned at her sister. "Well, she's a lot older than us, which means she can buy us beer before we're legal."

Mandy swatted their butts. "Over my dead body. Go make some coffee for everyone, you little ragamuffins." The girls scampered off. "I don't know where they get that cocky attitude."

Nathan shrugged. "Beats me."

"So how are you doing with all of this?" Mandy asked as Moira joined them.

"I'm happy for Jane." He shot a look across the kitchen, where she and her grandparents sat at the table, holding hands. Kyle had settled in the chair next to Jane. Nathan was pretty sure the guy was in as much shock as his daughter. He didn't know Jane yet, but he'd soon realize she would never cast judgment on his past. She'd start from today.

"You do realize," Moira said, "this is all because of you." An honest smile graced her expression. "If you hadn't fallen in love with Jane, she'd never have found her way home."

"It is kinda," he wanted to say crazy, but instead he said, "incredible. Jane probably didn't tell you about the accident."

Mandy shrugged. "She got hit by a taxi."

"No, not that. A few years ago, before she came to Vegas, she was trapped in an avalanche. Her two best friends died in Jane's arms. They dug her out of the snow three days later."

Mandy and Moira's mouths both gaped.

Nathan considered how life had a strange way of doling out challenges. "It's a miracle she survived. I served twelve years on the teams and I'm still breathing. Many of my SEAL brothers aren't. I made my way to Vegas, crawled up the corporate ladder, and put up with Bonita's drama for five years. But I'd do it all over again if I knew I'd meet Jane. Good luck brought me across Steven's path. Through a maze of impossibilities, Jane's a woman who always wanted a family and finally found hers."

Mandy's eyes glistened, and so did Moira's.

"It isn't about me. It's about Jane's strength. She never let adversity crush her spirit. After meeting the Porter brothers, I can see where she got it."

Flanked by both women. Moira and Mandy threw their arms around his neck and hugged him. Nathan grinned and hugged them back. When he looked up, Dane and Steven stood with their arms crossed and sported narrowed eyes.

"Okay," Nathan said, clearing his throat and stepping out of their embrace. "Think I'll check on Jane."

Moira clapped her hands and said, "Right! Who wants dessert?"

The kids erupted with a chorus of agreement. Dane placed his two boys on the ground, giving them a reprieve from bedtime, then he winked at Mandy. Without pause, she gave him a dramatic raise of one eyebrow, but didn't overrule her husband's decision.

After dessert and an hour to let the sugar fix run its course, the children went to bed. The Porters escorted Nathan to the front door. Jane and Kyle walked hand-in-hand to the car. Nathan lagged behind to give them a minute of privacy.

Moira winked at Nathan. "Don't forget next Saturday," she said. "You're in charge of barbequing the ribs, and don't forget that family secret sauce."

Nathan gave her a friendly, two-finger salute. "We'll be here."

As he approached the vehicle, Jane and Kyle had their foreheads tipped together. Kyle gave her a fatherly kiss on the cheek. "I'll pick you up at five on Friday."

She grinned. "Sounds perfect. See you then."

"Night, Nathan," Kyle said. "And don't let my brothers get to you. They're just kidding around."

While Jane settled in the passenger seat, Nathan rounded the front of his car. "No worries, I'm used to it. Good night."

Driving toward Jane's place, the front headlights illuminated the dry, deserted road. The glow of Henderson's urban area in the distance splashed the horizon with a dense glow. Nathan glanced at Jane, who sat quietly with her lips tilted upward in a smile.

"Got a date with your dad on Friday?"

She shifted onto her left hip, but her eyes focused on the driver's window. "He and Moira volunteer at a rehabilitation center for people struggling with addictions. Ky...my da...Kyle wants to give me a tour. You're invited too."

He didn't mind taking a back seat for a while. "Nah. You need some time alone with your old man. You like him, don't you?"

"I do," she said wistfully. "It's crazy. I'm a grown woman, but I couldn't stop holding his hand."

"A totally natural response, sweetheart. Inside you is a little girl who grew up without the affection and unfaltering love of a father. By the sound of him tonight, his paternal instincts kicked into high gear when I read the results of the test. That man was heartbroken because he'd given you up for adoption and overjoyed at finding you again all at the same time."

She uttered a quick gasp. "Oh, my goodness. You asked me to marry you today."

"I did, but finding your father trumps a poorly executed proposal."

"Your timing was perfect, Nathan. And I accepted."

He liked teasing her and said, "Was that before or after you got confirmation that I'm hot?"

She chuckled. "I was just kidding."

"Hmm. It seems like a Porter trait." He wanted to steer clear of the topic of marriage before she questioned his proposal to Bonita, which he'd done in Paris. Not the Las Vegas Strip locale, but in France.

"How did you propose to Bonita?"

And...bam. "Dinner. Drinks. Nothing special." Jane and Bonita were two completely different women. "I promise, I'll propose again."

"But why? I already said yes."

Darkness draped the desert on either side of the vehicle as they headed toward town. Nathan kept his attention on the road while considering his response. Jane deserved memorable. Quaint. Simple but memorable. "Because I want a do-over without your family hanging on my every word. I know I've got rough edges, and I'm not exactly a romantic type of guy, but I want that moment to be special. It's you and me, babe, until the end of our days."

"What if I say 'no'?"

He chuckled, but his guts rolled a little. He'd wait until her vision returned because he had a feeling that when she finally saw him, she'd have questions. "Guess I'll keep trying until I wear you down."

She snorted and faced the front windshield. "You're not a

quitter, that's for sure, Mr. Selkirk. But Kyle's a little concerned. I admitted we've only known each other for a few weeks. He thinks we should wait."

He hoped like hell that she wouldn't tell him to hit the road at first sight. For twenty minutes, they drove in comfortable silence until Nathan turned onto Jane's street and parked in front of her townhouse. He shut down the engine and sat back, observing the quiet neighborhood. He looked forward to the day when they shared the same address.

"We're here."

Jane removed the seatbelt and placed her hand on his arm. "Thank you for being my rock today. Every day."

He kissed her soft lips. "I love you, Jane. And as much as I respect your father's wishes, there's no way I'm waiting six months to marry you."

She smiled and placed a warm peck on his mouth. "Coming in?"

"Um, only if you promise to let me show you how much I've missed you since you dumped my ass."

She squinted. "I had to think about my employees' welfare."

He cracked open the driver's door. "Bullshit. You dumped me because of the difference in our financial statuses. It was friggin' torture not seeing you every day."

"Oh, come on," she scoffed. "It wasn't that bad." Jane felt around to unlatch the door.

Nathan got out of the car, but before he shut the door, he bent over and said, "Not that bad, huh? I highly recommend you come up with a safe word before we get inside the house."

She laughed, obviously thinking he was kidding.

He wasn't. In a few short minutes, he would teach her a lesson: pleasure came in many forms, including blissful torture, and he planned to keep her breathless.

CHAPTER EIGHTEEN

T he MRI tech placed headphones over Jane's ears. The protective wear didn't completely diminish the rhythmic thud of the equipment scanning her brain. Twenty minutes later, the technician extracted her from the claustrophobic confines of the machine.

Blood tests followed.

Ocular tests.

Three hours later, she met Dr. Nelson in his office. Nathan sat on her right side, and Kyle sat on her left.

The neurologist palmed his chin while reviewing the reports.

Nathan tapped his heel on the floor while her father's thumb swept back and forth on her hand in a comforting motion.

A month ago, she didn't have friends, family, or a boyfriend. Because a taxi driver missed the posted signs and sent her flying, she'd gained everything, but lost most of her vision.

"Sitting on pins and needles here, Doc," Kyle stated.

Finally, Dr. Nelson laid the images of her brain scan on the desk. "Jane, I'm going to refer you to a neuro-ophthalmologist. The visual pathway is complex. They specialize in the brain's role in the visual system."

Nathan sat forward. "What do *you* see in the scans?"

"It looks to me like there's ocular damage. Could have been caused during the brain surgery or by the accident. Because Jane's field of vision is deteriorating, it's cause for concern. I see signs of bleeding. If that's the case, surgery could fix the issue."

The doctor's diagnosis put her in a holding pattern. "How long do I have to wait?"

Dr. Nelson sat back in his leather chair, the metal springs sounding off with a squeak. "The situation warrants attention now. At this point, Jane, you're considered clinically blind. I'll have you in to see the specialist within days."

Instead of asking what the chance of her vision returning was, she stood. "Thank you."

"You're welcome. And thank Steven and Moira Porter. It's their generous donations to this hospital over the years that allowed us to recently expand the eye care department. It's the best facility in the Southwest.

"I'll do that."

Kyle wrapped an arm around her shoulders as they walked out of the office. "Don't worry, honey. This is just another step in your recovery."

"Thanks for coming with me."

"I never got the chance when you were growing up. My fault, of course."

"Kyle, we talked about this. It's not anyone's fault. You did what you thought was right at the time."

"I'm not blameless, honey. If your mother and I weren't high twenty-four-seven, everything would have been different. But I'm thankful our mistakes didn't have any lasting physical effects on you."

"Straight four-oh grade point average!"

He chuckled. "Runs in the family."

Her escorts led her through the maze of hallways and out into the sunshine. Another gorgeous June day.

"It's noon," Kyle said as they stopped in the parking lot. "Why don't you two follow me back to the Grand Palms for lunch?"

Nathan didn't jump in with an answer.

She stopped abruptly and pivoted. "Nathan?"

"He stopped to answer his phone," Kyle said.

A few seconds later, Nathan joined them. "I gotta get back to the Jade."

"Sounds serious," Jane said.

"There's always a catastrophe to deal with. Kyle, do you mind driving Jane home?"

"No problem."

"Appreciate it." She felt a peck on her cheek. "Talk later."

"Bye."

Her dad slipped his arm around her elbow. "Is he okay? Seems a little on edge."

"Not sure what's going on."

The barbeque last Saturday was a big hit. Nathan had fun. They both did. But that night, he'd gone home instead of staying at her place. He'd called late Sunday afternoon but didn't come over. Normally, he couldn't wait for an invitation. On Monday, he'd said he had to work late. They only spoke for a few minutes before he ended the call.

Kyle guided her through the parking lot to his car.

"Maybe I'm crowding him out," Kyle said. "I don't mean to, but you're my daughter. I missed so much of your life."

"That's not it. Nathan understands what this means to me."

He closed the door once she'd settled in the passenger seat.

After snapping his seatbelt into the buckle, Kyle started the vehicle. "The incident at Oasis Secrète with Bonita made *her* look bad. Not him or you."

Friday morning, Mandy had called and told her what had transpired at the restaurant on Thursday didn't take long to hit entertainment headlines. Her aunt read the tagline. *Bonita Williams' ex-husband blinded by love.*

Someone in the restaurant that day gave a play-by-play to a reporter.

Explosive revelations! Witnesses said a heated exchange took place in Sin City's exclusive Oasis Secrète at the Grand Palms resort. Is Nathan Selkirk committing adultery, as Bonita accused only last week? Court records prove her performance was a ruse for her own promiscuous activity. They're divorced! The source said Nathan Selkirk, a Las Vegas executive, is blinded by love for a visually impaired mystery woman. Making a scene without cameras rolling, Bonita pounced on Nathan's new sweetheart while she ate lunch with billionaire Hollywood mogul Steven Porter's wife and sister-in-law. We learned the actress is expecting and schemed to pin the pregnancy on Nathan. With Bonita's plot revealed, Nathan's new gal pal delivered a harsh warning and had the actress running from the restaurant with her tail between her legs.

Whoever spilled the story must have been sitting close by, Jane thought, because the article ended with a bombshell.

Not much is known about the mystery woman at Nathan's side, but sources revealed Selkirk's new girlfriend is the long-lost daughter of Kyle Porter, brother of Steven Porter.

Nathan thought the article had done Jane a favor. Bonita desperately wanted a role in one of Steven's movies. She'd struck out so far. With the news that Steven was Jane's uncle, Bonita would pour gasoline over her chance of ever acting in one of his films if she targeted Jane. With the weight Steven carried in Hollywood, he could end Bonita's career entirely.

"Kyle, I need to meet up with Miguel after lunch. Want to grab some greasy cheese burgers on the way home instead?"

"Whatever you want. And I know we're picking up thirty-two years after the fact, but if you want to call me Dad, I'm okay with that."

"Just okay?" she teased.

He laughed. "Fine, you cornered me. I want that, but not if it makes you feel uncomfortable."

Nothing about her father made her uncomfortable. "I can't wait to see what you look like, Dad. You said I look like my mother, but do I have any of your traits?"

Jane felt the car slow to a stop. She saw a red light ahead, but only through the tiniest hole in her vision.

"Your grandparents think so."

"Like what?"

"You have your mother's eye color, but they're shaped like mine. Guess I'd have to say your intellect, too. Your mom was beautiful. Creative. But she didn't do so great in school."

The light turned green, and they slowly picked up speed behind a line of cars. "Do you think she's still alive?"

"Hmm, I've been kind of wondering that myself. She had a nice family. They weren't wealthy, but they had a decent home in the burbs of Denver. Clea did as much damage to them as I did to mine. Left them brokenhearted."

"Why'd you break up?"

The signal light indicator blinked as he made a right-hand turn into a strip mall, probably for a drive-thru.

"I wouldn't call it a breakup. I got arrested for possession. Spent three years in prison. She stopped coming by for visits. Once I was released, I headed to her folks' place. They told me she'd disappeared a year before and didn't know where she was. Without her, there was no reason to stay in Denver, and I headed back to LA. I stayed clean for a while, but started dealing drugs for cash."

"You think they lied to keep you apart?"

"Maybe. Don't know. I was twenty-five by then. I had another stint in prison and five years before I cleaned up." He rolled down the driver's window. "What do you want, honey?"

"The works," she said, her stomach grumbling with hunger.

"So that's a green salad with tofu and water on the side."

She laughed. "Noooo."

After munching on cheeseburgers in her kitchen, Dad stowed the bags and wrappers in the trash under the sink. "If you want, we can try to find your mother. It's possible her family is still in Denver. She had older brothers and sisters. Someone might know what happened to her."

Jane had lucked out. Her father had kicked the addiction and straightened out his life. Her mother might not have fared so well. She might be dead or, worse, still using.

"I'm not sure. There's been so much going on lately. Maybe we should wait."

"Probably a good idea. On another note, you're not working today, are you?"

"Light duty. I want to catch up with Miguel. I've been sloughing off."

One of the cats jumped on her lap. Running her hand over the animal's sleek coat, she could feel it was Piper. The cat meowed and rubbed her head against Jane's chest.

"Why don't I come along?"

"Dad, I think you'd look pretty goofy slinging compost in a suit."

"Hey, I'm not like your uncles, who won't roll up their sleeves. Steven and Dane haven't done a hard day of labor in their lives. I know what sweating from something other than workout equipment is like. Besides, I want to revel in my daughter's accomplishments."

A warmth she'd never known seeped into her heart. She stood, rounded the table, and wrapped her arms around her dad's broad shoulders. "Promise you'll be around for a long, long time." She tucked her head next to his.

Kyle patted her arm. "Wouldn't want it any other way. And,"—he got to his feet then held her hands—"the Palms needs a new landscaping company soon. You're it."

"Daaad, that's nepotism."

"Like hell, it is. The Palms is your uncle's resort, and I make the executive decisions. That means it's a family-owned and operated business. I drove by the Royal Jade to check out your work. It's top-notch. You really have an eye for—shit. Sorry."

She shrugged. "I'm a realist. If my vision doesn't return, my business is finished. I'm finished."

"Hey." He cupped her cheeks. "Throwin' in the towel isn't something a Porter does. Not even a black sheep of the family like me. If you have to change course, then you'll reinvent yourself. I bought a place three years ago. It's not a mansion like Steven's, but it's comfortable and huge. You can move in with your old man until you figure out what's next."

She chuckled. "I think Nathan might have something to say about that."

"Listen, I know I haven't earned the right to give you a father's speech yet, but I'm doing it anyway. I like Nathan. He's got his shit together and cares about you. Steven vouches for him too, but he literally just got divorced, and you've only known him for a few weeks. Give it a few months at least."

Kyle might not have been her father for very long, but when she listened to his plea, she knew he was right. They needed time. Nathan had been distant since Sunday, but she didn't know why.

"You have a point. I guess waiting a little would be wise."

"Wanna move in with me now?" he asked with enthusiasm.

She laughed. "Dad, I've passed the Barbie stage, and the last thing I need is a curfew."

He snorted, then hugged her. "Okay, okay, I get it. You're a grown woman who needs her privacy. But the door is wide open, my girl. You walk through it any time you want."

"Thanks. We better go. I need to make a pit stop at one of my suppliers. He's reneging on the price we agreed on over the phone for a shipment of palm trees I ordered. I need to straighten that out."

"Is he now?" Dad's tone dropped with displeasure. "Well, let's pay him a visit, shall we? Need to use the bathroom. Be out in a second."

Jane tugged on the patio sliding doors to make sure they were locked. Then she strode down the hallway to the front entry by fingering the left wall to keep her bearings. When she stepped outside to wait, her cell rang.

"Jane," Nathan greeted. "Sorry, I missed lunch."

"You didn't miss much. We picked up burgers and ate at home. Dad's driving me to meet up with Miguel on a work site."

"Sounds good. Listen, I'm going out of town for a few days."

Jane waited for him to explain, but the line remained quiet. Since they'd met, he'd gone from caring and concerned to elusive. This was unfamiliar territory for her. Like a light switch, he'd turned off.

"Jane, you still there?"

"Still here."

Was she supposed to question him? Or was this another side of Nathan she didn't know existed? If he'd done this to his wife—shut her out without explanation—Jane understood why Bonita became frustrated. It didn't feel very good at all. She had plenty on her mind, but her heart shriveled with disappointment. Some guys did this. They laid out the red carpet, then pulled it out from under you.

"I better go," he said in a flat tone.

"Hope everything is okay. Have a good trip wherever it is you're going. Talk again sometime." She disconnected the call. Hurt and pissed off.

****

Nathan sat at his desk, closed his eyes, and laid the phone down. Barb knocked on the door to his office, then entered.

"Flight's arranged. I texted you the information. Departure time is six p.m." She paused. "Anything I can do for you or Jane while you're gone?"

He shook his head. "She doesn't know." Since receiving Tony Bale's message on Saturday night, he'd barely kept it together.

Barb inched her way to the guest chair and slowly sat down. "Why doesn't she know?"

"Because it's part of my past. She has enough to deal with."

He'd been working on autopilot. The news had left him numb. Tony's message was the type guys like him get from time to time. Expected and unexpected all at once. But this time was different. Ian Kelly, aka Razor, was Nathan's best friend. Razor had stayed with the SEAL teams. He was on his last deployment before retiring. One fucking deployment.

"Sir?"

He glanced at Barb. "What is it?"

"When my dad died unexpectedly last year, you marched my butt in here and made me talk about him. I'd bottled up my grief because my mom was a wreck and I needed to keep it together. I remember being so angry that he'd died. You helped me vent that anger."

Nathan turned his chair around to face the window overlooking the strip. "There are plenty of team guys to vent with in San Diego after we bury Ian. That's why I'm going. For him and his wife, Angela. Jane's condition has worsened, but finding her father keeps her mind off of that. She doesn't need to hold my hand or see me grieve."

"No, sir, she doesn't *need* to, but she's not self-centered like Bonita. Yet you're treating her like she is. I watched a few of those videos floating around that were taken at Oasis Secrète when Bonita made a scene. Before the blowout, I saw how you acted with Jane. Those photos the blackmailer took revealed the same thing. I wish a man looked at me that way. You're in love with her. She means something to you."

He slowly turned his chair to face his admin assistant. "You're saying I'm a bastard because I don't want to let her see me grieve."

Barb folded her hands. "If you haven't told her about your best friend being killed in action, it's worse than not seeing you grieve. You're shutting her out of an important moment in your life." She shrugged. "Bonita was a Class 'A' bitch. No question. It was obvious you didn't love Bonita. Eventually, she saw that too."

He respected Barb. In the kindest way possible, she told him he wasn't without blame. And it was true. In the early days, Bonita accused him of being cold and illusive. He hadn't been that way intentionally, but his actions revealed his misgivings about marrying someone he didn't love.

With Jane, he was trying to protect her, but using the same technique. She didn't ask him where he was going. *Hope everything is okay. Talk again sometime.*

While he stared at the dark, stained top of his desk, Barb quietly left his office and closed the door.

Had he put distance between himself and Jane for her benefit or his? He didn't know the answer. She hadn't flown into a melodramatic rant like Bonita. A twist of concern punctured his numbness. Jane's words registered. *Talk again sometime.* She knew something was wrong, and in typical Jane fashion, didn't question his behavior or demand he divulge anything. She just set him adrift.

Nathan snapped his phone up and scrolled through the multitude of contacts, then dialed.

****

Jane removed her ball cap and swept an arm across her forehead. Eighty-five degrees and blue skies.

"Still like hard labor?" she asked, grinning.

Dad had done exactly what he said he'd do. Stopping off at the wholesale nursery, her father had gone all businessman on the owner. By the time they walked out, she not only had her palm trees, but a thirty percent discount plus free delivery. Dad had some kind of magic ability to talk circles around the guy. Definitely something she could learn.

After introducing her father to Miguel and the team assigned to the apartment complex in east Henderson, Dad tossed his suit jacket and tie, then rolled up his sleeves.

"*Mija*, you have a visitor," Miguel said.

"Who?"

Dad stopped shoveling Champagne rock over the garden bed. "It's Nathan."

A few more feet of the half-inch tan and pink rock to spread, and they could call it a day. Her team had finished mowing the grounds, removing the weeds, and planting the zinnias and snapdragons in the front gardens.

She kept shoveling rocks in the general direction of the garden bed.

"Jane. Do you have a minute?" Nathan asked.

Normally, he always touched her to let her know he was close. A kiss. A hug. A gentle caress. Not this time. Was he here to dump her in front of her staff? Maybe he got a taste of reality from Dr. Nelson and realized life with a blind person wouldn't be much fun.

She kept digging.

The shovel came to an abrupt halt. Nathan must have grabbed the handle. She sighed and dropped her arms to her sides. "If this is a private conversation, it can wait. If you want to call me after your trip—great. If you don't want to call me again

233

—no problem. Can I have my shovel back, please?" Her brow flexed, hearing the blade dig into the rocks and the whisk of stones tossed onto the bed. "What are you doing?"

"We have a plane to catch. Let's finish the job, get you home and showered, and we should make it to the airport in time."

"We? You've barely spoken to me since Saturday night. Now you want me to hop on a plane. I don't know what's wrong with you, but I'm not going anywhere."

"Is there a problem?" Dad asked.

"Yeah," Nathan said.

Swoosh. The rocks clattered over the ground.

Scoop. Swoosh. Clatter.

"Nathan?" Dad's tone heightened, as if disturbed by what he saw.

Scoop. Swoosh. Clatter.

Something was definitely wrong. "Dad, can you give us a second?"

Scoop. Swoosh. Clatter.

"No," her father said sternly. "Come here, honey. I think we should give him some space."

The blade ground into the pile of rocks. *Scoop. Clatter.*

Without her sight, she couldn't read the situation. "Nathan," she said calmly. "I can't see your expression. I don't know if I'm supposed to be scared, concerned, or walk away. I don't have sight, but I have ears."

Scoop. Swoosh...clatter.

Scoop...

Jane waited. The warm afternoon wind swept over the sweat on her bare arms and face. A bird whistled in a nearby Carob tree planted about twenty feet behind her.

"San Diego," he said in a thick, gravelly tone.

This wasn't about Bonita, or her, or breaking up. But there was a Navy SEAL base in San Diego. Tony and Lumin lived in San Diego. She worried her lip.

The shovel fell to the ground with a *clank*.

"When I entered BUD/S, I met a guy. Ian Kelly. We went

234

through hell but graduated because we wouldn't let the other quit. Worked on the teams together. Deployed together. He met Angela, fell in love, and married her. When his first son was born, we were in Syria. He wanted to be by her side, but we were hunting a bad guy. I saved his life. He saved mine. Then I left the teams..." Nathan's voice choked up, and he paused. "I talked to him two months ago. Workups were finished, and he'd decided that after this deployment, he was hanging up his Trident. Coming home to Angela and the kids for good."

Jane's heart twisted into a tight little pebble. The punchline had yet to come, but it was obvious. She stretched her arms out.

"He's coming home," Nathan said, his words strained. "And we're gonna bury him tomorrow."

Tears welled in her eyes. Nathan's arms cinched around her body, and she heard his stuttered breath. She squeezed him in a tight hug. From what she'd learned about SEALs, the connection with their teammates was a brotherhood. Bonded for life. Losing his best friend was devastating.

"I understand. Believe me, I do." When she'd lost Celia and Kate, her world had crumbled. They were like sisters. Family.

Nathan stepped back, palming her upper arms. "I'm supposed to put my pain in a box and lock it away. That's what we do for fallen brothers. Men like Ian, like me, accept the risk. There's no question or regret. But he was so close to retirement, Jane. He was supposed to come home to Angela. I keep asking myself, why now? I'm numb. Pissed off. Empty. I can't close the box. I shut you out so you wouldn't have to see it. Convinced myself that it was for you, but it's not true. There's something wrong with me. Because I've done it before. For different reasons."

"Nathan, I did exactly the same thing when Celia and Kate died. But I didn't have anybody to shut out. You can't force grief into a box. It crawls inside when it's ready and shuts the lid. If you want space, you can have it, but if you want me beside you, I'm here. That's kinda what you do when you love someone who's hurting."

Nathan kissed her tenderly. "I love you, sweetheart, and yes —I need you beside me to get through this."

"I don't mean to interrupt," Dad said. "Nathan, I can't imagine what this loss means. My deepest condolences. Honey, I'll take care of your cats. You two better get going."

"Miguel," she called.

"Go, *mija*," he said, standing behind her. "*Señor Selkirk. Mi más sentido pésame. Nosotros compartimos tu dolor.*"

Nathan cleared his throat. "Thank you, Miguel. I'll have her back in a few days."

CHAPTER NINETEEN

J ane stood among a crowd of military personnel who'd mustered together for Ian Kelly's outdoor service. The sea of dark uniforms looked like a black blur. Two rows of foldable chairs beneath a white canopy waited for the family next to where the casket would sit during the ceremony. Ian's wife wanted Nathan to stand next to the family. Without hesitancy, he'd agreed to give his best friend's eulogy. A man by the name of Thane Austen would present Angela with a folded American flag and the Navy's condolences, which was tradition during a military service.

A brisk ocean breeze snapped at the canopy. She held Nathan's hand and wished with all her heart she could see him in his uniform, which he'd opted to wear in respect of his best friend.

A hum of sullen, respectful conversation mingled with the early summer day as those who gathered took their places.

Tony and Lumin found them, but they'd stand with other retired SEALs behind rows and rows of currently active members during the burial service.

"Mace and Nina are here," Tony said. "Everyone's here from Alpha and Delta squads, Lieutenant. Retired, and those not deployed. We'll catch up with you later."

"Thanks, T-man," Nathan said.

"Are we close to the base?" she asked.

"Not far. We're near the shoreline on a grassy field. That's the Coronado Bridge in the distance. I can't tell you how many times Ian and I crossed over and under that bridge. Tired. Elated. Drunk. Scared. Proud." A reminiscent chuckle, laden with sadness, followed.

She squeezed his hand. "Are you going to make it through the eulogy?"

"I didn't think so this morning, but now that I'm here, standing on Coronado soil, I remembered something."

"Something Ian said?"

"Yeah. It was after we graduated. He said, *'Buddy, I don't ever want to come home in a box, but if I do, you make sure they get all the pieces and bury me near the water. Cuz we're Frogs, man. It's where we belong.'*"

"I wish I had a chance to know him."

"Me too, but he knew you."

She blinked. Surprised by his comment. "How?"

"Ian was the best man at my wedding. He asked me three times if I was sure I wanted to go through with it. As we were about to take our places, he slapped me on the back and said, *'Don't worry, Rider. I'll be your best man next time, when you really fall in love.'* Two years ago, when I saw you at the Jade, I told him. Told him everything. He laughed and said, *'You finally found her.'* As soon as he retired, I was going to bring you out here to meet him and the family."

She smiled. "I'll get to know him through you."

"Lt. Selkirk," a man with an authoritative voice greeted.

"Admiral Austen. Been a long time, sir." Jane turned her head toward the voice. "This is my fiancée, Jane St. Eval Porter."

She smiled at the way Nathan showed her family respect by mentioning their name.

"Nice to meet you, Jane."

She wasn't certain whether he'd lifted his hand for a shake. There was a pause, and then the admiral quickly said, "This is my wife, Kayla."

"Nathan," Kayla greeted. "Pleasure to meet you. Thane shared plenty of stories with me last night. We're glad you're here."

"T-man came to Vegas recently. He helped me solve an issue. He got me up to speed, Snow White. It's an honor to meet you."

She chuckled warmly. "Jane, do you mind if I stay with you during the service? Nathan and Thane are required to stand closer to the casket."

Jane liked the idea. "Sure."

Ian's family arrived, as did the hearse. Kayla must have figured out she couldn't see and quietly, from time to time, described the events as they happened.

The service began.

An officer barked out a roll call with Ian Kelly's name. He called again, but of course there was no answer but the wind. Tears swelled in her eyes with the poignant meaning.

Admiral Austen's speech and presentation to Angela thickened her throat, but when Nathan stepped up to give the eulogy, Kayla clasped Jane's hand as if to give her support, and she appreciated this woman's gracious sign of concern.

Ian's widow and her three children sat directly in front of Jane. She wondered how Angela didn't fall to pieces. Even with her lousy vision, she saw the woman kept her shoulders straight and didn't move a muscle.

Jane knew Nathan as a lover and Operations Director —a civilian—but standing before his brothers-in-arms, she witnessed the echo of who he'd once been. Outstanding. Dignified. A warrior who'd served his country by fighting alongside his men. This was the commanding voice of an officer in the United States Navy SEALs. Nathan's speech was inspiring, heartbreaking, and cloaked in admiration for his best friend. With her keen sense of hearing, sniffles and subdued throat clearing came from every direction.

Silence ensued once he'd finished. Then Jane heard a *thwack*. Like a fist pounding wood. Seconds later, another *thwack*. Then another.

She lifted her chin and turned her ear toward the sound.

Kayla leaned closer, their shoulders brushing. "You're hearing the men who served with Ian pounding their Tridents into his coffin, followed by a salute.

That just made her tear up even more. When the men finished, Kayla said, "He's receiving an honor volley. Three shots."

Even with the warning, Jane jolted when the first volley fired. Kayla knew what was coming because this wasn't her first military funeral. The notion stole the breath from Jane's lungs. Nathan survived his service on the teams. She hadn't known him then, but cold reality settled in her veins. Grateful he'd survived and terrified that during his years of combat, at any time, he could have come home like Ian. A profound urge to hug Nathan and make sure he was alive held her captive.

The service ended and she stood, overwhelmed by emotion. "Thank you, Kayla."

"The first one is jarring, as are the second and third. It doesn't get any easier. Because my husband is the Commander of the West Coast Chain, he feels it's his responsibility to attend them all. It doesn't always happen, but because he served as commander of the west coast teams here in Coronado, we always try to be here."

Jane swept the tears from her cheeks.

A woman's arm slid around her shoulder. "Little overwhelming, isn't it?" Lumin asked.

Glad to hear a familiar voice, she turned and gave her a hug. "How, as wives, did you live with the weight of your husband's job on your shoulders? You must be made of steel."

"Nope. More like fire and ice," an unfamiliar voice said.

Lumin introduced the woman. "This is Nina Callahan. Mace's wife and our good friend."

She nodded. "Lumin talked about you and Mace. And so many others. Nice to meet you."

"You too, Jane," Nina said. "Nathan had retired from the teams by the time I showed up, but Mace says he was one helluva good lieutenant. You live in Vegas?"

"We do."

Suddenly, there was a flurry of 'How you holding up, Angela?' and other comforting condolences by the women. They all knew each other.

Nathan's low timbre cut through the crowd. "Angela, this is Jane."

She lifted her hand, not exactly sure which direction to face with so many people around.

"Thank you for coming, Jane." Cool, slender fingers with a slight tremble accepted her hand for a shake. "It means a lot that Nathan was here. That you're all here."

Ian's widow had to be paralyzed with grief. Jane knew words of compassion didn't penetrate the wall of pain, but she said, "I'm so sorry for your loss. I'm sure you have amazing support, but if there's anything you need, don't hesitate to ask."

Conversations hummed all around her, but the crowd seemed to thin out.

"Marg. You came!" Angela's voice lifted with surprise.

A delicate hand rested on Jane's left shoulder, and Kayla said, "That's Margaret Cobbs. Her husband was killed in action. He was my husband's swim buddy and best friend. They served together for twenty years."

If anyone could understand what Angela was going through, it'd be Mrs. Cobbs. "This must be hard for Margaret to relive," Jane commented.

"She's got us. So does Angela. No one understands like a team wife."

Nathan's past and his time on the teams were completely foreign to Jane. Since she'd met him, he'd briefly made reference to those years, but never in any detail. "Ian's death affected Nathan deeply. I think it will for a long time."

Kayla gently squeezed Jane's arm. "Thane still struggles with Pat Cobbs' death. Eventually, they come to terms with the loss but never really accept it."

"Do you see Nathan?"

"He's with Ian's parents right now. Ian's father is a thirty-five-year Navy veteran."

"Oh, God. His parents must be distraught."

Kayla hummed in a lighthearted tone. "Actually, whatever Nathan said, Mrs. Kelly is smiling."

"I'm not surprised. Not that long ago, I was in an awful place. Nathan made me smile, too. I just wish I could return the favor.

But I feel completely useless."

"You'd be surprised," Kayla said. "Men like ours rarely show their weak spots. It goes against some kind of instinctual law. They're trained to ignore pain and restrain their emotions. It's not something they leave behind when they come home from a mission or retire from active duty. It's part of them forever. Any woman who loves a SEAL needs to read their withdrawal like sign language. There's a reason behind the silence. Berating them or demanding they spill their guts never works. All we can do is stand beside them when we sense there's trouble."

Kayla described exactly what she'd witnessed with Nathan. He'd withdrawn, trying to deal with the loss of his friend. She'd stepped back, giving him space, not knowing what had transpired. If this happened again, and surely it would, she'd deal with his silence differently. There were so many layers to the man. She didn't have to dissect each one, but tell him she would listen when he needed to talk.

"Thane and Nathan are coming," Kayla said. She gave her shoulder an extra squeeze and stepped away.

"Sweetheart," Nathan said, clasping her hand. "We're heading over to Breakers for the wake. You okay?"

She palmed his arm. The feel of his uniform was different from the suit jackets he normally wore. "I'm stunned." They walked across the spongy grass, holding hands. "Is it wrong to tell you how deeply I love you? Or how proud I am to walk beside you. Until now, I knew you were a remarkable man, but you're more than that. You're beyond belief. I can't tell you how happy I am that the taxi sent me ass over teakettle."

Nathan choked out a laugh.

The admiral's deep voice said, "I'd marry that woman if I were you, Rider."

Her mouth gaped, not realizing the admiral and Kayla walked beside them. She felt her cheeks heat with embarrassment.

Nathan didn't skip a beat. "I intend to, Ghost. The sooner the better."

****

When they reached the infamous bar that Nathan described as a favorite watering hole for SEALs and other service members from NAB Coronado, he steered her toward a table. In minutes, Lumin and other wives joined her. Nathan checked on her often, but she shooed him off to reunite with his teammates. As the night waned, it sounded more like a party than a wake, which meant the healing had begun. There were bursts of laughter and lively conversation from the men.

Kayla introduced her to Margaret Cobbs.

"I remember when Nathan was assigned to Alpha Squad," Marg said. "He was a few classes behind my husband, Patrick, and Thane. They deployed together twice before Nathan shifted to Delta Squad."

"I didn't know that," she said. "To be honest, I don't know anything about his life on the teams. But today certainly was a wake-up call. I'm so sorry you lost your husband."

"Patrick and I have three daughters. Before he was taken from us, we had so many amazing years together. Because of their profession, our husbands are home and then gone again. But Patrick loved us, and when he was home, we made the most of it."

"Just in a few short hours, and what I've learned, I have so much admiration for the wives and these men. Today must have resurrected difficult memories for you."

"It did. But I have good friends. A team wife is never alone, especially during a time like this."

Jane listened to the women talk about their children and their lives. Their independence became extremely apparent to her.

"Hey." Lumin tapped her on the shoulder. "Moira told me the incredible news about you and Kyle. It's a miracle."

Jane smiled. "I'm still in shock. Within hours, I went from having no one to having a family. Kyle and I have spent every day together, getting to know each other."

"I'm just a goddaughter, but Moira and Steven have always had my best interests at heart. They've always treated me like family."

"We're blessed," Jane said.

A woman named Rebecca, who arrived late, sat across the table from Jane. With the low lighting in the bar, she couldn't see much at all.

"Someone said you're here with Nathan."

"Yes. I'm Jane." Rebecca's strong perfume assaulted her nose.

"I thought Nathan was married to a movie star. He and I dated for a long time when he was on the teams. I didn't know he was single again. Lucky me."

Nina piped up. "Got a hearing problem, Rebecca. He's with Jane."

"Jesus, take a pill, Nina. I'm just kidding, but I'm gonna find Nathan and say hello. We had some hot times together. See ya, ladies."

Drained of energy and half asleep, Jane considered returning to the hotel, but Rebecca's statement put her on edge. "Um. Should I be concerned?"

Nina snorted. "That's Rebecca Horton. A two-faced slut that makes the rounds with the single guys. She's in her late thirties and getting a little long in the tooth to be playing Frog Hog games."

"Frog Hog? That doesn't sound very complimentary," Jane said after having a sip of water.

"It's not," Lumin explained. "They're groupies. They normally hang out at bars, but she's been around so long that she thinks she's part of the crowd. At one time, all our husbands were bachelors. Rebecca was always willing and able to...you know."

"Then I'm in good company, huh?"

The women chuckled in unison. "You are," Nina said. "There isn't an operator in here, married or single, that doesn't know her routine."

"I'm not overly concerned, but I could really use my eyesight right about now."

Lumin gave her a little nudge with a shoulder. "Don't worry, you've got eight pairs of eyes watching for you."

"Did Rebecca find him?"

"Mm. Yup," Nina said. "Accosted him with her D cups and plastered herself to his arm. He just gave her a peck on the cheek, and…now he's peeling her off. All good!"

Relieved, she covered an enormous yawn.

"It's getting late," Lumin said. "Jane, I can drop you off at the hotel on my way home. I have to relieve the babysitter of duty."

"Would you mind? I'm burnt."

"I'll let Nathan know we're leaving," Lumin said. "Be right back."

Jane gathered her purse and fiddled with her sweater to find the arms. The other women sounded like they were getting ready to go home as well, with the sound of chairs being shoved under the table.

"Jane. Are you and Nathan flying home tomorrow?" Kayla asked.

"Day after tomorrow. I think Nathan wanted an extra day in case Angela needed him."

"Thane and I aren't flying back to Hawaii for a few days yet. Why don't I call you and we can meet for brunch?"

Before she could answer, Nina said, "I'm calling dibs. Brunch at our place, but you're helping me cook, Kayla."

"Deal," Kayla answered.

Nathan returned with Lumin. "Sweetheart, I'll take you back to the hotel."

"Take a load off, big guy," Nina said. "We got it covered. We'll drop Jane off at your room."

His large hand palmed the back of her neck. "Are you sure, Jane?"

He wasn't exactly slurring, but he'd had a few. "Just make sure that slut Rebecca keeps her distance."

"You saw that?" he asked with surprise.

"No, but I have eight pairs of eyes that did. And *she* won't have any eyes left if she tries that again."

"Don't worry, darlin'. I only got eyes for you." His warm mouth lingered on her lips.

The women, in unison, all said, "Aw."

He laughed. "Take care of her."

Somewhere in the wee hours of the morning, Jane woke when Nathan slid under the covers and pressed his firm chest against her back. His hand slid under her arm and cupped her bare breast in his palm.

"Everything okay?" she mumbled.

He kissed her shoulder. "It is now. I love you. Everyone loved you."

"Love you, too," she said, patting his hip. "Now, turn around because you reek of booze."

Nathan shoved his nose into her hair. "I am sooo gonna marry you."

CHAPTER TWENTY

A week later, Jane was back in the hospital with an IV taped to her hand. Aunt Moira and Uncle Steven had just left the room after a quick visit. Jane's nerves sang with anticipation. She was going under the knife again. Or, more accurately, a laser.

The neuro-ophthalmologist, a friendly woman in her forties named Dr. Steddler, had determined the cause of Jane's blindness. They had to perform a delicate operation to close three ocular tears. Two in her left eye, and the third in her right. Because of the blood leakage, blockages had formed in both eyes. There were signs of infection, which she said should clear up with antibiotics.

Dr. Steddler had treated several people with similar issues, and most of the surgeries had been successful. To avoid any problems, Jane would be fully sedated.

"Hey, honey," Dad said, sitting on the left side of the hospital bed, clasping her hand. "You're going to breeze through this. Within two days, your vision should return to normal."

Staring up at the ceiling, she saw relatively nothing. "Keep your fingers crossed. I need all the positive mojo I can get."

Nathan cupped her right hand, and his thumb caressed the pulse in her wrist. "Sweetheart, we're going to be right here after the operation. Promise you won't dump me the second you see my face."

She laughed at his teasing. "I promise."

Hospital staff arrived to take her to the OR. Nathan and Dad both gave her a kiss. She didn't want to let go of their hands and held on when they had to back away.

"See you soon," she said, as they rolled her from the room.

After the operation, someone gently prodded Jane from her

sleep. She blinked, her eyes feeling gummy.

"You're in the recovery room. You doing okay?" a male voice asked.

"Thirsty," she said.

"Once you're back in your room, they'll get you something to drink."

Jane blinked again, her vision blurry, but she smiled. "I can see colors."

The attending nurse patted her forearm. "That's good."

Did this mean her vision would come back, or was this all she had left? Minutes later, she felt the hospital bed moving. Jane squinted at the lights in the hallway but saw the off-white walls streaming past. After a quick ride in an elevator, someone shunted her down another long hallway until they arrived at her room.

Her heart pattered with excitement. She wanted to see her father's and Nathan's faces.

Dad and Nathan swarmed her bed.

"How are you feeling, honey?" Dad asked.

"Sleepy."

Nathan kissed her forehead. "We spoke to Dr. Steddler. She closed the tears. Now we wait."

"You guys go home. Staying here is like watching paint dry."

The specialist wanted her to stay in the hospital one night for monitoring. At three in the morning, after another deluge of antibiotic drops, colors seemed sharper, and she could make out the defined edges of the monitoring equipment, the pale green curtain around her hospital bed, and the noses, cheeks, and eyes of the nursing staff.

Jane shuffled to the bathroom in her private room at four a.m. She hit the light switch and had never been so happy to *see* a toilet in her life.

By seven in the morning, a nurse escorted her to the eye care wing for tests to check her eye pressure and ascertain there were no more leakages.

Checkmarks across the board.

Dr. Steddler nodded at the results. Sitting on a stool with wheels, she swiveled to face Jane. "It looks good."

"The blurriness is almost gone. I can see you and everything in this office. Thank you."

"My pleasure," the specialist said. "Would you like me to call your father?"

Jane slid out of the examination chair. "No. I'll take a cab." Since the accident, she'd relied on people for help. She needed a breath of independence to feel whole again.

After being released from the hospital, Jane arrived home twenty minutes later. She stooped to check her plants at the front entry. The leaves looked a little curled. "You guys need some fertilizer."

As soon as she opened the door, Peony and Piper ran down the hallway.

"Hey girls!" She picked up both cats, and they nuzzled her chin. Jane took a second to gaze at her humble home. Her ratty but comfortable reading chair with discolored arms sat in the living room. The bookshelves rammed full of paperbacks reminded her that she needed to thin out the herd and visit Goodwill to drop off a few boxes. All the photographs on the wall of Celia, Kate, and herself were bittersweet memories. Over the last two months, she doubted she'd ever see them again.

Standing in her kitchen, Jane rinsed out the coffeepot and added fresh grains. Her ability to do the simplest tasks independently made her smile.

While she waited for the coffee to perk, she called her dad.

"Jane! Everything okay?" he asked.

"Perfect. I'm at home."

"I was just about to head out the door for the hospital. Nathan bring you home?"

"Nope. I had a bunch of tests this morning. The doc sprung me early. I got here under my own steam."

"Does that mean—?"

"Sure does! I can't wait to see you, Dad. I'm not allowed to drive for a few days, but I'll grab a taxi and meet you at the Palms for lunch."

He chuckled. "Honey, I'm so happy for you. I'll meet you in the lobby at noon."

"I'll be there!"

She disconnected the call, nervous all over again, but couldn't wait to see her father. Jane gulped back her coffee. She'd have a quick shower, then call Nathan.

Jane bolted up the stairs without holding the railing. Stripped down, she stepped under the rain of hot water in her shower, thankful she didn't have to feel around for the soap and shampoo. She swiped at the tiles and mangy-looking grout. The next thing on her to-do list was cleaning the house.

Standing in front of the vanity mirror, she towel-dried her hair. With a sweep of her hand, she cleared the steam from the glass. Two inches of hair had grown back and stood up in goofy little spikes. Thankfully, the doctor accessed the veins through her eyes instead of shaving her bald.

Back in her bedroom, she dabbed the dampness from her arms and legs.

"Jane!"

Her heart thumped madly. Nathan had let himself in.

"Upstairs!" she yelled back. She heard the heavy footfall of him running up the stairs. The moment of truth. The bedroom door cracked open. "Wait!"

Nathan stood on the other side of the half-closed door. "What's going on? I went to the hospital and they'd already released you. Why didn't you call me?"

Jane wrapped the white bath towel around her body, her nerves popping with anticipation. "Nothing's wrong."

With her loss of vision, she'd created an image of Nathan in her mind. The nurse's description of him as hot and handsome didn't exactly help define a picture. She'd made one up based on his voice, the way he'd touched her, and his concern. Every woman's idea of handsome was as vast as an ocean. She knew he was blond, had green eyes, and a rockin' hard body.

"Can I...come in?" The sound of uncertainty surfed along

with his request.

The sun streamed through her open window and laid a swath of sunlight across the white comforter on her bed. Why was she so nervous?

She exhaled to calm herself. "Yes."

But he didn't open the door. "The operation was a success. You can see, can't you?"

"Everything!" she answered. When only silence returned from the other side of the door, she asked, "Are you coming in?"

"Sweetheart, I want you to take a deep breath, okay?"

"Why? Did you grow two heads?"

"Not exactly," he answered.

The door swung open, and Nathan stepped into the bedroom. Her pulse shot through the roof. At least six-foot-four and stunningly good-looking, a dark blue pinstriped suit jacket streamlined his firm physique.

The expression on his unforgettably handsome features was distinctively wary.

Instead of elation, her mouth gaped and her heart raced. Jane's knees quaked, and her pulse skipped every second beat.

"Oh my, God!" she shouted. "You! You—you lied to me!"

Nathan slammed his eyes shut and exhaled. "You remember."

Was he kidding? "Rafael Park," she nearly shouted, feeling lightheaded. *Holy shit! Her fantasy guy, the man she'd remembered so vividly since that day, stood in her fucking bedroom!* She also recalled her first thoughts as they spoke briefly in the park. At the time, Jane instantly knew she'd never be enough to have a relationship with a man like him.

Nathan swallowed thickly, his tongue sliding along his bottom lip, emphasizing the minute cleft on his chin.

An image of him had carved itself into her gray matter that evening. "I saw you a year and a half ago."

A resistant smile crooked his lips. "You promised not to dump me at first sight," he teased.

She wasn't amused. Not at all. "It's not first sight, is it?"

He cleared his throat and straightened his enormous shoulders. "I was jogging in the park, and you were walking. I stopped for a breather. When I looked up, I couldn't believe it was you. You looked right into my eyes and..."

Why had he said they'd never met? "I said, *Fresh air is good for the soul. Enjoy your run,* didn't I?"

He nodded.

She blew out a stuttered breath. "Your eyes are so mesmerizing." She shook her head in disbelief. "I wondered if I'd ever see you again. Then I berated myself for being stupid."

"Stupid? Why would you feel like that?"

She bowed her head and shrugged. "You said you'd watched me for two years. That means you knew who I was when we met in the park six months after I got the contract at the Jade. Why did you lie?"

Nathan strode across the room and curled his strong fingers around her bare arms. "When you were struck by the cab, I vowed to make sure you were safe, then keep my distance."

"I think you should have."

Nathan clasped her hand and drew her over to the bed. She sat on the edge of the mattress, and he put one knee on the carpeted floor in front of her, then cupped her folded hands. It was so strange to see his large hands and, at the same time, feel his warmth. His chiseled jaw and heart-palpitating features had the same effect on her now as they did in those fleeting moments at the park.

"That day, you never looked back, Jane. There were only two reasons for that. You already had someone in your life or didn't like what you saw. Once I'd learned you weren't involved with anyone that only left the latter."

"I didn't turn around because there was no point." Jane slid her hands from his grasp.

Nathan gnawed on his inner cheek, his eyes sweeping back and forth across her features. "I panicked. A little. I wanted time for you to get to know me."

Get to know her? What the hell for? "No wonder a movie star

married you," she railed.

The glint in Nathan's eyes dimmed, and he chewed on the edge of his bottom lip.

She couldn't explain why her heart felt so heavy. Jane had formed an image of Nathan in her mind, but not this image. Not a man of his caliber. He wasn't polished at all. A rugged aura emanated from Nathan, vibrating with a universal raw-sex appeal. Way, way, waaaay out of her league.

His jaw flexed as if clenching his teeth. Finally, his gaze dropped to the carpet. "I was right, wasn't I? You never looked back because—"

"*Because* you were like walking past a billboard of a supermodel in Times Square. I don't stop to ogle billboards. Kinda useless. I mean, look at you! That's a thousand-dollar suit." She pointed at his wrist. "That's a Gucci watch. I wear faded jeans, and T-shirts covered with dirt and sweat by the end of the day. What the hell is the matter with you?"

Was she pissed because she'd fantasized about the man in Rafael Park for months, like a teenage crush, or because his attraction to her made zero sense?

"Nothing's the matter with me." Nathan's mouth twitched, the start of a smile curtailed. He sat back on his heel and tilted his head to the right.

Her sense of touch had been spot-on. Nathan took excellent care of himself. She remembered that day in the park when he'd worn a sleeveless shirt and jogging shorts. The man had solid muscle from top to bottom.

"You're frickin' crazy," she spouted.

"If you want me to dissect all the reasons I think you're beautiful to me, I will."

She remembered the drizzle of sweat that coursed from his temples and slid down his chiseled jaw. Damp bangs stuck to his forehead and his pronounced cheekbones. The way his eyes had penetrated her soul caused a monumental uptick in her pulse.

"You made a friendly comment. So did I, and that was that," she said.

"I should have told you the truth before now. With everything we've dealt with since the accident, I didn't want to —"

"To what?"

"Rock the boat. When we met in the park, I almost caved and ran after you." He bowed his head. "Just to talk with you for a few more minutes. But it was useless. I had a ring on my finger."

A small chunk of disbelief tumbled to the ground and lay gasping for life. Her heart scurried out and snuffed the evil tidbit to death. "Do you remember when I spoke about the man I'd seen in the park? Not the one I dated briefly, but the one I teased you about."

"Yeah, I remember. You said I must have met someone in my past that I'd instantly lusted over."

"I was thinking about you when I said that," she admitted. "Someone I was never supposed to see again. We're starting at square one. I know you, but it feels like I don't. Does that make any sense?" This guy, of all guys, had been her mystery man. A fantasy. "I take it all back. You need to go. Find yourself a Miss Universe to marry."

Shoving herself off the bed, he had enough strength in his forearm to hold her thighs down and she couldn't budge.

Keeping her legs pinned to the mattress, Nathan dug a hand into his suit's inner pocket. "I had a feeling you'd have a hard time, so I brought this." He retrieved an eight-by-twelve-inch sheet of paper and laid it on her lap. "Look at it, Jane."

"What for?" she said, glaring at the window. "Listen, I have to clean the house and meet Dad for lunch."

"Jane! Just look at it."

Slowly, she shifted her gaze to her lap. Nathan had kept a high-res photograph the blackmailer had taken of them in the Italian restaurant. The scarf on her head hid the bandage she'd worn. She'd been blind, but Nathan's eyes were riveted on her, and a charismatic, sexy smile pulled at his lips. She stared at the photo for a long time.

"That's us," she finally said.

He crossed his arms and perched them on her knees. "That's us." He set another photograph on top of the first one. "This is us too."

A photo taken at the instant he'd kissed her. Nathan built a bridge between the man she'd imagined and fallen in love with and the man kneeling in front of her now. The same man. Nathan slowly laid eight more photographs on her lap. Of them laughing. Of him holding her hand. In essence, it was proof that he cared.

Jane's pulse finally returned to an even gait, and she raised her eyes to Nathan's face. She looked beyond his characteristics and remembered his actions. The way he'd kept returning to the hospital to spend time with her. Kept her company. His comforting touch and the timbre of his voice when he'd read to her. The distance he'd gone to protect her from the fallout of his divorce.

Nathan's thumb swept back and forth on her bare leg. "Every minute we spent together, I learned more about you. I love the way you look at the world, Jane."

"You were going through a divorce."

Anger glinted in his eyes. "Don't. You're not a rebound. If you want to start all over again, fine with me. No problem. I'll pick you up for our first date. Tonight. Five o'clock."

"Why are you pissed?"

He strode to the window and stared through the pane. Jane's unit sat at the end of the complex. The bedroom window looked over a small playground.

"I'm not angry. I'm confused. I knew you'd be shocked, but I didn't think you'd take one look at me and tell me to hit the road."

He seemed genuinely hurt. The man had plenty of alpha qualities, but she didn't see any signs of a butt-hurt ego. "Nathan, you're too good to be true. Don't be a fool. Whatever this is, it can't last."

His chin tipped upward, and his jaw carved into a sharp edge. With a pivot of his heel, his gaze shot across the room, puncturing the excuse she'd created to protect herself.

"You have cold feet!" he said, as if he'd made an earth-shattering discovery. "You're scared I'm going to leave, so you're pushing me away now to save yourself the heartache."

"No." Was she? Probably. Definitely.

"Yes, sweetheart, you are. Your parents left you at the hospital. An avalanche took your friends' lives. The people who fostered you never adopted you. Everyone who's ever been important has abandoned you in one way or another. They hurt you, and you think I will, too."

Nathan crouched at her feet again. A rugged but understanding smile sent her heart into a confused, chaotic beat.

"You're right. That's what *will* happen. I won't place a bet that I know I'll lose."

"Then wager on love." His incredible eyes locked on her face. "Because I do love you. I'm not going anywhere, Jane. Not without the intelligent, beautiful woman I want to spend the rest of my life with. You're my other half. You know it's the truth. I know you do."

Nathan's words chipped away at her concerns. She closed her eyes, scooped her fingers around his hand, and pressed his warm palm against her cheek.

"It's me, darlin'. The same guy who loved you from a distance for two long years. Open your eyes, Jane."

She blinked and did as he asked.

"I'm the same guy who can't believe how lucky he is to have found you. The same man who loves you even more today."

He could have abandoned her, but he hadn't. "I still think you're certifiable, Nathan Selkirk, but after everything we've been through, if I saw you in the park today, I'd turn around for a second look."

Creases at the edges of his penetrating eyes deepened. His fingertip traced her collarbone and aimed for the twist of the towel between her breasts. After releasing the damp fabric, he pressed her shoulders down to the mattress.

While laying a line of blistering kisses along her bare stomach, Nathan shunted the jacket off his shoulders.

"I want to see you in your uniform," she said.

"Can I make love to you first?" he asked, a cocky grin tightening his chiseled jaw as he loosened the buttons on his shirt.

When his white cotton shirt separated, revealing the hills and valleys of his abs, her blood boiled. "I can't believe it's you. This has to be some crazy mistake."

He shook his head. "Everything happened the way it was supposed to happen. From the day I first saw you until this moment."

Nathan removed his clothes, and Jane's gaze strolled over every muscular ridge of his physique, pausing on the rigid body part that had brought her so much pleasure. Her cheeks heated, and she glanced nervously into his eyes. He watched, his incredible green gaze filled with desire. Nathan had a tattoo on his right bicep. A green frog squatted under the curl of a breaking wave, and a skull with red, thorny vines sprouted from its eyes and mouth.

When he leaned over, pressing his palms to the mattress on either side of her shoulders, she trailed her finger over the tats, peeling Nathan from an untouchable billboard to a warrior who'd served his country.

"Are you sure I woke up after the accident?"

His hungry gaze glided across her body, stalling on her peaked nipple. An intense, achy need shot to her core. Nathan slid a strong, masculine hand up the outside of her right leg, and he pressed a tender kiss to the inside of her left knee.

His piercing eyes locked with hers. "We both did, Jane."

****

Two months later

Kyle Porter sat in his office at the Grand Palms. His guest wore a black leather jacket and shades hooked on the collar of his

T-shirt.

"You're sure of this?" Kyle asked, laying the paperwork the PI had given him to preview on the desk.

"Absolutely," Dwayne Dawson said. "I did the research myself." He nodded toward the file folder. There are four current photographs in there as well.

Kyle slid the red folder across the desk and hesitantly opened the cover. He hadn't set eyes on her for thirty-one years, and his pulse tripled. "Thanks, Dwayne." He closed the folder.

"Anything else I can do?" the PI asked.

He shook his head. You found the answers I was looking for.

Three days later, with his stomach in knots, Kyle got out of the rental car and headed for the business entrance. He hadn't stepped foot in Denver since he'd left at twenty-five. The late August day held a hint of fall in the air.

A painted green plaque with *Lundgrin Nursery* hung over the doorway. Potted fall flowers and shrubs sat stacked on either side of the entry. To his right, piles of fall lawn fertilizer sat against the yellow exterior wall. Half-wine barrels and wheelbarrows marked with price tags were decoratively placed on a rock-covered garden bed.

He gripped the metal handle and opened the glass door. Seeing a sales desk to his right, he detoured. A young woman with fawn-colored eyes and brown hair smiled at him.

"Afternoon. Can I help you find something?"

"Hi. Is Mrs. Lundgrin in?"

The woman nodded. "Sure. Do you want me to call her up here?"

"No. Just point me in the right direction."

"You can find her through those doors," she said, looking toward the end of the garden shop and into a greenhouse with rows and rows of benches covered in planted pots.

"Thanks."

Kyle strolled through the store and into the spacious greenhouse covered in white plastic to protect the plants. A few customers wandered the aisles. In the far right corner, a woman held a hose and watered the plants.

Well, fuck, he didn't expect a thready pulse and a bead of sweat to cover his brow.

He made his way past the rows of seasonal plants and stopped a few feet behind the woman, who leaned over the plywood bench and picked up a clay pot. Straightening, she turned it in her hands and inspected the ten-inch-tall pink chrysanthemum. Wearing a tank top, her dark auburn hair teased her bare, slender shoulders. She wore it shorter than he remembered. But he certainly remembered that gorgeous heart-shaped ass, filling out a pair of jeans.

"Clea?"

She turned with a friendly smile, and then her expression melted with shock. She blinked and blinked again. The clay pot slid from her gloved hands and broke into pieces when it landed on the concrete floor.

"Ky—Kyle?" she said in a breathy voice. "You're alive!"

Um, okay. He gnawed on his bottom lip for a second. "As far as I know."

Clea shook her head, her pale green eyes wide with disbelief. "How?"

He shrugged. "Healthy diet. Exercise. Good genes." Shock had frozen her to the spot. "I'm guessing your parents told you I was dead."

She nodded.

Jesus, after all this time, she was still beautiful. A few creases edged her eyes, like his. They were fifty-one, after all.

Well, he was here for a reason and said, "When I got out of prison, I went to your folks' place. They said you'd run away. Didn't know where you were. I headed back to LA."

Clea's shoulders dipped. "I didn't run away. I was in rehab." She paused. "Failed twice, but finally got my shit together." A slip of a smile coated her mouth. "You—you look good."

He wanted to set her mind at ease. "Yeah, I ah—I'm clean too, Clea. Wasn't easy."

"No, it wasn't," she said, her gaze darting to the shards of clay pot on the ground. "How did you find me?"

"I hired an investigator." Kyle shoved his hands into his front jean pockets. "He told me you still lived in Denver." He gazed around the large greenhouse. "Said you married and had two sons, and this business."

She tipped her head and grinned. "And divorced."

"Yeah, he might have mentioned that, too. Sorry."

She pulled off the gloves printed with flower petals from her hands. "I divorced *him*. Caught him having an affair with the woman who approved our loan for the nursery. He dumped her, too. We haven't seen him in years." Her brows knit together. "Did you marry?"

"No. Never settled down. But six years ago, I reunited with my family. Things are good with us."

Clea's beautiful eyes slanted with a smile. "I'm glad. My parents forgave me, but things have always been tense with my siblings." She shrugged. "I'm happy to see you, but why are you here?"

The moment of truth had arrived. He crossed his arms and cleared his throat. If she was shocked at the sight of him, he figured he'd better be prepared for what came next.

"Because I promised someone I love that I'd find you. If you were still alive and had been as lucky as me to get a second chance, I'd introduce you."

Clea fingered a loose curl behind her ear. "Okay. Mysterious, but okay."

Kyle held his breath and twisted. The woman standing a few feet behind him turned and stepped to his side. Jane clamped onto his hand, her fingers trembling.

"Clea—" His old girlfriend's hand slapped over her mouth, her eyes wide. "Clea, I'd like you to meet our daughter, Jane."

She gasped. "I—I." Her brow notched with tight lines, but she couldn't avoid what her eyes must be telling her as she looked at a younger mirror image of herself.

"Hi—Clea," Jane said. "I can see you're shocked, and I'm terrified, but I just wanted to see you. Once. We'll go." Jane took a step back.

Clea's eyes slammed closed and then reopened. Her gaze slashed back and forth between him and her daughter. "How did you find her?"

Kyle slid an arm around Jane's shoulder. "We found each other. Imagine my shock at seeing a young woman who looked exactly like you. It was a total fluke. We're not here with any expectations or to turn your life upside down. No one adopted Jane. She was raised in foster care. It's kind of ironic that she owns her own landscape business and you own a garden nursery. Anyway—we'll go. Once the shock wears off, if you want to—"

"Don't go!" She reached out both arms. Jane grasped her mother's hands. "I don't know what to say. You must hate me."

Jane smiled. "Not at all. Dad told me everything. I don't blame him or you."

"How long ago did you find her?" Clea asked, turning her bewildered gaze toward him.

"Not that long. In June. But I'm never giving her up again. Jane and I both live in Las Vegas."

Clea shook her head as if still shell-shocked. "I was twenty-one when I got clean. I wanted to find you, but my parents convinced me you'd have a better life with the people who adopted you." Tears welled in her eyes. "But you weren't adopted."

Unsurprisingly, Jane swept her mother into a hug. "It's okay, Clea. I grew up in a good home. I graduated with a degree in biology, majoring in botany. And I run my own business."

Sniffing, Clea stepped back and inhaled a deep breath.

"Mom." A young man in his mid-twenties joined them. He read the scene and took an extra-long look at Jane. "Everything okay?"

Clea held her hand out, and the young man with dark hair and green eyes, the same as Jane's, took her hand. "Everything's fine, honey."

Jane shook her head. "You don't have—"

"This is my son, Cash," she said, winking at him. "When they were old enough to understand, I told my boys that I'd had a daughter when I was nineteen."

"Holy shit," Cash uttered. "You look just like Mom."

Kyle was happy to stand back and let the shock wear off and the union between Jane and her mother and half-brother unfold.

"Sorry we sprung this on you, babe—Clea," Kyle corrected. "But there's another reason we came."

Jane dug out a small envelope titled with gold lettering from her back pocket and held it out to her mother. "If you want—no pressure."

Clea opened the envelope and pulled out the white stationery. She grinned. "You're getting married."

Cash stood about six feet tall. He wore a white T-shirt, work boots, and jeans with dirty knees. Obviously, he worked in the nursery with his mother. His eyebrows arched. "Getting hitched, huh? Who's the dude?"

Jane grinned at her half-brother. "His name is Nathan Selkirk."

Cash raised a shoulder, and his thick biceps flexed. "Mailman, cop, what?"

Kyle sensed Cash was a good kid, but he had a healthy dose of cockiness.

Jane crossed her arms. "Why? Are you expecting a letter or an arrest warrant?"

Not expecting the fast comeback, Cash laughed. "Ouch. You bite like that all the time?"

With humor etched in her eyes, she said, "Only if you deserve it."

Kyle's gaze slid to Clea, and at the same time, her gaze strolled over to take a gander at him. He had no clue why her husband would screw around. The guy had to be a bona fide fuckup. Back in the day, even under the influence, Clea made him crazy. He couldn't keep his hands off her, hence the reason Jane had come into the world. Thirty-plus years later, and the woman still made his cock hard and his heart do crazy shit.

UNQUENCHABLE CRAVINGS: WAGER ON LOVE

Clea's gaze flashed back to her daughter. "It doesn't matter what he does, Cash. When you truly love someone, they own your heart forever." Her cheeks tinted with color, and she glanced at Kyle. "We'd love to come to your wedding. It's in Las Vegas?"

Jane tipped onto the front of her sneakers. "Yes. You don't have to get a hotel room. You can stay with Nathan and me, or with Dad. He has a big house. He's got plenty of room."

"Okay, we'll work out the details later. Can you stay for dinner?" she asked.

Jane eyed her half-brother. "I don't know. Does he eat with his hands or cutlery?"

Cash slapped a palm over his chest. "Wounded. Damn, girl. I call a truce."

Jane broke into a laugh. "So soon?"

He rolled his eyes. "Come on, I'll show you the way."

"First, I want a tour of the nursery."

"Interested in plants?" he asked.

"I have a landscaping business."

"No, shit."

The kids wandered toward the back exit of the greenhouse. Clea stepped up next to Kyle. "She's beautiful and smart."

Her bare arm brushed against his elbow, sending ripples of excitement through his veins. "Just like her mother."

"Do you have a plus one for the wedding?" she asked, watching the kids exit the greenhouse.

A skitter of hope lodged in his heart. He'd had plenty of brief relationships with women over the years. Finding a willing woman for sex wasn't an issue for him, especially these days. But committing to one woman never crossed his mind.

"No. You?" he asked, turning to face her. The neckline of her blue tank top revealed the soft swell of her breasts. When they were young and limber, making love to Clea was mind-blowing. He'd bet all he'd acquired since straightening out his life that the embers burning in his gut meant something. His gaze met hers, waiting for an answer.

A demure smile turned her lips upward, and her green eyes lit a fire in his belly.

"No one special," she said. "My boys and this business have had my full attention until now."

His fingers itched to follow the graceful curve of her cheekbone and thread through her thick hair. "As Jane mentioned, I've got plenty of room. You're welcome to stay with me when you attend the wedding."

Clea glanced toward the back exit. "I've lived with a hole in my heart for years, Kyle. We should have never given her up."

"I know how you feel, but it's only because we're on this side of life looking back, babe. You'll be amazed at the incredible woman Jane became. We did the right thing at the time."

"Did we?"

"Hey." He palmed her cheeks. "Yes. We did. When the paternity test proved I was Jane's father, I was riddled with guilt, but I instantly put it behind me because I didn't want the future tainted with my mistakes. Nathan, Jane's fiancé, is one helluva guy. I'm going to walk my daughter down the aisle and thank God for bringing her back to me."

Clea's slender fingers rested against his chest. "I thank God he brought you both back."

"Hey! Mom. Dad. You coming?" Jane yelled from the doorway.

Clea hooked her arm around his elbow as they strolled past the budding plants. "Is it just me, or do you get the feeling our daughter wants to play matchmaker?"

"Don't know, but when I walked in here and saw you leaning over that bench, thirty years evaporated."

She grinned, and his chest tightened with fond memories his addiction-addled mind hadn't erased.

"Are you trying to tell me if I accept your offer to bunk at your place, you won't keep your hands to yourself?"

They exited the greenhouse and wandered past rows of saplings of different varieties toward a two-story home with a large wraparound deck. He paused, and she turned to face him. Kyle's gaze calmly swept across her features, but his body erupted with heat. There wasn't a hope in hell he'd wait that long to reignite what they'd once shared.

"Babe, I think you know the answer to that already."

CHAPTER TWENTY-ONE

Three years later

A thunderous round of applause filled the massive banquet hall. With the overhead lights dimmed, spotlights shone on Nathan as he stood behind a podium.

Round tables draped with royal blue cloths covered the hall. Employees of the resort, from security to cleaning staff and every department in between, occupied the seats.

Jane sat to the left of her husband on a stage where tables draped with white clothes, tucked end to end, stretched for thirty feet on either side of them.

With the meal finished, the audience quieted. The *clank* of cutlery and dishes removed by hospitality servers signaled the next phase of the event.

Aunt Moira and Uncle Steven sat to Jane's left. Vince Laker and his wife, Lacey, were seated next to them. Other smaller investors had a place at the head table, as did the resort executives of each department.

Jane's closest friends and family sat in the audience near the stage. Dad gave her a wink while he sat next to her mom, the gold bands on their ring fingers glittering under the lights. Her half-brothers, Cash and Paul, were at the same table. Dane and Mandy Porter sat at the head table because they'd invested in Nathan's dream. Four tables with Navy SEALS and their spouses watched, including Tony, Lumin, Admiral Austen, and his wife Kayla.

Nathan raised his hand to quiet the crowd and spoke into the microphone.

"Tonight we celebrate three years of commitment and hard work. Tomorrow is the grand opening of the Royal Breeze Casino and Resort."

Another roar of applause echoed off the walls.

"I couldn't have done this without—"

"Dadeeee!" their son yelled from Jane's lap, loud enough that it reached the microphone. Laughter swelled like a wave throughout the room.

Nathan grinned and stooped to pick up their two-year-old son, Jaxon, holding him in his left arm. Jax's chubby little arm shot into the air like a prizefighter. "My son thinks I did this all on my own."

Another roar of applause shook the room.

Jane's heart swelled with pride, and she clapped as hard as everyone else.

"The truth," Nathan said, "is that no man is victorious on their own. Serving in the United States Special Forces, I survived a few close calls to teach me that lesson. It takes a qualified team and determination to succeed in any mission. Every man and woman in this room plays a part in the Royal Breeze's success. We will reshape the reputation of Laughlin."

After a short applause, Nathan continued. "There are two men in particular who are responsible for this incredible destination. They stand out because they're risk-takers and believers. They see desert sand and envision an oasis of luxury and a world-class resort. Vince Laker and Steven Porter. These two men *believed* in me. And I owe eternal thanks to my beautiful and talented wife, Jane. She is my rock."

"Maamaa," Jax said in his sweet voice.

"And my son, who just wants his old man to tuck him in at night."

A titter of polite chuckles followed.

"When I look out at the sea of faces here tonight, I see family, not employees, executives, and investors. I welcome you all and thank you for breathing life into this dream."

Nathan raised his wineglass to another round of applause.

More speeches followed by Vince and Steven, and then the bar with glittering lights and elaborate ice sculptures opened, serving complimentary alcohol to the guests. A rock band picked things up a notch, and people hit the dance floor.

The media invited to the event interviewed anyone who would stand still, and the click of photographs was a continuous stream of flickers.

By midnight, Jane's feet ached, not used to wearing heels. The children of guests who weren't local were upstairs in the hotel rooms, tucked in bed with a slew of babysitters and nannies watching over them.

The hotel was sold out for two months, as was the four-hundred-site RV park.

Sitting in the Vista Oasis, an area Jane had designed with soaring palms, trimmed boxwood hedges, water features, and stone pathways that led to teak tables and comfortable cushioned seating, she arched her head back and sighed.

Surrounded by her friends, family, and the wives of several SEALs who'd come to enjoy the evening, she smiled up at the stars. Aunt Moira, Aunt Mandy, Kayla—Admiral Austen's wife—and Nina were in a deep discussion about Canadian politics since that's where they'd all been born.

Jane's mom placed a hand on her thigh. "Holding up, honey?"

"My feet are killing me."

Patio lights glinted in her mother's pale green eyes, identical to her own.

"Your father and I are so proud of you and Nathan. This place is incredible. What an accomplishment!"

"I couldn't have done it without you, Mom."

A few months after she and Nathan married, her mom moved in with Dad. She'd left the nursery operation in Denver to her sons, since horticulture was in their blood too. Jane and her mother went into business together with a silent partner, Moira Porter. They bought a tract of land and three years later, they were the largest nursery and garden center in the state.

Her parents' wedding had been relatively small. Only family. A quaint, dignified ceremony where Jane, already pregnant and crazy with hormones, couldn't stop crying. Dad's speech at his wedding revealed the hardships of addiction, the will to keep trying, and his enduring love for Clea, which brought everyone to tears.

Jane scanned the familiar faces of her family and the SEAL team wives she'd gotten to know better over the last few years.

"You know who's incredible. All of you," she said.

Dad arrived and stood behind Mom's chair, draping his arms over her shoulders and whispering in her ear, making her cheeks tighten and blush at the same time.

"Honey, we're going to head home," Dad said.

"'kay. Coming back tomorrow for the grand opening?"

"You be—what the hell?" he muttered, looking over Jane's shoulder.

Aunt Moira stopped talking and sat up straight, as did Aunt Mandy.

"Nice resort," a voice said from behind Jane.

Jane lashed the straps on her temper. Bonita had not been on the guest list. She pushed to her feet and shared a glance with Aunt Moira before turning around.

Nathan's ex-wife stood in a sequined red dress, hanging onto the arm of a guy wearing a tux who looked like he'd been cut from the pages of Gentleman's Quarterly.

"I just had to drop by and see it for myself," Bonita said, her ruby-red lips pinned in a practiced smile that resembled more of a sneer. "I'm so happy I pushed Nathan to believe in himself. I knew he'd own a resort one day."

After their exchange at Oasis Secrète, the tabloids said Bonita had lost the baby. Moira heard through the Hollywood grapevine that the actress had received a leading role in a new movie at the same time.

Jane's friends, seated at the tables, quieted. All heads turned their way.

When Jane didn't respond, Bonita primped her blonde-styled updo. "I just thought I'd add a little star power to Nathan's big night. I was so proud watching him make his speech." Her forehead creased with mock sympathy. "I know my presence must be uncomfortable for you, but I'm such an important part of his life, after all."

Aunt Moira and Mandy had given her some pointers over the last three years. What Jane really wanted was to tell Bonita to shove her pride up her ass. Instead, she lacquered a smile on her face. "Well, isn't that kind. Bless your heart."

A few snorts from the table erupted from the women who knew *exactly* what that meant.

At that moment, a herd of men rounded a group of palm trees lit with thousands of tiny white lights. Nathan was in the lead, and he had Jaxon in his arms.

Bonita gasped, and her heels clicked on the stone tiles. "Oh my goodness, there you are!"

Nathan stopped, and his brows knit together, seeing his ex-wife hurtling herself toward him. The other men, including the SEALs, swelled past Nathan to join their wives.

Jax lifted his head and pointed at Jane.

"Oh, he is such a darling," Bonita gushed. "He has your eyes."

"He has Jane's eyes," Nathan said, his features drilled into a stern look. "Jane, sweetheart."

She joined her husband. Jax rubbed his eyes, his cheeks rosy red from crying. "Aww, sweetie."

"Maamaa."

Nathan shifted their son into her arms and she cuddled Jax, who lowered his chin to her shoulder.

"Why don't we take our boy home?" Nathan said. "We have a big day tomorrow. Besides," he leaned over and planted the hottest kiss on her mouth, causing the SEALs to hoot and holler. "I can't wait to put you to bed."

When they unhooked their gazes from one another and planted a look on Bonita, a bitter glare twisted her features. That was until Steven and Dane Porter rounded the corner.

Bonita's expression lit up, and she aimed for Steven like a fly to sticky paper. "Steven," she gushed, her heels clickity-clacking on the stone path. "Congratulations on another historic success. How are you?"

Jane shook her head. "Psycho," she muttered under her

breath.

Nathan chuckled and raised an arm. "Good night, all. See you back here tomorrow for the big day."

****

Jane shut the bathroom light off and strode across the low-pile bedroom carpet. Nathan lay against the cotton pillows, the sheets tucked around his bare waist, with Jax sound asleep on his chest. It melted her heart the way Nathan looked at their son.

"I'll put him to bed," she said, caressing Jax's blond mop of hair.

Nathan carefully cradled his son and got up. "I've got him."

Jane slipped under the covers and sighed, wiggling her aching toes while scanning the muted brown and green tones of their bedroom. Picture frames filled with family sat on the mantle above the gas fireplace. Across the room, a moss green lounger with a beige blanket draped over the back sat next to a reading light. Instead of buying a home, they'd built one. Close to Uncle Steven's and Aunt Moira's place. It had every modern convenience and plenty of extra bedrooms for guests, but it was a home, not a cold monstrosity.

Nathan had sold his residence on Dragon Peak three weeks after Jane's operation to restore her vision. He'd brought her over to see his old house before changing titles.

She'd bit her lip versus uttering, "Yuck." Although the backyard was pretty spectacular.

They'd toured the house he'd shared with Bonita and finally ended in his bedroom.

Nathan, with a glint in his eyes, had backed her up to his bed. "I want to leave one good memory in this house."

She'd grinned, knowing exactly what that hungry look in his eyes meant. "Any ideas?"

Unbuttoning her blouse, he'd nodded. "I spent two years dreaming about you while I slept alone in this bed. Seeing your smile every Tuesday kept me sane." He'd slid the blouse off her shoulders and unclasped her bra.

"I get the feeling you have something specific in mind." Her heart beat with a hectic rhythm whenever he looked at her like that.

His lips spread into a wide, handsome smile and he tackled her, sending them rolling onto the satin white comforter.

They'd christened his old bed three times that night.

When Nathan returned from putting their son to bed, he left their bedroom door ajar, and Jane watched her husband's sure-footed stride cross the room. Wearing a pair of blue pajama bottoms, her pulse got thready as she admired his smooth, hard abs and broad shoulders.

He rolled into bed and shut off the bedside light, dipping the room into darkness. Nathan turned onto his side and caressed her hip.

"Every time I look at our son, I'm reminded how much I love you," he said in his deep timbre.

With the lights out and her eyes adjusting, it reminded her of the days when they'd first met and she had no vision.

"I feel the same way."

His warm palm splayed across her stomach. "How's our little girl?"

"She can't wait to meet her daddy." Their daughter was due in five months.

"Hmm, I can't wait to hold her in my arms."

"Seeing Bonita tonight brought back memories of our early challenges. Glad those are over."

Nathan groaned. "That woman is so desperate to be seen, she'd come to a letter opening. I wasn't surprised she showed up."

"She looked green with envy to me." Jane tucked the pillow under her head. "Think she has any regrets, because I'm not giving you back."

He chuckled and rolled Jane on top of his firm body. "I used to think blinded by love was just a poetic phrase. Until I saw you, Mrs. Selkirk."

"And you bamboozled me."

Nathan's lips brushed against her mouth. "That's not what I want right now."

His shaft thickened beneath the thin fabric of his pajamas. "We're already pregnant."

He slid her silk negligee up and over her head, then palmed her ass and lifted his hips. "Let's practice for next time."

Jane leaned forward and kissed her husband. She'd gone from an empty life to one filled with family. The cab that struck her on that April day was a small price to pay for the happiness she had now.

The End

MESSAGE FROM NATHAN

I want to extend my thanks to Nat's readers who enjoyed the Hard to Catch series. Steven, Dane, and Kyle Porter are sitting around the kitchen table with me, enjoying a beer on a hot Nevada summer afternoon. We consider ourselves extraordinarily fortunate men. Not because of our success in business, but because four amazing women put up with our blunders when it came to issues of the heart and loved us anyway.

Are you wondering how I proposed to Jane? When her eyesight returned, I took her for another ride on the hang glider and proposed at five hundred feet. I nearly dropped the ring before getting it on her finger. Not my slickest moment, but a SEAL never quits. I hope it's a moment she'll remember when we're old and gray, but just in case, I remind her every day how much I love her.

From the entire cast of A Warrior's Challenge series and the Hard to Catch series, we hope you found adventure and enjoyed sharing the pages of our lives with you.

ACKNOWLEDGEMENT

To those readers who love a little sizzle between the covers! (In the book, people. Sheesh)

To my patient husband, whose heart always remains true.

To Robyn F, who beta reads my crazy novels with a smile.

ABOUT THE AUTHOR

Natasza Waters

Natasza Waters debuted her first romance novel in 2011 for readers who enjoy a cup of romance with a twist of steam. After majoring in English, Natasza's life altered course. After thirty-four years of service in the Coast Guard, a few crow's feet, and deeper laugh lines, she now spends her days crafting stories. Readers can look forward to romance, action, and suspense in her award-winning novels.

Follow her on Amazon for new releases.
Drop a review at BookBub or Goodreads
For new books and cool swag sign up for her newsletter https://nataszawaters.com
Facebook https://www.facebook.com/natasza.waters
Twitter https://twitter.com/NataszaWaters
Email Nataszawaters@gmail.com

BOOKS IN THIS SERIES

Hard to Catch

A sassy, light-hearted romance trilogy of three brothers who meet three intriguing, spicy women who dare them to burn their bachelor cards. Action and humor clash head-on.

Unquenchable Cravings: Gamble On Love – Book 1

A Warrior's Challenge series crossover. In Code Name: Nina's Choice, we briefly meet Steven and Moira Porter. Who are they?

What starts as seduction ends in adventure. During a business trip to Las Vegas, Steven Porter's attention is drawn to the woman sitting at his blackjack table. When synchronicity and irony join hands to box him into a corner, it's a cat-and-mouse game as he tries to hide his identity from Moira. Within four days, she ignites an unquenchable craving, and he's faced with the decision of his life: Treat her like the other women in his past or gamble on love.

Unquenchable Cravings: Last Chance On Love

Mandy McPhearson vividly remembers the mischievous prank Dane Porter played at her best friend's wedding. A year later, the searing kiss still sizzles when she disembarks the corporate jet, and the strikingly handsome, single father of two is waiting.

Unquenchable Cravings: Wager On Love

Jane's landscaping business thrives thanks to her contract with the Royal Jade Resort in Las Vegas. On a warm April morning, she steps onto the roadway at the valet entrance and wakes up in the hospital, nearly blind. When a guy from the Jade drops by, Jane suspects he wants her to waive any injury claim against the five-star resort. Nathan doesn't divulge much other than he's a retired Navy SEAL and works at the Jade, but he keeps coming back. Jane's vision might be gone, but her other four senses are falling for a guy she's never seen.

BOOKS BY THIS AUTHOR

Join The Adventure!

A Warrior's Challenge Series

Code Name: Ghost
Code Name: Kayla's Fire
Code Name: Nina's Choice
Code Name: Luminous
Code Name: Forever & Ever
Code Name: Redemption
Code Name: War of Stones

A Warrior's Passion Series

Cricket Under Fire
Dixie Under Siege

Hard to Catch Series

Unquenchable Cravings: Gamble on Love
Unquenchable Cravings: Last Chance on Love
Unquenchable Cravings: Wager on Love

Contemporary Romance

His Perfect Imperfection
Twila's Tempest
Committed to Chase

Sealed With a Weekend
Bordering on Love

Paranormal Romance

Legend of Spiralling Cedars

Vyro Creek Series

Arizona Lightning
Arizona Thunder

www.ingramcontent.com/pod-product-compliance
Lightning Source LLC
Chambersburg PA
CBHW021959010726
47494CB00003B/812